Dedication

To the Chairman who was always my guiding light on how life's journey should be lived. Your wisdom left an indelible mark for all that were privileged to have known you. We all still miss you.

Acknowledgement

My thanks to William McKenzie for invaluable information on missile silos and providing me with many understandings of the DIA (Defense Intelligence Agency). Also, I'd like to acknowledge the good people at Quantico Virginia, who are too numerous to cite individually but who assisted me in writing this book. Next, I'd like to thank Nan Fremont, who has always been a good friend and associate. Her background in journalism and her tiresome readings and critiques of my storyline, not only assisted but offered great encouragement through recommendations on character development. Also to all of my friends who read my manuscript from cover to cover and encouraged me to stay the course of living my dreams to tell great stories through writing novels.

KEN PETERS

CUBA'S NUCLEAR PIÑATA

Castro's attempt to blackmail America
with a stolen nuclear warhead

Cuba's Nuclear Pinata

Castro's attempt to blackmail America with a stolen nuclear warhead

print ISBN: 978-1-09839-980-1
ebook ISBN: 978-1-09839-981-8

CONTENTS

Summary

It's 1992. Clinton has ascended the Presidency, the Cold War is over, and the West is offering aid for democratization and the dismantling of former Soviet nuclear arsenals. Fidel Castro is left in the lurch with his former Soviet benefactors now bankrupt, and Castro has one last ploy to bring the West to him.

PREFACE

Since about 1959, Fidel Castro's reign has been brutal. While many have visited this tiny Caribbean Island, few have really seen the tyrannical world as seen by Peter Kennedy. The years had been fruitful for Castro but with the closing of the Cold War and his lost alliance with the USSR, with Russia now in its own world of turmoil, his world was becoming a desperate one. With food shortages and almost total fuel depletion, desperation was consuming him. With no allies of any financial consequence, his question of how to maintain was becoming ever more absorbing. Since the change in Nicaragua, Panama, and his defeat in Grenada, the chance of finding anyone to come to his aid was bleak.

Few people ever really tracked those missiles back in 1962 during the days of the October crisis. The boats were loaded, without any international inspection, and it was assumed that all the missiles were intact. But the truth was, which only Castro knew, some of the thirty Soviet missiles had had their warheads removed. They'd been kept a secret, which no one, excluding Castro's brother and a few others, now dead, had ever known:

the fact that he had possessed, for more than three decades, seven nuclear warheads. Now, with all sides closing in on him, the plan to finally put these secret warheads to work had become Castro's last resort.

Peter Kennedy was a private consultant in the world of biotechnology. During the war over the Falklands, he was approached for his help while working overseas by the DIA (Defense Intelligence Agency). Previous to his working in the corporate world, Peter was a professor of economics. As such while working overseas for a large American healthcare company in South America, he frequently worked in the various ministries, securing favorable trade situations for the importing of goods from the company that employed him. It was at that time that Peter stumbled upon the world of black work. Peter was approximately thirty-five at the time and had always felt guilty that he somehow missed the Vietnam War. As the years had gone by, he met many veterans and became acutely ashamed that he never did his part. Sure the war was unpopular but reality was many men served and many men died, and Peter, he hadn't done very much for anyone other than himself. It was on a Christmas night in Buenos Aires, while attending a party at the US Embassy, that he was first approached. He had no idea whom he was talking to, but after Peter confessed his guilt to these two embassy staffers, one of them asked, "How'd you like to finally do something for your nation?" Peter's obvious answer was sure what's involved. They explained that they simply needed some information on Argentina's fuel reserves. They said it should be easy for Peter since he worked for a private company, visited the ministries daily, and was a former economist, with obvious interests in the economies of the nation. It didn't take long and it wasn't particularly hard for Peter to get what they wanted. After he delivered the information, there were many pats on his back by the agents involved, a private dinner to celebrate their success, and he was made to feel that he had truly made a significant contribution to the efforts of ending the war over the Falklands. Of course, Peter was told that this event was to be kept secret, that as far as anyone in the outside world was concerned, this event had never really taken place and no one would ever know about it.

But the DIA doesn't work that way, and Peter's file was just put into storage until they could use him again. Recently in 1992, a defector from Cuba had given the DIA information about the possibility that Castro had seven nuclear warheads, stolen leftovers from the Cuban missile crisis. The question was, was this defector telling the truth or was he creating a fabrication which would not only guarantee him political asylum but also a constant flow of lifestyle and money in his newfound American home? So the question now became for the DIA, confirmation. Next, the how-to question. It happened that one of the old embassy staffers from Buenos Aires who was in on the interrogation had a recollection and a remembrance, and that was Peter's calling. It was decided, after the staffer, a guy named Henry St. John, told the story of how they recruited this guy before during the Falklands, that they could do it again.

Peter didn't know it but he was once again to be recruited by the DIA; only this time, he wouldn't be volunteering, they would be drafting him, whether Peter liked it or not.

Chapter 1

The Journey

The ship was damp and old. This was the kind of freighter that had seen its day more than forty years ago. It was harbored outside of Cardenas, about forty miles east of Havana. The captain was an old seaman. His face weathered by the years, his body shunted by the time at sea, the lack of exercise, and in general his age. He didn't know what his cargo was going to be; he only knew that contraband was his game and whatever the market would bear, buy or trade, was how he made his living. His ship was under a Salvador registry and they had trade relations with almost everyone, but most important with the US and also with Cuba. Today he received word from one of his contacts that he'd be carrying cargo from a wealthy Cuban, who'd be paying top dollar to get a whole load of his personal valuables out of Cuba. The story was logical, after all, almost everyone who had any valuables knew the end was only a matter of time, one or two years at most. Castro had become fanatical in seizing people's property just so his regime could stay alive and acquire money any way possible. With no real trade, the country was in shock. Next to no one drove anymore unless you were one of the elite, otherwise it was walking or a bicycle. So the next logical step was the seizing of personal property, even amongst those who were in the Castro circle. It no longer mattered if you knew someone, when your time came, there was a letter or a knock at the door or some messenger; whatever sooner or later, everyone's time would come. That's how it had to be because Fidel was not going to knuckle under to the West. So it was not unusual that a ship's captain used to trading in contraband should not question the fact that someone rich was trying to get his or her valuables out of Cuba.

The crate being loaded into the hole was large but again nothing unusual, unless of course, the fact that the goods seemed to have a contingent of bodyguards with it. Nevertheless, the captain thought, *I guess everyone is just as corrupt as everyone else, afraid someone would steal their treasure even aboard his ship.* Now while the captain dealt in contraband, such as stolen goods and also items that would arrive in America in an undeclared status, he didn't consider himself a thief, but he understood the types of people he served, and they for the most part were thieves themselves. How else did they get so rich under Castro? He was in his cabin, getting ready to get things in order, charts, radio frequencies, and what last-minute checks were needed before departure, when the head of the security team for this precious cargo he was carrying came into his cabin.

His name was Fernando Martinez.

"When will we be getting under way?" Fernando asked.

"We're only about an hour from departure," said the captain. "I'm just getting all of the requirements in order so we can depart."

"You know, Senor Martinez, when we travel this short distance to Miami, the fact that we will be leaving Cuba is for sure a guarantee that we will be stopped and checked by the American Coast Guard. So it is important, senor, that everything is in order, or perhaps your precious cargo belonging to your *heffe* will be looked into. Is that what you want?"

"Okay, but please try to keep on schedule; we have people expecting us in Miami to receive our cargo," said Fernando.

This, the captain thought was strange. Why would someone be worried about the arrival time if their cargo was just valuables? Well, who knows, maybe they were worried about a hijack. After all, these things did take place but never to his ships, for in all the years at his trade, he had developed an arsenal of arms via his various deals. *After all*, he thought, *a man does not succeed in this business unless he is prepared*. This was a rough world and, more importantly, a rough business.

It was now 10:00 a.m. and if they left before eleven, they should have no problem in arriving in Miami to clear customs before dark. While this freighter was old, the captain had had its engines redone, and she could make twelve knots with no problem; a key feature needed in the contraband business—good engines and, even more importantly, speed.

At departure time, the sun was high, almost noon. The heat was starting to become overbearing. Nothing for the captain, but for the *norteamericanos*, it is always too much. The water was calm, the lines were cast off, and they were under way. After an hour, Senor Martinez came into the cabin. He asked a lot of questions about the procedures upon arriving in Miami. Would they come on board or would they just review the manifest?

The captain said, "They will probably come on board. My reputation, you know, she's not so good, but they know me and I have nothing to hide on this trip, and this they will read in my face."

Later during the journey, Senor Martinez stood on the bow of the ship, looking out over the water, contemplating what the procedure would be when they arrive.

After they'd cleared customs on the dock, Martinez will see his cousin, Juan Lopez. He hadn't seen him since the last time he was out of Cuba, some three years ago. How fortunate it is to be able to leave when you can. *It is good to be the cousin of Fidel*, Fernando thought.

Ah Lopez, that crazy *muchacho*, too long! He was fond of Juan, but he knew that this time he could not let his fondness for Juan get in the way.

I hope he will be organized this time, not like when we were transferring that ten million in cash. How stupid could one be to buy suitcases without latches! *Well, he is a cousin and after all,* he thought, *family is the reason why his life in Cuba has been so good to him.*

About seven miles from Miami, they started to see lots of ships in the vicinity they were travelling. Suddenly from out of nowhere came the blare of a bullhorn, "Cut your engines, stand fast, and prepare to be boarded, this is the United States Coast Guard." When Senor Martinez heard the blare of the horn, he froze. *Why*, he thought, *why would they be stopping us so close to the Miami port? Could the captain's reputation be that bad?*

After all, the ship had a Salvadoran registry and flag. Were they being watched when they left Cuba? Could someone know about their cargo? Surely no one could know. This was not only a secret now but had been for over thirty years. Surely it couldn't be. Fernando was sick with fear. He knew what this mission meant. He also knew what his fate would be if he failed to deliver the cargo and get it planted. He would have no choice; either live in exile and become a refugee in the US and lose all of his status, wealth, and power in Cuba or return to Cuba and be assassinated one night by one of Fidel's secret squad, *los hombres de muerto* (men of death).

His mind was ablaze with a million bizarre thoughts and recriminations. What was happening? At that moment, the captain of the coast guard vessel was now on deck, talking to the ship's captain. There seemed to be a disagreement. Hands were moving, gestures were being made, he could not, for the fear and apprehension, even think about getting close enough to hear the conversation. He watched their mouths move and the pointing to some papers. Suddenly as quickly as it all began, it was over and the captain of the coast guard vessel was leaving to reboard the Coast Guard Cutter.

Once the coast was clear and the engines started back up, Senor Martinez went immediately to see the captain.

"What was all that about?" Fernando asked.

"Oh, it was nothing, just the usual drug-check inspections. That coast guard captain, he should have known better, me, I never carry drugs, the world carries drugs and so that's what they look for. Me, I know better, stolen goods, people trying to sneak into Miami, much, much easier. So stupid, he must be a new captain because everyone knows I no carry drugs, it's bad business."

Upon reaching Miami at around six thirty that evening, everything seemed back on track. Senor Martinez had long since calmed down about the near scare with the US Coast Guard.

The INS people came on board to inspect everyone's papers and then the customs people stood on the dock to watch the unloading of the ship. At about 7:00 p.m., one of the customs people called up to the captain, asking if they could have a word before they started to unload. The captain walked down the gangway to the dock to speak with the agent. Again with nerves soaring and butterflies in his stomach, Senor Martinez watched. *What now*, he thought.

After ten minutes, the captain returned and said, "We have a problem." Fernando could not believe it. *What's next*, he thought, *God, dirty money was so much easier and smaller too.* Having done dirty deals before, such as laundering drug money, he hadn't given much thought about this when Fidel approached him. Only this time he were to be caught, there would be no high-priced lawyers or bail. There would be no special considerations like for Manuel Noriega. No appeals, for this would be a crime where all of America would want a real taste of strong-arm justice.

There would be only a federal penitentiary or the death penalty for acts of war against the United States. When the captain proceeded to explain the problem, Fernando could not believe it.

The captain said, "Do you see this guy down there, he has all sorts of problems with the union workers, what time they've got to be done before they get overtime. Next, it's his brother's daughter's birthday this evening, and he really wishes a favor of me: he wants me to wait until tomorrow in the morning to unload. You see, Senor Martinez, when one of these guys asks you for a favor and you're in my kind of business, you kind of go along with it. It's called good relations with people you often hope will look the other way sometimes. So I'm very sorry, senor, but you see, this is one of those times I just can't say no."

Martinez did not know what to do; there were schedules, contacts, people, and timing. This was no drug money laundering task; this was a very dangerous situation, he thought.

While standing on the deck, he looked over and saw Juan Lopez. He immediately headed towards the gangway to see his old friend.

Lopez's greeting was warm; with a huge hug, he grabbed Fernando and said, "*Que pasa, Mucho Tiempo.*"

"Hello Juan, it's good to see you."

"And it is good to see you."

"Let's get right to business," said Fernando.

"Before business, my friend, first it's a little pleasure," Juan said. "I have some *chicas*, ladies, for this evening. It has been too long, my friend, since we had a fiesta together."

Fernando pushed his arms down, as if to say, this is business first, we will party later. "We've got a little problem and we have to talk," said Fernando.

Juan asked, "What's the problem?"

Fernando proceeded to tell him about the customs agent and all the rest about the captain. What Fernando wanted to know was would it all hold together for tomorrow in the same sequence, with the same people.

Juan said, "*No hay problemas.*" Juan continued, "Most of the people we've got in on this are either criminals or a couple of the Mariel flotilla people who have no love for America. A lot of these people really got the shit when they came here. You know, kept in jails, treated like real animals. They've got no love of America."

"You haven't told them anything, you fool, have you?" Fernando asked.

"No man, not to worry, these guys think it's the usual, drugs."

"How are you? Did you explain the size of the cargo?" Fernando asked.

"I told them it's just a larger than usual shipment, concealed inside other items to make things look better," Juan said.

Fernando thought for a moment, *God, I hope this fool has it all together, this is serious stuff.* "Okay," Fernando said, "let's talk. Do you know somewhere we could go to discuss the movement of the materials tomorrow?"

"Sure, man," Juan said, "I know a place that has cafe *Cubano* better than you get in that poor, forsaken country of yours where nobody has nothing."

Fernando said, "Soon we will have everything and more. The Americans will be at our feet, making any deal they can to eliminate confrontation."

"All these years of living in the shadow of the United States, they will soon treat us with respect, even if our friends from Russia and other parts of the world have surrendered. We, my friend, will be the ones they will talk to. They will fear us like they fear the Chinese and the Koreans. We will make the terms and they will fear that Fidel just might let this one go off. But enough of our day, it is not far off."

When they arrived at the cafe, Fernando became deadly serious. They found a quiet place in the corner to sit and talk. It was your typical South Miami Cuban café—lots of chatter in Spanish, locals abounding, and lots of lovely Latin women. It reminded him of home, only here he was a nobody, at home, people stepped aside for him, and after he completed his task at hand and Fidel had finally made the West come to terms, he would be even more powerful at home, but for now, he had a mission to complete and that was all he could focus on at the moment.

"Listen," Fernando said, "this is serious business, we're talking a nuclear warhead being planted right here in Miami. I mean enough nuclear power to level most of the city, *comprendo* amigo?"

"Jesus," Juan said.

"Yeah, now let's get started," Fernando said. "I want to know how many people we've got, what is the route we're taking, and how it's going to get to Miami International Airport."

It was 8:00 a.m. when Juan met Fernando at the Sheraton Bal Harbor for breakfast.

Juan said he checked at the dock earlier and the cargo should be off the boat on their truck by nine thirty.

Fernando was outraged. "Why are you not there to oversee the unloading?"

"Calm down," Juan said. "It is far better that we let the longshoremen do their job as if it were just a normal day unloading the usual. The way I see it if something goes wrong, the further away we are from the cargo, the better."

Fernando thought, *I guess he's right. Perhaps Juan has grown and matured here in America since we last had contact.* Fernando was feeling better and at least had the stomach to enjoy his breakfast.

It was now nine thirty, and as Juan had said, the cargo was loaded on the truck at the dock and they could now proceed. Senor Martinez saw the captain, signed the release papers, and they left. The truck was a rider rental, eighteen feet long, and had enough space inside to hide the cargo which was about six feet square in a very strong wooden crate marked "fragile perishable antique" diagonally across the sides. Juan and Fernando drove in the front cab, while the four bodyguards who had accompanied Fernando on the journey the day before, stayed in the back with the cargo.

Their first job was to get out of the port authority and head to the airport. Fernando was not familiar enough with the highways of Miami, so Juan drove.

This did not make Fernando feel any calmer, as Juan still had that carefree attitude about him and that made Fernando even more nervous. He didn't even know if the warhead was stable. *Jesus,* he thought, *what if this bomb goes off.* Suddenly his stomach was starting to act up again.

As his anxiety rose, he could think of only one thing—getting the job done and then it's back to Havana. As they drove towards the airport, Fernando began to revisit the discussion they had in the cafe the evening before.

Fernando began, "Okay, let's review this again."

Juan interrupted, "Listen, man, it's straightforward, first we pick up the uniforms at a warehouse outside of the airport. These aren't fake, man; they're the real thing. My cousin Julio ripped them off."

"Jesus Christ," Fernando said, "no one else was to be involved, only you and I, and those four *muchachos* in the back." Fernando turned serious and said, "And what did you tell him the reason was for these uniforms?"

Juan answered, "I told him it was for a drug job. You know, trying to lift a shipment the customs agents seized at sea." Fernando thought to himself for a moment, *More loose ends to be taken care of when this is done.*

Fernando began again, "After we get the uniforms, what about ID badges?"

"*No problema*, man, we got those too," Juan said.

"Okay, let me get this, we get to the airport; we go to the customs agents entrance gate. Then, once we're through the gate, we go into the holding area."

"Yeah, yeah," Juan said. "It's easy. After we arrive at the gate, they will look at our IDs. We'll tell them we're bringing in a transfer of goods from Fort Lauderdale. Believe, man, these IDs are real. The only thing needed is a picture change and we'll be doing that at the warehouse when we suit up. I've got a Polaroid there and everything else we need."

Juan continued, "We leave our four buddies at our changing point. After we're through the gate, we go to the storage area."

Fernando interrupted again, "And how do we unload this huge crate?"

Juan jumped in, "That's the beauty, man, they'll unload it for us." Juan laughed and said, "Can you believe this, man, only in America, like the song man. Then we just sign the papers that get us into the deep storage area with a phony case number which will never be called up, because the case number doesn't exist."

Fernando asked, "And how did you come up with a case number that would pass for real?"

"Easy, man. After you called me and explained the job, I came up with this plan and came down here. I got some recently arrested drug dealer's name out of the newspaper, and I said I was a lawyer.

"I told them I was here to make sure that the evidence the customs people were holding against my client was still here and untampered with.

"While walking through deep storage, I lifted a recent case number from a label and changed the last digit. Hey, man, this is America, my client's got rights. Like I said, man, 'only in America,' I love it."

It was 11:00 a.m. when they arrived at the airport. They had to drive around to the back part of the airport where cargo, storage, and airport security were located. Upon entering the cargo area, Juan became lost. Fernando's stomach was starting to act up again. Although it was still morning, Fernando could feel his palms begin to sweat. *So close*, he thought, *please let me just get this done and get out of here.*

Juan should have remembered the way; he was here before. How could he not remember? Finally, Juan got to the customs agents gate. There were two customs agents there. The gate was wide enough for only one car to pass through at a time. The fences on either side of the gate were eight feet high, with circular razor wire on the top, stretching as far as Fernando could see in either direction. Inside, the area was wide open for the most part, with a few small buildings to the left and right of the entrance. The area looked like what it was, the back side of the airport, the part commercial travelers never see. About three hundred yards straight ahead was a large hangar. Fernando wondered if that was the destination of their cargo.

The agent speaking to Juan asked about the papers. "Where were you dispatched from?"

Juan answered, "Fort Lauderdale, it says it on the papers, doesn't it?"

Fernando froze and thought, *Shut your mouth, you idiot.*

The agent answered, "Juan, I can see that. I asked about you two. I've never seen you guys before." Fernando's hands began to sweat more. His stomach was doing flips at this point. *Why is this guy asking about this?* Fernando thought, *This is Miami, there must be 3,000 agents in southern Florida.* By the time Fernando left his thoughts and returned to listening to the conversation, he could hear Juan talking about his transfer down here from New York and about how goddamned cold it was up there and how lucky these guys were to have never known the cold wind working outside at Kennedy International in the winter. The agent laughed and said, "Well, the grass always seems greener on the other side, wait till you have to live through a summer down here."

"Look," the agent said, "drive straight out to that huge hangar over there, honk your horn at the door, and it'll open. I've initialed the papers and they'll unload the cargo for you."

"Great," Juan said, "thanks." They drove straight ahead, and Juan said, "See, it was a breeze, *como no*!" Fernando was still sweating. He wasn't sure if it was the heat or his nerves at this point. They arrived at the large garage door and honked their horn as instructed.

The door opened, another agent walked out and straight ahead. Fernando could see what looked like acres of rows of stored crates, four levels high. There were hand trucks and motorized forklifts, everything you'd need to place anything anywhere at any height. Juan got out of the truck and handed the papers to the agent. Fernando looked out of the truck at Juan and thought, *God, he looks real.*

Well, Fernando thought, *I guess it will be this easy.* The agent called for some guys who were sitting around a lunch table, listening to the radio, and reading newspapers. A big guy got up and went over to the forklift to start it up. At the same time, two others went to the back of the truck, opened it up, and began to slide the crate forward to the edge where the forklift could grab it.

By this time, Fernando was outside of the truck near the rear with Juan watching the operation. The crate shifted a little as the forklift got under it. Fernando's body tensed and shifted at the same time, in the same movement, as if he were connected to the crate.

God, please no accidents, he thought. But all was well and the forklift lowered it down and proceeded to head to the back of the warehouse.

Juan said, "Take it easy, guys," and he turned back to go to the front of the truck. Without incident, they got in and Fernando continued to watch the forklift as it travelled down the center aisle. Juan started the truck and began to back out. Fernando relaxed and smiled inside himself; this went well, it will all soon be over, and I'll be back on my way to Havana and to my rewards. He felt bad about Juan, but what could he do. What must be, must be.

There was a crash in the distance, Fernando tensed. He looked down the aisle, panic erupted immediately.

Suddenly the agent outside the truck yelled, "God, damn it, can't you guys learn how to set those things down gently?" He laughed and looked up at Juan and said, "Clowns, all of them, they think this is a go-cart haven back here."

Juan laughed, said, "Yeah, see ya." They backed the truck out and turned it around and headed for the gate. As they passed through the gate, they slowed down and waved at the first agent.

As they passed, the agent yelled, "Hey, don't forget."

Juan stopped and nervously said, "Don't forget what?"

The agent smiled and said, "The weather, enjoy it if you can, it's supposed to be 97 today."

As they drove away, Fernando thought how well it all went today. Fidel will be most pleased that all went without problems. He felt bad about what had to come next but he had no choice, too much was at stake. The future of Cuba was what really mattered.

Even though Juan was Cuban, he no longer really understood Fidel and the way of life that must preserved in Havana.

The rest of the capitalist pigs who have abandoned Fidel will see there were other ways than to turn to capitalism and the West. He'd known Juan since they were little boys. He was his mother's cousin's son. They used to play together when they were just five years old. They lived next door to each other in a small barrio five miles outside of Havana. That was 1965, a few years after Fidel had come to power. They were much alike then, but as they grew older, Juan cared only for his personal gain; he never understood what Fidel had created. Whereas Fernando's mother, who was a strong supporter and was also related to Castro on his mother's side, always preached to Fernando from when he was very young, "We owe much to your cousin Fidel. He threw out that pig Batista and his foul group so that decent hardworking people like us could share in what truly belonged to the people of Cuba."

As Juan grew older, he thought only of himself and the pleasures of life. He ascribed to the party program, but never in his heart. It was for that reason that as the years passed and he became a young man in his early twenties that he decided he wanted to go to the United States. At that time in the early eighties, he partook in the Mariel flotilla. He sneaked aboard one of the ships carrying a load of Cuban criminals, which Castro delighted in sending to America. Once in Miami and held by the immigration people, he was able to demonstrate to the US officials that he had family there and that he would be able to have a place to live. He was then released and was able to establish himself in the land of plenty. What the land of plenty meant to Juan was just that, plenty for Juan. It didn't take him long to get in with the right people and find his way into the world of illegal cons and scams.

He kept in touch with Fernando always, as he still considered him close although he cared not for any of Fernando's ideologies. So it was logical that when things evolved as they did, Fernando knew that Juan could be of great use to him. He also knew that Juan would do as he asked, were there enough money involved. Sadly, Juan never really understood how devoted Fernando was to his life in Cuba, or he might have realized that his destiny was to be so tragically altered.

Driving through the streets of Miami, Fernando told Juan to take him back to the Sheraton Bal Harbor Hotel and drop him off. He told Juan to go back to the warehouse where the others waited and to stay there. He would go to the bank and get the money and be back by dark.

Just as Fernando got out of the car, he stopped and said, "Oh, don't forget to bring your cousin Julio. I want to pay him and thank him for those wonderful uniforms; you should not have to give him from your share, and you've done a great job, Juan."

After dropping off Fernando, Juan could not wipe the smile from his face. He could think only of what a half a million dollars was going to do for his lifestyle. Life had been good all these years, but never had he been able to do a covert job where the payoff was so much at one time. He thought if he were smart, he could put some away and still buy a new Porsche and have all the women he could handle. "Ah, life is good, and now I will live it like the best do."

Fernando arrived at the warehouse after dark as he said he would. The warehouse was in a commercial area, quite isolated at night. When he came inside, they were all there—Juan, Julio, and the four *caballeros* that had accompanied him and the crate from Cardenas. He patted Juan on the back and said once again, "Great job, Juan."

He put the briefcase on the table and asked them all to gather close by. They all approached with great anticipation. None of them had ever seen this kind of money before.

Juan laughed as he came closer, saying, "It's going to be a party tonight."

Fernando opened the briefcase facing himself, reached in, and pulled out a steel black Glock 9 mm automatic with a silencer and shot each of them.

The look on Juan's face was of disbelief. "But we are brothers," Juan said, but before he finished spewing the words, he fell to the ground like the others. He was the last to be shot and with his last breath, he asked, "Why, Fernando, why," and he exhaled.

Fernando put the gun back in the case, closed it, and turned to the door. As he reached the door, he turned back, looked, and said, "I'm sorry, Juan, it's how it had to be." Fernando felt great remorse. He was torn by what he had done, while at the same time his belief in the revolutionary ideologies by which he'd grown up told him he had had no choice. If the plans were to succeed, for the greater good of all, this was the way it had to be. He would say a rosary for Juan and see to it that his mother truly did get his share. Fidel would never know if some of the funds from the account in Miami were rearranged; after all, Juan had paid for Fidel's success with his life. Could anyone ask for more or give more?

His instructions from Fidel were clear. When all was completed, he was to fly to New York to the Cuban Mission on

Lexington and 38th Street in New York. There he would make contact with a man named Ortega. He was to tell Ortega only that the bank account was in place and nothing more. Ortega was to provide him with a diplomatic passport.

From there, Fernando was to go directly to Kennedy International and fly home. Fernando had never met Ortega, but he understood from Fidel that Ortega was the one who would contact the United Nations and tell them of the six nuclear warheads that Castro had and his willingness to negotiate with the US for their surrender.

Chapter 2

Conscription

Henry St. John was driving south on the George Washington Parkway. It was a piss-poor day. The rain was pouring down, all of the leaves would drop from the trees now, and he won't even get the chance to enjoy the fall colors. The world should have been perfect but it wasn't. The problem he had today was the news on CNN this morning about the six nuclear warheads which Castro announced he had now.

Christ, ninety miles offshore. This wasn't like the Ukraine or North Korea; this was right in our backyard. *God, like the missiles of October all over again*, he thought.

Henry was a good guy; he just ended up in the wrong place, at the wrong age, and at the wrong time. During the autumn of 1970, Henry was beginning his senior year at Long Island University in Queens, New York. He was neither pro the Vietnam War or anti the War. His goal was not even to finish school but to drop out and be an actor, a talent which would serve him well later in life. Unfortunately, due to the war, he was staying in school in order to hold on to his student deferment.

During the fall, that year, the American public was up in arms with what some would call early political correctness. It seemed that most of the draftees were from minority groups out of the inner cities and the media played this event and was dragging it on for quite a while.

Eventually the establishment was forced to develop a more equitable plan for the draft: that was the lottery. Birthdays were drawn at random that year. During the national event and depending on the number for which your birthday was drawn, you were either very close to being drafted or you were home free.

Although they wouldn't meet each other for another ten years or so, a young man named Peter Kennedy drew number 288, while Henry St. John unluckily pulled down number four. Their paths would develop in totally different directions over the coming years; however, their fate was preordained to be intertwined one day.

In light of Henry's low number, Henry decided to sign up in the hopes he could get into a unit that would not be Vietnam bound. Anything that would insure he didn't go overseas was a reprieve.

He eventually got called and enlisted into a signal core unit. During his physical at Fort Hamilton, he met someone who reaffirmed he'd made the right choice, that this unit would never get to see action but would spend its tour of duty up in

Boston. Henry was fairly naive at the age of twenty and wasn't too sure what the program was going to be when he arrived for his induction.

After he was sworn in, some different men came around from different sections of the military recruiting people for special assignments. They said they were looking for guys who wanted to learn languages. When Henry heard this, he immediately raised his hand and volunteered.

What Henry didn't realize was that he wouldn't be learning Spanish or French, it was to be Russian and Vietnamese. But by the time Henry learned this, it was too late; they owned him.

As time went by, Henry liked what he did; after all, while he dealt with some pretty weird characters, he wasn't going to Vietnam to fight on the ground. For all this, he was thankful and tried to adjust to the people and the life being required of him.

During the interview process for this language training, he learned he was actually working for a branch of the military known as the Defense Intelligence Agency under the wing of the NSA, the National Security Agency. When he was first interviewed, the men he met were pretty gruesome. He became convinced they only recruited guys with a bad attitude and who never smiled. They were kind of like Jack Webb on the old television show *Dragnet*. Only these guys weren't on TV; this wasn't television, and these guys had a license to kill.

He did his basic training at Fort Meade, where the NSA was located. Each branch of the DIA went through the NSA for training sooner or later. That's where he met Willie, Major William B. O'Connor.

Willy was his nickname and he preferred it that way. He was a soldier's man. Willy wasn't tall. He was broad however and forever wore the traditional military buzz cut. His face, however, smooth at age fifty-five and perhaps it was that young, still innocent look which was the soft side of his soul. It gave you the feeling that he cared. He always cared more about his troops than the official political muck. For this reason, the major had a loyal following. This also did not escape his superiors. They saw that the major could often inspire men to go far and beyond, no matter what the danger, and that was important when you wanted men to do what they ordinarily wouldn't.

Being Henry's mentor, he was a great influence and helped Henry with his transition to life in the DIA. After all, Henry's aspirations were acting, not to be a spy. However, as time went by, Henry saw a beautiful synergy between his gift for acting and his newfound language skills.

Willy was kind of a middle-of-the-road guy, not as gruesome as the usual DIA type but nevertheless, he liked the spy business. With Willy's help and time, Henry rose in the ranks and learned all he needed to be good at his job; he even started to become a bit gruesome. Henry was single and never married. Part of his single life evolved due to his job; there was no time and space to be able to give a woman what she'd most likely want. Henry wasn't too sure what they wanted anyway. His success rate with long-standing relationships never exceeded much over a few months. For the most part, he had a general aversion to marital commitment. He didn't like the concept of checking in, either in his personal life or professional one.

During the Falklands War, the DIA was looking for people to go down to Argentina to do some snooping for the agency. While the US was not involved in the conflict, they were very much involved with the British military. At that time, Henry was in middle management at the DIA, and he heard about the recruitment for people to head south. He got to his old mentor Willie, who by now was senior. He was a section head in the air force's branch of the DIA. When Henry told Willy he wanted to go, Willie said okay. He'd make sure Henry would lead the team, assisting in information gathering on Argentina's air strength. This was Britain's greatest concern, since Argentina had sixty-six French Mirage jets, and that was a concern for the British.

It was during this assignment that the paths of Peter Kennedy and Henry St. John would finally cross. Henry recruited Peter to do volunteer work. Peter was a frustrated baby boomer who didn't go into the service and always wanted to contribute to his country to ease his conscience for not having served during the Vietnam War.

Peter worked for a US healthcare company in South America. Over the years, he made all sorts of contacts with government ministry people in Argentina. He was able to question people and gain valuable information without any trace back to the US government. While the idea hadn't hit Henry yet, Peter had served him well then, and considering today's announcement on CNN, Peter would serve him well again. This Henry would now remember considering the meeting he was about to attend today.

He was on his way to the Pentagon to pick up some other DIA officials who had expertise in varying areas. Most of the senior defense department officials in the establishment were working with the presidential administration to address the current crisis announced today. The people Henry was picking up today, however, were not part of the establishment trying to solve the issues of the day. They were specialists, part of Henry's team. Henry was part of a covert group known as SIREN. This group was controlled out of NSA, reporting directly to the assistant director, who also ran the group. All of the members of SIREN were involved in cover positions in various branches of government intelligence and what they did was black work.

Today while the establishment was grappling with the political aspects of the new Cuban missile crisis, Henry's team was off to a safe house in Fairfax, Virginia, to view the problem from another perspective.

When they arrived at the safe house, it was 9:30 a.m. and the first thing on the agenda was to make a pot of coffee and settle in for the day. They had a lot of work ahead of them and getting comfortable was important. Attending the meeting with Henry was Joel Johnson, Spencer Briggs, Eliot Brackston, and

Barry Henson. Each of them had a specialty which would be required for the plan to be executed.

The day before, when the US ambassador received word from the United Nations of Castro's communication with them, Ambassador Connolly immediately contacted the White House secretary and told him to inform the president. The president then called the Joint Chiefs of Staff and convened an immediate meeting. In attendance at the meeting was General Richard Lee Anderson of the army. The meeting went as one would expect. Everyone gave the president what information they had and their opinions on the situation.

Without exception the majority opinion was we need to negotiate as soon as possible. The sentiments of all but General Anderson were that, like the other countries in Eastern Europe, all we had to do was buy off Castro. After all what Fidel really wanted was the money, for without that, surely, he would eventually be overthrown. For if he could not contain the people, his Marxist world as he knew it would come to an end. For Fidel, as it was with all communist governments, they realized their future was in keeping the party line; it was never in their economic system. Any economist who studied comparative systems knew that the only thing which kept those governments in power was brute force, not their wealth or economic power.

But General Anderson introduced what should have been obvious to everyone, but it wasn't. The fact was that Fidel Castro was not the leader of a fledgling democracy trying to put in place a new government. He was the leader of one of the last communist regimes in the world, and he had a long-standing bone to pick with the United States. That was Kennedy's Operation Mongoose in 1962, when we tried to assassinate him.

General Anderson put forth to the Joint Chiefs of Staff the view that Castro wouldn't yield the weapons until he truly brought the US to its knees. Mostly everyone disagreed with the general. They all felt that no matter what we gave Castro, it was nothing compared to a confrontation. The general tried to gain sway with the group by putting forth another thought.

"Gentlemen," he said, "this man is not putting forth the idea of democracy. He's maintaining that his system of governing is right and he's not going to change that. How do you people expect to rectify this with our new friends in the Eastern Bloc. Would the Ukraine or any of the other countries we've just negotiated with be able to stay with their reform movements? After all, if we show them that we are willing to supply aid in return for their weapons, what would stop some of their conservative movements from putting forth the idea that reform was not needed in order to negotiate with the West?"

The general continued, "What about the human rights issues and all the groups around the world who would say we were supporting a brutal government? I implore you to understand this is a different situation with a different man. The world today and all who we deal with see a direct relationship between our support and their alignment with democracy. Let's not forget, we don't give aid and support countries just because they have weapons. We do it because we as a nation aspire to a certain way of life, to a constitutional government, to freedom. That's not what Fidel Castro offers his people. Gentlemen, there has to be another way, and if we don't know it now, we will have to think of it. In the meantime, we must stall."

His speech was received well by all. He further compared this type of deal with Castro akin to the arms-for-hostages deal with Iran, not good public policy especially with CNN and the rest of the world press. Anderson indicated further that the discussion today would surely make the headline news and the media will have a field day. That the present administration would be crucified by the press for making a deal with Castro without the political changes.

It was clear to all there that US could not provide the same type of aid to Cuba that they were providing to the Eastern Bloc countries unless Castro was removed, or he changed his policies. The latter was not likely, and the former would be difficult.

Henry walked into the living room at the safe house and asked who'd made the coffee. "It's terrible," Henry said.

Joel Johnson answered, "Is that what you brought us here for, to discuss how bad my coffee is?"

Henry said no. He went on to explain about the phone call he received last night from General Anderson. He explained about the Joint Chiefs' meeting the morning before and the outcome. After going into detail about yesterday's meeting, he said,

"So it's going to be our job guys to get us out of this one. General Anderson is giving us the full throttle to go ahead. It's time to get down to business. You've all been brought here because of your expertise; now it's time to put it to the test."

Joel Johnson was forty-four years old. He was a communications specialist, with multiple degrees from MIT and Stanford. There wasn't anything from a ham radio to microwave transmissions that he didn't know about. He was married but never had kids due to an infertility problem his wife had. Their marriage fared but never flourished, so his wife had her career as a nurse and he had his, a communications electronics freak, with all his toys paid for by the government.

Spencer Briggs's area of expertise was in nuclear armaments. He was forty-two, and never married. His skill in detonation devices was renowned within army ordinance circles. He advised and assisted many of America's metropolitan police departments as a bomb specialist when disarming potential dirty bombs.

Eliot Brackston was a specialist in field maneuvers. He was forty years old and just barely took part in Vietnam. He enlisted when he was eighteen and had the army pay for his college education after he did his three-year hitch. He was married with two kids and a lovely wife. His wife was an attorney and managed both, a fulfilling career in law yet had time to be a good mother. Eliot had worked closely over the years in South America with allied countries of the US, training ground troops in military ground tactics. His niche specialty was surprise incursions.

Barry Henson, the last of the group there this day, was a retired marine. Barry was fifty-three and his arena was Cuba. He was there before the fall of Batista. Afterwards, he became a Lt. Colonel based in Guantanamo Bay, Cuba, for five years. Cuba was an obsession for Barry. He had studied it intensely since the rise of Castro. He knew almost every inch of the terrain. He was also involved as an advisor during the Bay of Pigs Invasion. His knowledge would facilitate much of what would have to be accomplished if General Anderson's plan was to be successful.

"Boys, what we've got here is some serious shit," Henry said.

"Last night after I met with Gen. Richard Lee Anderson, I believe I've come up with a plan to address the issues our friends are fumbling over at the White House. When the general finally convinced the Joint Chiefs of Staff that they had to stall, he contacted an old friend of mine, Major William B. O'Connor. I in turn received a call from Willy last night, asking that I get directly over to Fort Meade for a very early morning discussion. Real early, like 2:00 a.m.

"Last night I committed you guys to this one, so prepare yourselves and contact whatever family you want and tell them we're going to be away for a while. All your cover positions will be handled by Major O'Connor, Willie. For all intents and purposes, will be at a training center in Eastern Europe, helping Uncle Sam get some things straightened out over there. Your supervisors will be told you're going to be gone for about a month or so.

"The plan as I see, boys, is major surgery. We're going to cut off Fidel's balls so his voice will be a few octaves higher when he sings the star-spangled banner for us. In other words, we're gonna go in there and disarm those missiles, so our buddy Fidel doesn't have anything to bargain with anymore.

"Each of you have specialties that will serve the team and our goal to neutralize the warheads.

"Joel, your job as you'd expect will be to create some sort of stealth landing. Obviously, they watch us as much as we watch them. With Castro's announcement, he'll surely have all defenses on, and getting in without detection by radar or any other of their CENCOM network will not be easy. As you know, they have all the technology the Soviets had and I'm sure it's all in working order. You've got about five days to figure out how to get us past them. We can be brought in by sea or by air, that will be determined by what you believe is the best way to obviate their defenses.

"Spencer, your job is to research our archives and get a handle on disarming those babies. The Pentagon has all the bird shots of those missiles. They'll be able to give you whatever you need to know. After we photographed them back in 1962, we did a very thorough analysis, as you know those boys do, and they have a complete profile of everything you'll need to know. Part of the data they got when we picked up one of the Soviet

KGB boys who was on his way to Siberia after a boo-boo he made. From the report Willy showed me, it seems he preferred coming over here as opposed to the permanent winter chalet they were offering him.

"Eliot, it will be your job to train us all for the rigors we'll be going through once we get to Cuba. No matter what Joel comes up with, be it sea or air, we surely won't be arriving too close to the missiles. I believe we can count on the fact that Fidel has them well under guard. So no matter the means of arrival, we're all going to be on basic maneuvers, and boys, if you guys are anywhere near the shape I'm in, we're in trouble.

"Eliot, I've made arrangements with the boys down in Quantico for us to have a couple of weeks there for a heavy-duty workout.

"I chose Quantico for two reasons. First because I felt it would be better to be away from Fort Meade; the further we are away from General Anderson, the better, at least that's the way Willy wants it. Second is Barry. Being a retired Lt. Colonel, our friend here still has lots of contacts in the corps that may be handy for information Barry may need. So, I figure, Barry's got a job to do, we've got to train, they've got great facilities, what more could you ask for."

"God," Joel said, "couldn't you get us to somewhere a little nicer? This is the first time in a long time I'm getting away and you pick Quantico."

"This isn't a pleasure trip, Joel, in case you've missed this discussion I've been having here," Henry said.

"Quantico is essential for Barry. It will be his job to navigate the SIREN team once we're in."

"Sure," Barry said, "It's one of my favorite pastimes, don't you! It's what I do all day at NSA or did you forget they've now got me listening in. It's boring work but it's going to sure come in handy for this one."

Henry cut in again and said, "Barry, I didn't bring you in on this one just for your Cuban accent. Your job is going to be to navigate us through the territory. This, as I mentioned before, is a big part of the reason why we're training in Virginia. While we're all working out during the day, each of us will have homework at night. Your homework, Barry, is going to be to brush up on all of the maps they're holding down there and make a comparison of what the birds see on their flybys and what we have in the way of maps left over from the Bay of Pigs Invasion."

"Guys, this is going to be a tough one, like I said before. But this time, we're going to finally beat Fidel at his own game.

"If the US government can stall for the approximate four weeks, we need to do this, we'll finally beat this bastard at his own game. We missed him during the Bay of Pigs, and he's laughed at us ever since."

Barry cut in again and said, "What makes you think we can get in and do this? I mean, he's going to be watching things pretty tight, and even with all our skills and if we get in, we're going to need time to do the job." "How much time do you think we'll need?" he asked Spencer.

Spencer answered, "The way I see it without having seen any schematics, we'll need at least one or two hours. It won't be easy. This stuff's going to be old. We don't know what kind of condition they're in. I mean I don't feel like I want to be moving too fast with thirty-year-old warheads."

Henry then said, "Well, that's where a very special wrinkle is coming in, boys. I've got a distraction for Fidel; he's called Peter Kennedy."

Henry then proceeded to tell them about Peter and how they met and his plan for using Peter again. He briefly gave them Peter's bio and what he's been doing over the years and said, "Boys, this guy's perfect for the decoy, and Fidel will never suspect a thing. Today is Fidel's lucky day; we're about to put him into the biotech business. We're going to get him to buy off that the CIA is as willing as ever to illegally facilitate an undercover biotechnology business just like some of those clowns started when they were financing Saddam and putting him in the chemical business. He's got to believe that if the American government was willing to do that in exchange for some hostages, we'd certainly be prepared to trade technology for his missiles to avoid a world confrontation. Believe me, he's going to bite this one, hook, line, and sinker. Boys, the party's just beginning."

The next day, Henry got into his office over at NSA early.

When he got in, his administrative assistant, Nan, was sitting at the desk.

"Well, it's been a dog's age since I've seen you here this early," Nan said. "The last time I saw you in before 9:00 a.m. was when you were preparing for the hearings on the Grenada fiasco."

"We've got lots of work to do, Nanette, so come in my office and let's get started."

Nan knew something was up when he switched to calling her Nanette. Nan was thirty-five, small, petite, and she wore her hair in a short Peter Pan cut. Never married and had no children, her life revolved around her career. Nan was raised on a farm in a small town just outside of Santa Barbara, California. Her parents were traditional; her father worked from sunup till sundown on their chicken farm and her mother tended to the children. She had a twin sister and an older brother, and while they were all living in different cities, they remained close, as that was part of the family tradition. Nan possessed those small-town values that made her something out of a Norman Rockwell picture. Her traditional values gave rise to a devout commitment to honesty. This often gave rise to conflicts in some of the projects she worked on, after all working at the NSA was at times covert. She was a civilian employee at NSA. She had all the clearances required and had been with Henry for seven years. She was a transfer from California, where she worked at Edwards Air Force Base. Her skills were more than secretarial. Nan could think like a man and act like a woman; that's what made her so valuable. With the types of assignments Henry was involved with, he needed someone who could take charge when he was away. Henry also needed someone who knew how to cover for him and that was really important. With covert operations, not everyone was always on the same team and knew what was going on. Nan had an uncanny way of juggling and keeping it all together. One of her specialties was research, and that's what Henry needed today.

"Nan," Henry said, "we're about to begin an assignment and I need someone special to act as a decoy during the entire operation." He continued, "There's someone I want you to hook on this one, but I don't yet know how we're going to get him. So, I want you to get started today on this guy."

Henry briefly gave Nan the bio on Peter Kennedy and how they first met. He explained the entire program they were going into, in light of Castro's recent revelation to the United Nations. He further explained where Peter was going to fit in and why he guessed he might have trouble recruiting him.

Nan asked, "Why do you think this guy Kennedy is going to be willing to get involved in this one?"

"I don't think he will go into this one, not voluntarily anyway," Henry said.

"So I ask you again, Henry, what makes you think you can hook him?" she said. "I mean he sounds like he's clean, so how are you going to recruit him?"

"That's where you come in, my compatriot," Henry said. "This is where you really excel."

"I don't get," Nan said, "He's not in government, he doesn't deal drugs, so what's the catch?"

Henry turned around, got up from his large leather chair, and walked to the window. "Nan," he said, "research is what you do best and with your data gathering about to turn blackmail into an invitation, you find something on this guy, something he can't walk away from."

Nan said again, "But this guy's probably clean, what makes you think we can find anything on him?"

"Nobody's clean, Nan," he said. "Everybody's got closets and in those closets are skeletons. He got to have some. Are you trying to tell me that you have none, Nan?"

Nan looked with a startled glare. "Sure, maybe I've got some, but there's nothing in my closet that you could use to make me do what you want this guy to do," Nan answered.

"No, Nan, maybe not in your closet but perhaps in your family's or an old boyfriend's or someone you knew. The point is," Henry said, "that no one has lived a clean and perfect life. We were all young, we all grew up, and we've all made mistakes. I'm hard-pressed to believe that anyone who's made any kind of decent income in their life has done everything by the book. Anyway," Henry said, "that's what I want you to research, find something on him or his family. Bring in extra people if you need. Just let me know and I'll clear the funds or personnel, whatever it is you need. One caveat to all this, Nan, is that you've got one week at the maximum to get me something."

"Okay," Nan said, "but I wish I was as sure as you that everyone's got a soft spot somewhere."

"Believe me, Nan, in the twenty-odd years I've been in the business, I've met very few people who didn't have a bone or two in their closet," Henry said.

Nan got up to leave the office to get started immediately. As she got up, Henry said, "Oh, by the way, call down to records and get me the complete file on our black work during the Falklands."

Nan said, "I really don't think they'll have it still; it's been more than ten years now."

"Then have records contact archives and put through an urgent retrieval request," Henry said. "Tell them, we need it for British Intelligence, that way if they ask you what the rush is, you can push it off on them. After all, we don't know what they're up to, we only know good relations are important and we aim to please our partners across the pond. Oh, and tell them before noon."

Nan left the office and closed the door on the way out; it was a habit Henry liked. In the spook business, you just kind of get used to closed doors.

Henry walked back to his chair and fell into it. He looked around the office and thought to himself of the timetables that would have to be met. He felt comfortable with the idea of contacting Peter Kennedy even before Nan had finished her research.

He reasoned contact this early would be good, if only in allowing himself the opportunity to get reacquainted with Peter. He needed to assess how Peter had grown. What kind of biotech contacts through business he might have in Cuba? After all, most companies were doing business with Cuba, if only through alternative channels.

It was noon and like clockwork Nan showed up with the Falklands file. Henry immediately opened it and turned to the section on freelance recruits. There it was, Peter Kennedy, Annapolis, Maryland. Eight years with Syntex Laboratories, current assignment, manager of scientific products for South America. He read further and found his US address. He picked up the phone and called information. They had a listing but when Henry inquired about the address, he'd found that Peter had moved. The operator gave him the new number and he hung up. He dialed the number, it rang, but there was no one in, just an answering machine. He left his name and number and asked Peter to call him as soon as he could. He said he needed a name which Peter would have regarding someone at Syntex International.

Next, Henry picked up the phone and called all the members of team SIREN. He told each of them to report to Quantico tomorrow morning by 0800 hours, "We're about to begin." he said, when they arrived, and Willie would be there to get them settled. Willie would have all of their assignments ready, and they should begin the rehearsal. He'd be there within one week and then they'd begin as a team. Target launch for the operation was four weeks and counting.

Henry got a call from Peter Kennedy that afternoon. Peter said he was surprised and shocked at the call. He said it kind of made his adrenaline pump, like it did back in the Argentina during the Falklands War.

Henry thought to himself, *Good he's remembering the rush and excitement of his secret work*. Perhaps, Henry thought, this will be an easier job of recruitment than he thought.

Henry asked Peter if they could get together for lunch. He asked Peter if he was still in the same field, biotechnology. When Peter said yes, Henry asked if they could get together for lunch as he needed some information about Peter's field and thought perhaps Peter could be of help.

Peter said, "Sure, where do you want to meet and when?" Henry suggested a place near the capital called the Monocle, a place he frequented due to the nature of his work. The Monocle was close to Justice Department. Henry's work often called for a close association with the boys downtown, and as a consequence, he was familiar with this restaurant as a quiet and safe place to meet. They agreed to meet the next day at noon and they hung up. Henry smiled and thought, *Okay, we've got the ball rolling. Maybe this won't be so hard after all.*

Peter was now forty-six years old. He was tall, about six feet two inches, had thinning hair but was generally in good shape. Working out was the only way Peter figured he could try to beat the aging game. He knew it was a losing battle, but his vanity kept him at it. He was single with two sons, one in high school and the other in college. His older son was on a football scholarship and the younger one was a ladies' man.

Peter grew up in middle America during the fifties. He came from a working-class family, and as most postwar babies, he was swept up in a college-bound direction based on the friends he had at the time. He graduated from the City University of New York with a degree in economics. Due to the Vietnam War, he chose to go into teaching in order to avoid the draft. Eventually Peter went on to graduate school to get his PhD and went on to teaching economics at the University of Arizona.

After a few years of teaching, Peter saw that financially this was never going to take him anywhere. At that point, he decided to get into the corporate world and try to make a real living. With his flair for people and his background as an economist, he fit well into the world of corporate development. He was articulate in the academic realm and most accomplished when it came to negotiating with people. It was while working for a large American healthcare company that Peter met Henry in Argentina.

Peter's wife died when the kids were young. The oldest was nine and the younger was six when it happened. He got an au pair through an agency to live in and help him with the kids. This allowed him to at least earn a living and continue a career.

He had had a few romances in his life since his wife passed away but being single with two kids did not necessarily present an ideal situation for most women. He hoped one day he would meet someone, but at the rate he travelled and with his commitment to his kids, there just didn't seem to be the time or space. As the kids grew, he did his best to provide love and a good home. The kids fared well, and the result was two fine sons that any man would be proud of. At the moment with the kids now older, he was travelling again. His current consulting job was setting up distribution for a generic pharmaceutical firm in South America, a job he was not particularly crazy about but it paid the rent.

What Peter really wanted to do was go back to teaching economics. But positions were hard to find, what with all the baby boomers out of work. The eighties were brutal to most of the middle management of corporate America. Peter was happy to be under contract and to have talents people were willing to pay for. Anyway, Peter thought, you could starve to death on a professor's salary.

Peter's mind at this moment was wandering all over the board. Perhaps it was that call from Henry St. John. *God, that was an exciting time*, he thought as he pulled into the valet parking lot at the Monocle Restaurant.

The Monocle was a beautiful old traditional Washingtonian restaurant. It was near the Supreme Court and Justice Department, so the patrons were typically the government type. The only difference was they were the white-collar government people, middle management, and up. The wallpaper was a dark burgundy; it kind of reminded you of a cross between a brothel and an antebellum southern home.

When Peter walked in, he looked around and saw Henry sitting near the bar in a corner booth. Henry got up and said, "Long time no see, my friend." The greeting was warm on both sides and Peter enjoyed seeing Henry. Peter was immediately reminded of their time together. Seeing Henry's face thrust him back ten years and the remembrances gave him a feeling of rejuvenation.

Peter truly loved the excitement of that chapter in his life. While what Peter had done, he did to serve his country and ease his conscience for not having served in Vietnam, he was, at the time, enthralled with the idea that he was doing something really special. Today while driving to the meeting, he thought to himself, *I wonder what Henry really wants.*

Peter liked the edge. There was something about the adrenaline that felt good. Back in graduate school, he rode in motocross races, and he liked soaring in gliders. Anything as long as there was a challenge, and he could test himself. Testing himself was where Peters excelled. To the edge, the scarier, the better, only Peter liked to know the limits. He wasn't crazy and didn't want to get killed, but a little excitement was a feeling he liked.

Deep down inside, Peter was hoping perhaps Henry wanted him to do something again. Whatever it was, the idea of reliving what was an exciting time in his life was making his heart pump.

Henry began by apologizing for getting him down there on a ruse. Peter interrupted immediately and said, "I kind of had a feeling it wasn't about some information on the biotech field."

"Well, in a way it sort of is," Henry said. "You see, we got a little problem with our friend Fidel as I'm sure you've heard by now. The whole God damned thing has been all over CNN and the rest of the media since this thing has been announced. What we've got here is a true communist who thinks he can deal with the West the way the Eastern European Bloc countries are doing right now."

Henry paused and started again, "You see, with Russia and Yeltsin, we're doing this missile deal for two reasons. First because we obviously want to get control of those missiles and secondly because Russia and those other countries are fledgling democracies.

"We're only bolstering those countries which are aspiring to reform their own countries. We can't very well expect Yeltsin to fight off the old hardline communist guard from taking over if we make out like we'll deal with anybody. This would be the hard-liners' opportunity to jump in and say, 'Hey, we don't have to go the reform route, we'll just trade the missiles for Western cash and aid or use them as bargaining chips with other countries who will do the bidding for him.'"

"So, you see, we can't really do the deal with Castro; he's kind of missed the point," Henry said. "So where this puts us is in a different direction and that's what the government is working on right now. The real reason I invited you here today is I could use you again."

Peter's heart soared at the idea that there was something here very exciting just around the bend. He couldn't hold himself back from quietly shouting, "So what do you want me to do?"

Henry sat back in the chair, stared at Peter, and thought to himself, *this is too good to be true; he's actually excited about the possibility of being involved again.* Henry paused and said, "We want you to go in there. It's part of a plan I have, what do you think?"

It was now Peter's turn to sit back and stare. Peter responded by saying, "I know I speak Spanish and I've travelled a lot, but what makes you think I could do anything in this situation? I mean, this isn't like Argentina where I just snorted out some information on fuel reserves. I mean, I'm no soldier of fortune."

"I've got two kids, and besides, what makes you think I could get information for you from Fidel Castro himself?" Peter said.

Henry spoke, "I didn't say it was information gathering. As a matter of fact, I don't think I said what it was I wanted you to do. But on that note, I will give you a brief outline of what the assignment would be."

"I can't tell you a lot, as obviously it's all classified, and until you're in, the details have to be, by the nature of this situation, secret."

"Before I begin, Peter," Henry said, "I want you to know what I'm about to tell you is very confidential. Like the IRS, we're everywhere and if I go further and tell you more, and should any of this get out, we'll make your life miserable. Do I make myself perfectly clear?"

Peter felt the adrenaline rush. He thought to himself, *hey, what the heck, I've got nothing to worry about. I'm not going to say anything, let's hear about this. After all, if it's too scary, I can decline and just keep my mouth shut.* "Okay," Peter said, "I'm listening, and I know the consequences if I open my mouth.

"Remember, I've got kids and a whole normal life to protect. I'm not interested in shooting off my mouth and having you guys wreaking havoc on my life. Go ahead, your secrets are safe with me," Peter said.

Henry began by describing what took place with that section of the CIA who were supplying Saddam Hussein with the chemicals through Miami before the Iraq War. He went on, "Your job will be a decoy, Peter. We'll set you up and get you in under the guise as a contractor of bacteriological agents. You're in biotechnology. You know a lot about cloning bacteria. It would be a piece of cake for you to make it look real. We'll be, in the meantime, planning a covert operation to get to the missiles and disarm them."

Peter looked at Henry and said, "Wait a minute. What makes you think you could set me up and he'd believe it?"

Henry said, "I can't give you the details now, but while the US and the UN are stalling him, he's going to get edging and start to think about the very thing we're planning."

Peter said, "Yeah, I know. Again, what makes you think he'll bite on me showing up at the time he's negotiating his missiles away and he's already sensing something's not kosher?"

"Don't worry about that," Henry said. "We've got that figured. As I said, I can't give you the details; I only want to know if you want in."

Peter looked down, and he thought to himself, *God, this is crazy. I've let this thing go too far. Do I really want into this thing*? He looked up at Henry and said, "Listen, guy, I'm flattered you were thinking of me, and to tell you the truth, when I got here today, I was excited at the prospect of being involved with you guys again. I mean, it was great. I loved what I did before, but this is a whole lot more, Henry, and I feel like it's out of my league."

Henry heard it all and he thought to himself, *Yeah, it was too good to be true. He likes the edge but not this close. So I guess it's going to be up to Nan.*

As Henry's thoughts cleared his head, he spoke, "Well, Peter, I can't say I thought for sure you'd be interested, but I was hoping."

Henry's thoughts turn to the next ploy, money. "There'd be money in it for you, you know. There'd be enough so that if we pulled this one off, you'd be set for life. You know about these covert things; it's not just what you read in books, we have funds."

Peter responded and said, "It's going to have to be a no, Henry; it's just out of my league. I'm sorry."

Henry heard it all. He just sat there listening and thinking to himself, *I'm sorry, guy, but we're pulling you in whether you know it or not.*

Henry spoke again and said, "Well, I tried. I guess we'll have to look at some alternative plans. I hope you'll sleep on it, guy. It could mean a lot to the kids financially and for you. Okay then, but remember, not a word of this or your life could get miserable, and I mean real miserable."

As they were departing, Peter turned to Henry and said, "Why can't you get someone else like me? I mean, if you can plant the idea and stage, it with Castro to make it believable, why not get someone else?"

"Because you were perfect," Henry said. "You'd been tested. You'd been out there before for us, so we know how believable you are. Besides, it's not just your Spanish, but your contacts in the biotech field. To pull this off, the decoy has got to really know the stuff; otherwise, if he's tripped up, it could be a fatal situation for that person and a failure for the mission. And the way I see it, we're going to have one and only one shot at this plan."

Peter said, "Well, I'm sorry. It's just out of my league. I wish you guys' luck and if I can help you in any way, just let me know. Oh and don't worry, like I said, this conversation won't go beyond today and us."

Henry shook his hand, turned, and said, "Be seeing ya."

The next morning when Henry got into his office, Nan was sitting there with a big smile. Henry saw this when he walked in and said, "tell me you've got something good, sweetie. I like that smile on your face."

"It's good," Nan said, "really good. Peter Kennedy's father is seventy-eight years old."

"Yeah, and that's supposed to mean what," Henry said.

"It means," Nan said, "if Peter's father were to go away to jail, the chances are he'd never see daylight again in his lifetime."

"This sounds good, Nan, keep going."

Nan continued, "Peter's dad was a longshoreman during the sixties and seventies. He retired in 1981. It appears by all records that his spending habits, while not exorbitant, clearly exceed his possible income. Further we've done a trace on safety deposit box visits and he visits them quite frequently."

"So the bottom line is this guy is hiding bucks and we could probably run him down and eventually get him on income tax evasion."

Henry asked, "But could we really get him?"

Nan answered, "Well, if given enough time, we definitely could. The point is, as I see it, Henry, Peter won't know that and this is the hook you could use to bring him in."

Henry liked it. He felt like he was seeing daylight and things would be coming together. With Peter in, he could now start to work on the rest of the operation. *Great*, Henry thought. He leaned over and gave Nan a peck on the cheek. He said, "Please don't consider this sexual harassment; you're just so good, it blows my mind."

"Okay," Henry said, "I'll get started on some of the other stuff and I'll contact Peter tomorrow and break it to him then."

As Nan left Henry's office, she felt bad about the sting, but it was her job and what she did well, research. She always took these things kind of hard. After all trapping people by blackmail was sort of counterculture to her Norman Rockwell upbringing, but as Nan saw it, dirty laundry was dirty laundry, and it wasn't her fault that Peter's dad had some bones in his closet. She closed her eyes and said, "God, save this crazy world we live in, and God protect this poor guy's butt."

Chapter 3

Fernando's Reunion

Fernando got off the plane in Havana at Jose Marti International Airport. Jose Marti, liberator and hero of Cuba before Castro's time. Fidel in many ways saw himself as his reincarnation. Fernando was quickly whisked away in a private car waiting on the tarmac. He was to be brought directly to Fidel. Castro's orders were clear and definitive, "I want him brought to me as soon as he lands."

While driving from the airport to the Capitol Building in Havana, Fernando's mind wandered back to the events of the last week. He felt good at what had transpired; he had succeeded.

The roads were desolate on the way into the city. Cuba today was short of cars as well as gasoline. Due to the US embargo on trade, parts for the repair of automobiles were scarce. Cuba's whole transportation pool of cars was primarily old Chevys and other American makes. Most of the other automobiles on the island were Russian made and those parts, even in light of trade with Russia, were near impossible to get a hold of due to the breakup of the former Soviet Union. Most of the manufacturing was broken up into the different satellite countries and now it was impossible to get any parts since you couldn't determine which country had what parts.

Upon nearing the city limits of Havana, the streets were empty too, except for the crowded buses that went roaring by. *Ah, but beautiful Cuba, it is so good to be back*, Fernando thought, *from its wonderful beaches to its high jagged mountain ranges.* From it's beautiful valleys, lakes, and rivers, it was a land of wonderful variety. It was no wonder that it was a fond vacation spot of the rich Americans.

Cuba was a country of many wonders, and prior to the revolution, Cuba truly was the playground of the affluent. As a country, it was quite large as compared to many of the other Caribbean islands. About the size of Pennsylvania, it offered everything one could want in a getaway only ninety miles from Miami. Now, under communism, Cuba had become quite attractive to Canadians and Europeans. It was a veritable bargain, from the cost of hotels to food and entertainment. There was no US Embassy in Havana anymore; however, there still was an American Interests Section there working out of the old US Embassy Building, now officially the Embassy of Switzerland.

The Special Interests Section was just that, the Americans' way of taking care of business without having diplomatic connections. When manufacturers and/or other US commodity companies, be they in sugar or cigars, needed to be assisted, that's what the American Special Interests Section did, assist them. It was and continued to be the hypocrisy of the US trade policy. Assist, but maintain the facade we don't do business with Cuba. Most Americans did business through Canada, but it was only enough for the rich to get richer, never enough to empower Cuba economically.

With the loss of over five billion yearly in financial support from the Warsaw Pact, Cuba was now literally falling apart. While driving into Havana, a city of just over two million people, the dramatic deterioration of the infrastructure was evident everywhere. The city had the power to both excite you and depress you. It was a city of what once was and now what wasn't. The sites of the old Spanish architecture were strong reminders of their founders. The more contemporary buildings of Art Deco design were all falling apart. Their paint peeling because Cuba lacked the resources to save an era that once made this country the jewel of the Caribbean.

As Fernando peered out the window, they passed the Museum of the Revolution, which was located in the former Presidential Palace of Batista, where you could see the motor launch "Granma" from which Castro landed to start the revolution in 1956. Next, they passed some bookshops and old department stores. While large and cavernous inside, the stores were almost empty. Once again reminding Fernando of the poverty and emptiness that was Cuba today.

They arrived in front of the Capitol at about twelve noon. A soldier outside the car opened the door and saluted Fernando. Fernando carried the rank of colonel, an easy feat when you were Fidel's cousin. The Capitol Building in Havana had been modeled after the US Capitol and had that grand look to it despite all the squalor surrounding it. As he went up the steps, his heart pounded with excitement. *Fidel will be most pleased*, he thought.

When he walked into Fidel's office, he saw Fidel standing there. He was wearing his traditional green fatigues. His beard was as prominent as ever, his trademark. Even for a man of his age, he looked strong and powerful. His persona, which had captured the masses, was unmistakable. He held a baseball mitt in one hand and a hardball in the other hand. He looked up at Fernando, slammed the ball into the mitt, and said, "Welcome, me amigo. I've been waiting for your return."

Fidel was still fond of baseball. In his youth, Castro was quite a baseball player. He had even once tried out for the Washington Senators farm team. Had he made the team that season, the world today might have been a very different place.

"So," Fidel said, "tell me of your success. Let us sit and have a fine cigar and speak of how great we are now."

Fidel tended to speak dramatically. It was part of his rhetoric. It's what Hitler and other tyrants of history fed on, the passion that was emoted when they spoke before the crowds. His tone was always strong and accented. When sitting across from him, even for a nonbeliever it was hard to not become impassioned when you listened.

Fidel continued, "Fernando, our country, our people are to be proud of you. With the success of your trip, our future grows better each day. They will negotiate now and if they do not, we will still have yet another tool."

"I have been in contact with Ortega, and he feels confident something is going to come of this and by whatever measure, we will be stronger and our position with the rest of the world will be better," Fidel said. "People will see that we take care of the poor and the unfortunate. That there are no enclaves of the rich. No ruling class."

While listening, Fernando thought, *We will gain many friends. Our friends in Russia and some of the other countries will see the way. This will give our old comrades new hope. These new fledgling governments of theirs will no longer flourish. The people will see this. The party will again rise because capitalism only breeds corruption and greed.* Fernando was totally absorbed in the cause, he was committed. Suddenly, his thoughts and his mind turned back to where he was, in the presidential office, listening to Fidel.

Fidel was repeating with a tone affirmation to his voice, "I believe all will go well; we will benefit much from this, *si, todo esta bien*."

Fernando began by recounting his arrival in Miami and their success in planting the warhead. He did not speak of Juan and the killing that took place. The thought of Juan brought some pain to Fernando. He knew that Fidel cared little for those who served us. As far as he was concerned, they were all traitors who left Cuba and abandoned the revolution. Fernando ended by telling him of his meeting with Ortega and his flight back to Cuba. Finally, Fernando asked, "So tell me, where we are today with the Americans and the United Nations?"

"Well," Fidel began, "Ortega has delivered the message as he was supposed to. The US ambassador has been talking with our mission in New York City. At the present time, they are going through the motions and are trying to think of ways to stall. It is, however, important to note that the Americans as well as the world press have done just what we wanted; they've blown it up, which has made the world shake a little at the thought that we have nuclear weapons.

"Soon we will begin negotiations and Cuba will regain what it needs, financial power. I believe they will have all sorts of conditions attached, but in the end, they will give in to a negotiated trade for the warheads."

Fernando looked at Fidel with all the hopes and aspirations of a twenty-one-year-old. His youth and energy for the revolution was still there. The power of the revolution was so great for him that he saw nothing else.

After hours of revolutionary talk, they both wearied of the day and the conversation. It was getting late and Fernando now longed to depart even his great mentor. He wanted to go home, see his family, and try to put his past week behind him.

While the cause was his life, the tasks he performed were more than he had expected. They'd taken their toll on him. When he first left for the mission, he was confident. He'd killed before but never someone so close. It took on a whole new meaning. Someone's life, whom you knew, was now gone. There was history. There were memories and that was something he'd never felt before with someone who had to die. All the others, while not many, were strangers or enemies, not someone you knew. While undaunted by his faith and beliefs, he now faced living with a contradiction in emotion and intellect. He was not sure if it would be resolved, but he knew he was tired and he longed for the comfort and sanctuary of his home and familiar surroundings.

There was silence at the end of Fidel's last words. They looked at one another a moment, as if to say without words, we wait now for the Americans.

As Fernando turned to the doors to leave, he looked back at Fidel, like a father, and said to himself, *I did it for the cause.*

Somehow though, he felt Fidel could not share or know his conflict. He walked through the heavy doors, leaving Fidel's office, the two guards outside saluted as he passed, heading for the grand stairs of the Capitol's entrance. While walking down the stairs, the fading sunlight of the day was coming through the massive doors of the Capitol's rotunda below. The sunlight of day's end shown. It reflected his own sense of dusk at that moment. The exhilaration of his arrival that day was now gone. He thought only of the drive to Mariana, home.

He entered the limousine at the foot of the steps to the Capitol and reclined in the rear seat. He turned to the driver and said, "*Adelante*, go." On the drive to his small town and home, he tried to close his eyes as they drove. The drive was not long, perhaps twenty minutes. He could not sleep; he just stared out the windows and read the signs on the billboards as they passed. Pictures of people in agrarian settings, working together on the collective. Larger than life slogans, words like "struggle," "victorious," and "conquering" were everywhere. The revolution was everywhere, now the question was "could it all be as it once was?" Fernando wondered; *Would the world be changed by his deeds?* Like all great things, only time would tell; patience was their ally.

Chapter 4

The Operation

Henry called Peter on the telephone and said they had to get together, that there'd been a change and he needed to see him immediately. It was now just three days since the announcement from the Cuban Mission delegate, Jose Ortega, that Cuba wanted a deal with the West, more specifically the Americans.

Henry told Peter to meet him around 11:00 a.m. that morning at the same restaurant they'd met at before. Peter responded by saying he wasn't sure he could get away. Henry made it clear that he had to find a way; it was extremely important, he needed him.

The urgency in Henry's voice was as powerful as it was compelling. Peter felt tenseness in his gut. There was a sense of urgency that gave Peter that edge that thrilled him. Perhaps, he thought, he could still help Henry out without being in too deep. In an odd way, uncertainty was part of Peter's personality and he thrived on it. It was part of what made him so good in the commercial world, the thrill of competing and winning against the unknown. He was disappointed that he had to turn down the opportunity before, but he knew it was way over his head. Peter liked danger, but based on the scenario Henry painted, there appeared to be a real chance that someone could get hurt or even disappear.

He cancelled all his morning appointments. He put on his coat and walked out the door. He walked to his car with a sense of mission which Henry had given him, only he didn't know that today for him would begin a journey that was going to alter his life in a way he was not prepared for.

He arrived at the Monocle Restaurant right on time. The valet took his car and gave him his ticket. He thought to himself, *Better he'd not forget to validate it this time.* That was to be one of Peter's last mundane thoughts for a long time to come.

When he walked in, Henry was sitting in the booth where they met at their last meeting. He walked over and sat across from him.

Henry began, "Thank you for coming, Peter. I'm sure it was difficult to get away on such short notice, but this is extremely important. Do you recall the first time we met in Argentina? At that time, my associate and I were trying to tell you of the significance of what we were doing down there during the war.

"If you remember, we discussed the fact that thousands of lives often depended on when a conflict could be stopped.

"Well, at that time you understood what you were doing and what it meant for the British forces. Enabling the British to find out in advance just how much petroleum reserves Argentina had which had shortened the war. In many ways you saved a lot of lives, whether you've ever given much thought to that or not."

Peter stared, he listened, and then said, "And I guess I really never thought I had made that much of a difference."

With all his strength and sincerity, Henry spoke, "You really did have a tremendous impact on what happened to a lot of innocent people, and now could you do that again, except for your own country?"

"Now hold on," Peter interrupted, "I know this thing with Castro is important, but like I said before, this is way over my head. I hope you didn't bring me here to try and sell this crazy plan of yours again?"

"No, Peter, I didn't. I brought you here to tell you that you're in and there are no choices."

"Listen," Peter said, "I told you before this is way out of my league. Surely you haven't been in the spy business that long that you can't understand the word no."

"The word no I understand, Peter," Henry said. "It's you who doesn't understand your position here." Henry continued, "Peter, we did a little research on your family and, well, we found that all things aren't what they should be."

"Now, I don't like having to do this, but you've got to understand my side of the world. In the business I'm in, we're sort of the policemen of the world, if you will. We don't necessarily like doing what we do, but we didn't create some of the maniacs of the world. I'm just doing what I've been trained to do, 'Protect and Serve.' Do you think we created Saddam Hussein or Idi Amin? These jerks just crop up. We didn't call up Radovan Karadzic in Serbia because we wanted some more insanity in the world. These lowlifes just arrive on the scene, and it's our job to either control them or stop them.

Henry's eyes locked with Peter's, and he said, "Listen, a lot of guys out there do this because they're off on some power trip; me, I do it because it's got to be done. Now we don't know what that maniac down there in Cuba will do, but we also can't afford to guess; there's too much at stake. We've got to stop him, and we can't take chances. Unfortunately, Peter, that's where you fit in."

Peter started to get up when Henry said, "We've got your father."

Peter stopped in his tracks and looked directly at Henry and said, "What do you mean you've got my father?"

Henry proceeded to explain to Peter about his father and his days as a longshoreman. About his pension and how much it was, along with the fact that the records show he lives above his means, albeit modestly, Henry added. After that, Henry explained how they could put his father away for enough time that, at seventy-eight years of age, he wouldn't be seeing daylight again.

Peter was outraged, his blood boiled, and all he could think of was "pricks, all of you."

He sat for a moment and thought. His mind raced. *Is this really happening? This isn't some spy novel or a screenplay out of the movies. There must be some way out of this, a law; surely, they can't just decide they're going to blackmail you and that's that. There are laws; I'll get an attorney.*

When Peter's thoughts cleared, he spoke. "Listen, Henry, this isn't the movies and my father's an old man. You can't possibly believe you could get a court to put away a seventy-eight-year-old man for the rest of his life for a little embezzlement. You said so yourself, it was only a modest way of life. He doesn't give off the picture you're typecasting."

"Face it, Henry," Peter said, "it would be a long shot for you to pull off putting away a senior citizen. The press would have a field day and I would be right there, telling the whole story to the world. You guys would be crucified."

Henry just stared at Peter and didn't say anything.

Peter returned the stare and knew that for all the words he just spewed out, it didn't amount to a hill of beans. He couldn't believe it, but somehow, he knew Henry was winning and he wouldn't be walking away from this.

Henry continued his stare. He then said, "We can put him away, Peter, and we will if you refuse. Peter, it's not so bad. You'll be doing it for America. You'll be okay. We're not going to hang you out to dry; you'll be covered and if at any time we think you're in danger, we'll pull you in. This is our business, Peter, we know what we're doing."

"Oh, and is that why Ollie North got caught with his pants down?" Peter said. "Where were you guys then, huh? Hey, he didn't do time, did he? No, but it was close. What would make me think you good old boys down at the agency would come to my rescue. Why should I believe you, after all, this whole thing is beginning to feel like I really am in a movie?"

Henry interrupted Peter's tirade, "Remember what you said in Argentina, how you didn't serve during Vietnam and the guilt you had over that? Well, now you'll be doing more than just affecting America's well-being; you're going to have an impact on the world."

Peter thought to himself and said, "Okay, so if I did believe you about my father, what exactly is it you want me to do?"

Henry began, "Do you remember a few years back how Reagan was forced to do an arms-for-hostages deal?"

Peter nodded.

"Well," Henry said, "we're going to make Fidel believe that the CIA boys are at it again. It's very believable; the boys at Langley do it all the time. Remember the chemicals Saddam was getting out of Miami? It's what the undercover boys do when we can't message things publicly. What we plan to do is plant you as a CIA man offering to trade covertly for the missiles. Only this time we won't be trading chemicals or arms but something much more powerful and enduring, biotechnology."

Peter exclaimed, "What, you are crazy, he'll never believe it."

"Yes, he will," Henry said. "You see, we're going to offer him technology that will provide him a new world power, economically speaking. We're going to make Fidel believe he's saving face by giving the warheads to the US without giving up his communist regime. Given all the commotion going on in the US Congress and the news media coverage over these missiles, our covert offer of biotechnology as an alternative financial solution to his economic problems should do the trick.

"We'll be offering him the chance to rebuild his nation; the chance to genetically engineer Cuba's agriculture. I mean, food is one of Castro's biggest problems. Ever since his bright idea to decimate his forests and plant strawberries, this guy has done about as much wrong agriculturally as anyone could possibly have done. He will finally be able to feed his nation, a feat which to date he has not been successful at since he lost his Russian backers.

"He'll even be able to generate trade and hard currency by exporting his new biotechnology. With his revolutionary ego, this will mean his chance to show the world how wonderful communism is. He'll say to the world, 'Look at Cuba, we did it all without capitalism.'"

"So you see, Peter, we have something he'll bite on, big time," Henry said. "Castro will see this as our way of saving face. He'll know when you get to him that this is the only way it can be done. With his mental profile and the way he sees the

Western capitalism, he will see this as nothing more than par for the course. Like I said, it's arms for hostages, it's all the same. So don't be naive, he'll bite. I mean the reality is we've done this before and he knows it, so why not again? It's just going to be a different kind of trade."

Peter asked, "And are you really going to give it to him?"

Henry answered, "Not unless it's a last resort. It's our goal for you to occupy him and tease him with a little of it, while we, my team, are going in to disarm the missiles."

Henry continued, "You've got to believe me, this is going to work. We're offering him much more than arms; we're offering him economic freedom, a membership card to the future."

Peter almost believed it. He thought, *Well, what difference does it make whether I believe this or not, they own me.*

Henry said, "You'll be leaving in two days. We've got to get you started quickly. At this point or soon, Castro's going to be looking to the United Nations for some sort of response."

"You'll be given a special passport and a contact at the American Special Interests Section at the Swiss Embassy in Havana. You'll be introduced to all the right people, and you'll be talking with Castro before you know it."

Peter shook his head, "You guys must think this guy is stupid. It's all too soon, he'll see something."

"No, he won't," Henry said to Peter. "He'll be contacted through his man at the Cuban Mission in New York; this is being played totally legitimate. The only people who will know about our intentions to land in Cuba and disarm the missiles will be you, me, my team, and two others at the NSA."

"Now," Henry said, "you go home, take care of your personal affairs over the next two days, and then you're off to lovely Havana." Henry laughed, "You'll love it there; Myer Lansky did."

Henry continued, "And remember, you're in now. Going to anyone and telling them about this won't get you anywhere. It will all be denied, and on top of that, your father will be learning to sing his own swan song. He'll be singing it as we take him off to his final resting place, a cell in a federal penitentiary."

Peter got up from the table. There was no handshake this time, only a parting question, "When will I be hearing from you?"

Henry answered, "The day after tomorrow."

Peter quickly thought, *The kids, what am I going to tell them, better yet, what am I going to do with them? Well, I guess that's the least of my problems; right now, I've got to first try to believe this whole thing.*

As Peter walked into the parking lot, he felt nauseous, like there was a vacant space where his stomach should have been. He couldn't believe it. He was either going to do this or his father was going away. The thought made him sick. He gave the valet the ticket for his car, he looked at it, and absentmindedly thought, *Shit, I didn't validate it.* This day certainly didn't turn out the way he thought it was going to.

As he drove away, he recalled that night when he first met Henry in Argentina, only this time the exhilaration and thrill of the moment had been replaced with his own fear. He was way out of his league, he knew it, and there wasn't a thing he could do about it. He looked at the falling leaves on Constitution Avenue as he left Washington, DC, for the ride back to Annapolis. He thought of the season, autumn, a time for football, and the coming of Thanksgiving. For Peter, however, this was now the season of fear and nothing more.

Chapter 5

Quantico

Henry went back to his office at the NSA. It was about 1:30 p.m. and he was somewhat fatigued by his morning visit with Peter. He didn't really like the idea of trapping him, but there wasn't much choice. He knew Peter was right; this was way over his head, but he too had no choice. Peter was the best candidate for the plan.

When he came into his office, Nan greeted him with a half-hearted smile. She asked how it went and she could tell by Henry's look that the trap was sprung, and Peter was now in. He told her what had taken place and how it all played out. She knew that although this was Henry's business and it had been for twenty years, he never liked using people.

He didn't say much more; he just went to his office. Nan pressed the security button to let Henry pass. Henry had a key, but Nan always hit the button to open the door when Henry was a walking zombie and that's what he looked like this morning.

He said he'd be leaving for Quantico the first thing tomorrow morning to connect with the team.

At 7:00 a.m., Henry awoke at his townhouse in Old Town, Alexandria, Virginia. He got up out of the bed and walked to the window and gazed out onto the Potomac River. He felt ready today, perhaps readier today than he had been all week.

He'd resigned himself to what had to be done. Over his twenty years in the DIA, he'd learned to put away emotion. He felt bad about Peter Kennedy, but it had to be done. While looking out on the water, he felt filled with the energy he once knew when he was twenty-five. He turned and went into the bathroom, looked into the mirror, and was quickly reminded he was now forty-five. "Ah what the heck, I'm still as fit as I ever was." He shaved and got dressed.

Today he would wear his winter greens. Since he was going to be at Quantico, he felt he'd draw less attention when he arrived on base if he fit in with everyone there. While he was no longer in the military proper, he still carried his rank, and when necessary, he wore a uniform.

It was a cool fall day, with a bright sun. He was invigorated as he walked outside and felt the cool morning air. He started up his Austin Healy 3000 and it turned, and it purred like a newborn kitten. He got onto I-95 south and headed for Quantico.

He daydreamed as he rode and went over some of the plans, he believed team SIREN would have. It wasn't his nature to second-guess the guys, but after enough years of association, he had some ideas of how they were going to plan this excursion. He passed the Potomac mills outlet exit and thought of America. Could Castro ever understand how good it was here in America? We had everything we needed, and they had so little.

It seemed so apparent that capitalism offered the incentives to succeed. Sure, we had our crime and other social problems, but Castro had them too. The only difference was in America if you wanted to get ahead, you could. In Cuba, no one could get ahead unless you were one of the favored party members. The world was not perfect, but at least here, you could make it if you set your mind to it.

Henry entered Quantico through the main gate. Henry loved the gate entrance with its two red brick columns and flat gray black beam running between the two brick pillars, reading "Crossroad of the Marine Corps." At the gate, two marine guards were standing in front of a hanging placard which displayed the marine corps logo encircled with the phrase "Marine Corps Combat and Development Center."

Henry flashed his identification card from the NSA. They saluted, and he continued on through. Driving in on Fuller Road, he passed the base golf course and saw a few diehards out there in the cool sun, getting in an early eighteen holes.

He drove past Neville Road, where Quantico town was, where you could get everything you needed without ever having to leave the base. It was a nice center to the base. A. M. Balognese and Sons had been there long before Henry ever knew about

Quantico. Mr. Bolognese owned everything from the tailor shop to the marine store, where you bought your dress blues. Henry saw the Command Post Pub and remembered the countless nights, while training at Quantico, where he had gotten blitzed many times beyond recognition.

That was when Henry woke up to realize what type of situation he had volunteered for. It took several years until Henry finally accepted and adjusted to a life with which he had now become comfortable and familiar.

As he passed Neville Road, he also passed on the right Butler Hall. In front was a statue of a marine from the 6th Regiment during World War I.

The first time Henry saw it, it struck him odd that the inscription read "In memory of the marines who gave their lives in the World War," built in 1921. It was the first time that Henry grasped what the marines were all about. They were a tradition, and they served and fought, no matter what, for their country, "Semper fidelis, always faithful."

It was a cold night about twenty years ago when he first noticed the plaque said "The World War." It struck him that they didn't know at that time there was to be another war just some twenty years or so later. Well, like he was saying to Peter; we don't create the maniacs, they just appear. Who would have thought in 1918 that within another two decades, we'd have the next maniac, Adolf Hitler, coming to power and threatening the world! Henry was now at Bldg. 2043, Vehicle and Weapons

Registration. *The Corps*, Henry thought, *why would they all three registrations together.* He pulled over and went in to let them know about today's meeting and gave them clearance papers for some of the weapons they'd be leaving with. While he didn't want to expose himself to any more people than necessary, he also didn't want to get stopped when any of them were leaving the base, should they be carrying anything.

Willie had prepared special clearance docs that ensured their group had the highest clearance, and no questions would be asked of them no matter what the circumstances.

Henry went through the traffic circle and headed towards Larson Gymnasium. He knew the boys would be in there, getting their morning workout. He pulled up outside the gym and went inside. As he expected, there they were, playing hoops as hard as any young jocks in a schoolyard game. Spencer saw him first and signaled with a gesture of his head to the others to see that Henry had arrived.

They all shut it down quickly and trotted over to Henry. "Hey," Barry said, "want to shoot a few?" "I don't think so, guy, but I will buy you guys' breakfast."

"Okay, you're on," Eliot said, "but have your wallet out because we've just done about two hours in here and, I believe I speak for all of us, we're ready to chow down."

They left the gym and headed into Quantico town to the Command Post Pub. Eliot was well-known there and he knew he could get them to make just about anything for him.

Neville Road ran down the center of Quantico town. It was like a small street in middle America. It had small stores, from eateries to a tailor to a laundromat.

The parking was vertical to the curb, and it just sort of reminded you of the fifties, when life was simple and direct. Kind of like the days when Dwight D. Eisenhower and Mamie were in the White House. When people didn't burn flags and the good guys were easy to tell apart from the bad guys.

Henry looked around at his team and said to himself, *with these guys, I know we're going to make it; they're the best.*

The boys from team SIREN ate with all the vigor of marathon runners. Henry was most impressed with their appetites in light of the fact that not a man jack among them was under thirty-eight years old.

The conversation was mostly small talk, nothing about the mission since they weren't in a secure location. They talked about the normal things in life, such as family life and what was going on in their homes. Henry rarely spent much time or talked with the members of team SIREN anymore, except when they were involved with government work. Other than their operations work through the DIA, they all led fairly distant and distinctive lives from one another.

After they finished chowing down massive quantities of food, Henry said, "Let's get going over to Newlin Hall. We've got a private room over there in the basement where we can be secure and get down to business. This isn't a holiday, guys, or didn't you all know that?"

Newlin Hall was the Marine Corps Telecommunications Activity Center and also served as the computer school at Quantico. The latest in satellite information and other telecommunication operations were quartered there. Most of the personnel on the base had no knowledge of the setup. This was strictly an NSA setup, and except for a handful of people at the MCCDC base, no other people outside of special covert operations had knowledge of this area.

The setup was established at Quantico due to concerns about information leakage around the NSA. With the way the American media conducted itself, it wasn't even safe to set up covert operations in the location where they were supposed to be.

In general, deep cover operations were always carried out away from the location of the agency to which those people involved belonged. It was crazy that even your own backyard wasn't safe, but that's what you had to do when operations went completely outside of the realm of presidential or congressional authority. Henry knew from the git-go that this operation was definitely outside, by any definition, of the law.

When they finally got to the basement of Newlin Hall, they found themselves getting off the elevator at the basement level, facing a steel door. None of the members of team SIREN had ever been here before. This secure area was built after the Iran Arms-for-Hostages Deal. It was at that time that those in deep cover operations first realized that even at NSA, all that seems secure, obviously, was not. It was for this recent historical fact that General Anderson at the NSA had instructed Maj. William (Willie) B. O'Connor to develop this clandestine site.

Henry produced a metal-type credit card, inserted into a slot on a steel wall plate, and the heavy metal door opened. Once inside the room, team SIREN was ushered into the room by a wave of Henry's arm.

The room was large, approximately sixty-by-forty feet. Inside there were computer terminals against the walls to the left and right sides of the room. There obviously were no windows and the room gave off the aura of what could only be viewed as a "Doomsday Room," a last holdout area in the event of a nuclear war. In the center of the room was a large walnut table with enough chairs to seat twelve people. Over the table were four microphones in a line, stretched equidistant over the length of the table. In the center, above the table, was a central camera setup with four lens fanning out in each direction, north, south, east, and west, so as to be able to view all and any participants of any discussions. At the end of the table, about twenty feet back were two large electronic maps, dividing the world in half, as global maps often appear when placed in a two-dimensional scale. The maps were made of glass and obviously used fluid electronic technology for motion tracking for live time events.

Barry spoke first, "This is what I'd definitely call secure."

Joel laughed and said, "Only the best for Henry, you know."

Henry asked them all to be seated around the table so they could begin. He briefly covered the history of the room and explained that except for those in deep cover operations such as team SIREN, few others in their security business knew of this place.

Henry wasn't at all concerned with team SIREN's knowledge of this site, because these boys were deeper and more loyal than even Oliver North, and Ollie was a pretty dedicated character.

Henry began by going over the plan as it was set up. He explained that Peter Kennedy was already in and what his launch time was as the decoy. He gave them all the dates for Kennedy's departure and his planned time for team SIREN's departure. He was now ready to hear from the team on how they were going to get into Cuba, disarm the "Nukes," and get out. He turned first to Joel Johnson since he was the communications specialist and it was his job to make sure they could land, hit the target, and get out undetected.

Joel began, "First, I want you guys to know that our intelligence in the area of Cuba's electronic security is far from up-to-date. What I've been able to gain is only solid up to 1991, before Gorbachev departed. This could all be good information, but then again, like Iran after the fall of the Shah, much may have deteriorated by now; we just can't be sure.

"We know from our operatives in Cuba that military parts in general have been on a steady depletion since the cessation of supplies from Russia. Our birds in the sky give us some infrared pictures that tell us where their motion sensors are for landing purposes. We know where their troops are and when and how often they move them. Our operatives inside tell us that rather than improvements, their security seems to be no better, if not worse, due to their economic situation. I feel fairly confident that we know what's going on and how to get in undetected. It is important however, gentlemen, that we understand that these calculations may be in error, although I doubt it."

"Well," Henry said, "based on all the caveats you've just presented, are you or aren't confident we'll make it and are you ready to risk your life on it? After all, if we can't even get in, the rest of our chances become a moot point."

Joel responded with an "affirmative."

Next it was Barry Henson's turn to speak. Barry started with a bold, brash grin on his face. "Listen," he said, "I know enough about Cuba to direct us to any location at any time. I've reviewed all my maps and compared them with whatever new information we've gotten via the birds. The roads haven't changed, and I know I can get us to ground zero without getting us lost. So for my part, if it's an Apache guide you want, I'm prepared to lead. My question is 'Have you located ground zero?'"

Henry responded by saying, "That's already been identified, and I'll be giving you the location site here today. Your only job is to keep us from getting lost. Our time on the ground is going to be limited to about six hours and we'll be travelling on foot."

Henry then addressed Eliot Brackston, as he was the field maneuvers (recon) man, and it would be his job to handle the terrain, so they didn't stumble and kill themselves in the dark.

Eliot spoke with confidence. He said, "We're going to be dropped by a CIA C-130, like they used at Entebbe. Our gear and landing crafts will handle the drop just fine. They should be able to get down to an air speed of about sixty miles an hour. A little rougher than a chopper drops, but a lot safer for the CIA boys to get in and out quickly. We'll be no more than a mile in distance from shore. We'll be scuttling our landing crafts within fifty yards of shore. As soon as you've given Barry the missile location, we'll be coordinating the best site to land.

"All of our equipment, ordinance, and other supplies are already on standby. My only need now is to have Barry tell me where we'll be landing. For that Barry needs the missile site. Other than that, once we're on shore, you guys along with our Last of the Mohicans guide, will be handled like my little babies, not to worry."

Henry broke in, "I haven't been holding the missile site information back, guys; it's just we didn't have a sure fix until yesterday when our operative finally got through."

Finally, Henry turned to Spencer Briggs and said, "Okay, Spence, you're last but not least, tell us, will the disarmament be a snap?"

Spencer started; it was his turn. "I've reviewed all the data on these warheads. They're relatively simple single devices compared to the multiple-head weapons of today. These babies are big and cumbersome, so goes the wonderful technology of our former buddies of the USSR. The warheads are covered by a simple shroud which shouldn't take more than five minutes to remove. The heads are about waist high and weigh about four hundred pounds. It will take two guys to pull them off.

The warheads are cradled in the guidance system; however, based on what I've seen from our files, we'll need to pull them off in order to get to triggering devices. There are cables from the triggering device to the code boxes. Unfortunately, the Soviets didn't build them to be easily dismantled. I guess they weren't too concerned about much more than launching them as compared to disarming them.

We've gotten the codes to the missiles via our agents inside Russia. It wasn't hard at all; chaos is truly the watchword over there these days. While they're on top of a lot, there's much that they have no handle on, at least that's the way our boys made the story out. Anyway, the connector cables are like serial port computer cables; they've got a special fit which goes only one way, you can't make the kind of mistakes you can with parallel cables. Their code boxes use simple thumbwheel switches, with alphanumeric codes. We simply pull the collars back on the cables, disconnect them, put the codes into the triggering devices, and we're done."

"Okay," Henry broke in, "I don't need a whole dissertation right now on how we disconnect a nuclear triggering device. I only want to know that you're prepared, and we won't be arriving with our thumbs up our ass. Well, gentlemen, it appears we're ready. Everyone seems to have his assignment down; I need only to give Barry the location site and the rest is history. Our sources have told us they're in a set of caves at the foot of Pico Turquino, their highest mountain, approximately 6500 feet high. Oh, and coincidently, it's very near Guantanamo, isn't that funny?

"So, boys, we'll be coming ashore within twenty miles of Guantanamo Bay. This peak is located in a jagged mountain range called Sierra Maestra. So it's good you're here, Eliot, because I understand the terrain is going to be pretty rough going."

"Would you agree with the assessment of this terrain, Barry?"

Barry answered, "You can count on that, Henry, these are some pretty rugged mountains. I climbed there once in 1959, before our buddy Batista left."

"So, Eliot," Henry said, "in light of this new information, you may need to rethink some of the equipment you've decided on."

"When I found out the location, I thought it was quite amusing. I guess Castro figured if something went wrong with these missiles, they'd be far from Havana and close to us," Henry said.

"I'll say," Spencer chimed in, "if these babies went off, with the trade winds of the Caribbean, our boys at Guantanamo wouldn't need floodlights on the perimeter fences, and the whole base would be glowing like a roman candle."

Henry laughed to himself and spoke, "Pretty funny, our boy Fidel. Well, if we pull this off, the joke will be on him, as we continue to watch his ideological revolution sink into the sunset."

Henry got up from the table and said, "Boys, we're about as ready as we're going to be. Each of you need to follow up on the last-minute details we've addressed here and wait for launch. I believe we'll be going in one week. You should all be going home and taking care of whatever personal matters need to be addressed. You've all been through operations like this before, and as usual, we need to be prepared for whatever the eventuality."

As they all left, they all knew what Henry was talking about, the fact that anyone of them, if not all, might not be returning if something went wrong. The air was confident but somber, nonetheless. They would all return home with the exception of Henry and tell their families they were going on special assignment and would be out of communication for a week or two. For Henry, there was only Nan in the office and his townhouse in Old Town, Alexandria.

Tomorrow was Henry's contact day with Peter Kennedy, and once Peter was in motion, so was the operation. There would be no turning back. He wouldn't use Peter and then leave him there; he owed him that much.

Chapter 6

The Voyage

It was eight in the morning and Henry was staring at the alarm clock, wondering just who invented this contraption or, better yet, who improved it to the point of total irritation. It had been two days since he told Peter he was in, like it or not.

He climbed out of bed and walked to the window as he always did to gaze out on the water. He supposed that had it not been for the view, he didn't think he'd be in this townhouse. After all, as a single guy, what did he need a house for; any apartment would do. He rarely entertained, and since he was not married, the space which he had in this house was much more than he could use.

He scratched his stubbly beard and thought about Peter. Today would be the start of the mission. Henry still felt confident that Peter could pull it off. Peter knew all about the biotechnology field and he'd worked under pressure before when he went on his information gathering tour in Argentina in 1980. At that time, he had to act extremely composed to ask the right questions without creating any suspicion amongst ministry personnel.

Henry smiled to himself and thought, *hey, what am I worried about? Peter's job was going to be the easy part; it's my job that's going to be the dangerous one.* Henry looked around the room and thought, *Better get started, got a big day here.* As he went downstairs, he continued to think about his part of the mission. He said out loud to himself, "Got it. Done it. Have it. Don't sweat it."

He poured a cup of coffee and took out his "To Do" list: Call Peter and have him meet me at his office. Call Nan and make sure the plane tickets are waiting at the office along with the special passport for Peter and the cash. He next picked up the phone and called Peter.

Peter seemed to be in a fair mood when he answered the phone. Henry had hoped that resignation had set in and Peter would be without anger. It appeared that way when Peter spoke. Henry asked if all his affairs were in order, mostly as it regarded the kids. Peter said all was okay, that an aunt was going to be staying at his house while he was away.

Henry asked if Peter was ready. Peter answered by saying that while this was blackmail and he didn't have much choice, he was nevertheless ready and would accomplish his mission. Henry told him to be at his NSA office by 10:00 a.m. and gave him directions as to which gate he was to go into. He told him that he needed to only give his name at the gate.

The guard would show him which entrance to park near and that Nan, his secretary, would be waiting outside to escort him to his office. Peter asked how he would recognize Nan, and Henry answered by saying, "Don't worry, she'll recognize you." They hung up and Henry went back upstairs to take a shower and get ready.

When Henry arrived at the office, he reviewed the checklist for a last time with Nan. Nan had the plane tickets, cash, and the special passport. It wasn't that Peter needed an alias, but for future purposes, it was probably better that the government didn't take a chance on messing up the guy's real name.

If something were to go wrong, like when the ex-CIA guy crashed in Nicaragua, it would be better if Peter was under a phony ID. Henry recalled that incident in Nicaragua and thought to himself, *What a mess that was!* That guy should have never been working under his real name. With the media today, once they nail you and spread your name all over the papers, your only choice is to move and start all over somewhere new with another identity. With Peter's kids and his family situation, Henry felt it was better to start off with a phony ID.

The second reason for a special passport was that this one was wired with a special microchip, which would operate as a locator at all times should Peter run into trouble. Henry couldn't predict what might go wrong, but if something did, he wanted to know where Peter was just in case they had to extricate him from a bad situation. Henry had seen things go wrong before and knowing the work they were involved in; it was always prudent to plan for the worst.

As Peter drove from Annapolis to the NSA offices, his intellect fought through a wide range of emotions. On one hand, he was angry at the thought that the government could do anything they wanted, when they wanted, to nail you. It was a sense of helplessness. He thought of his kids and what would become of them should anything happen to him. He felt sure they'd survive, but he couldn't help feeling a sense of emptiness at the thought.

On the other hand, there was a thrill at the idea that he was going on a dangerous assignment. His rational thoughts told him that this was still really way over his head, but his adventurous personality gave him that feeling of exhilaration, the edge that he liked so much. He asked himself how he could be excited about going on a covert government mission which he was blackmailed into. He shook his head to himself and just continued to drive down the highway.

When he arrived at the main gate, a marine guard held out his hand and motioned Peter to stop. Peter rolled down the window and gave his name. He told the guard that he was expected.

The guard looked at a list inside the guard station and returned. He told Peter to pull to the lot on the right and park in the visitors' area. He would then be right by the main entrance, where he could pick up his visitor's pass. What the guard didn't know was that this individual wouldn't be picking up a visitor's pass but would have an official NSA ID plate waiting for him in the hands of Henry St. John's secretary.

When he got out of the car, Nan recognized him immediately from the profile records she had seen during her research for Henry. She led him inside to a set of elevators and took him up to the fourth floor, where Henry's office was located. When Peter walked in, Nan passed him through her office to Henry's. She opened the door and Peter saw Henry standing at the window.

Peter spoke and said, "Not much of a view, eh?"

Henry answered, "No, but it's a window to look out of and that's just something I like to do. You got any peculiar things that you're always drawn to?"

"Yeah, danger, and that's how I got started with you, remember?"

"I do, Peter, and danger is certainly what you've got ahead of you, but not nearly as much as you think there is. Listen, we really don't have much time. Your plane will be leaving for Jamaica in two hours and from there you'll be making your connecting flight to Cuba, so let's get down to business."

Henry took out a manila envelope which Nan had left on his desk. On the cover was written "Operation Off Shore." Henry opened it and pulled out papers, cash, plane tickets, and a passport. He turned to Peter and said, "This is what you'll need to get started. You've got ten thousand dollars in US currency, round trip tickets via Jamaica, first-class, and a special passport with some instructions inside regarding your contact at the American Special Interests Section at the Swiss Embassy."

"When you clear immigration in Cuba, they will ask what your purpose is for this visit. This letter folded inside the passport shows that you have US State Department Trade clearance to work with the American Special Interests Section in Cuba. After they've cleared all of your papers, you're to walk outside and there will be a cab driver with a sign with your name on it. You're to go with him directly to the Swiss Embassy, and there you'll make contact with a woman named Theresa Feher. She will be your main contact and will get you to the right people very quickly. From there, you're on, and all the world, at least in Cuba, is your stage."

Henry didn't tell Peter about the special passport. He thought it was better to not raise any alarms about the possibility of Peter being found out or anything else going wrong.

Henry spoke again and he said, "Whatever you do, Peter, keep this passport on your person at all times."

Peter asked, "Why, is there something else I should know about?"

"No," Henry answered, "it's just important as an American that if anything goes wrong, you've got ID on you at all times."

Peter opened the passport and saw that the picture was him, but the name wasn't. His name in the passport was Peter Riley. Peter looked up and asked, "Why the different name?"

Henry told Peter that just in case there were any problems and the US Diplomatic Corp had to come to his rescue, it would be better for press purposes that they were using an assumed name. Henry didn't feel like raising any concerns by going into other situations where anonymous names came in handy, or people died, and the US government didn't want the media to ever find out that an innocent civilian was recruited or worse blackmailed into an assignment.

After Henry finished addressing the issue of the assumed name, he said to Peter, "Okay, it's time to go." They left the office and went downstairs to the parking lot. Peter asked if he was going to drive himself to the airport. Henry answered, "Just leave it here. We'll take care of it for you, until you get back."

They arrived at BWI about thirty minutes before Peter's flight left for Jamaica. Henry got out of the car, turned to Peter, and said, "Good luck, guy, we'll be seeing you in about two weeks. Don't worry about all the details. When you get there, Theresa will guide you all the way. Be seeing ya," Henry trailed off. Peter turned and walked away from Henry's view.

When Peter stepped off the plane at Jose Marti International Airport, he felt the intense heat immediately. Within five minutes while waiting to clear immigration, his shirt was soaked with sweat. The terminal was old and run-down. It was apparent that it had been a long time since this was the land of plenty. He cleared immigration quickly, got his luggage, and headed outside, looking for his contact. With his Spanish as good as it was, he knew that in many ways Henry was right; it would be easier for him than most, considering his language skills and his knowledge of biotechnology. He just hoped that all that Henry said about Castro buying into this plan was true.

Out front he saw a small Latin fellow, dressed shabbily, holding a sign with the name Peter Riley on it. The drive to the Swiss Embassy was fascinating for Peter. So much beauty and yet so much poverty. A world of what once was and now wasn't.

It was about a forty-five-minute drive into town. The fellow driving the car was about twenty-five years old. He was wise to the ways of the street and obviously lived better than most, evidenced by the fact that he had a car to drive and gasoline to put in it.

Peter asked him a few questions about how life was in Cuba now. The driver spoke with a most disenchanted attitude about life in Cuba today. He said he'd do just about anything to get out. Peter asked why he hadn't already. The driver answered by saying that while working for Senora Feher at the Embassy kept him here, it wouldn't be long before he'd get out. He went on to say that La Senora was going to make it better for him when his time came. He explained that in working for her, he was building up credits for when his time came.

He said, "You know, senor, life in America, she's good but better if you have contacts and money."

Peter asked, "How is La Senora Feher going to get you what you need when you get to America?"

"Senor," the driver answered, "here there is much that is difficult to do, but La Senora Feher, she is practiced in the ways of making things happen. I help her in many ways because I am Cuban and do not create questions when she needs me to get things done. For this, she is most grateful and for this, one day I will be an American but not a poor one."

They talked a little more about what was going on these days, but Peter mostly asked questions to find out more about La Senora Feher. He quickly deduced that this woman was something of an operator. This was logical since she was obviously running the covert operations down here for God knows which branch of the American government.

Peter's mind began to wander about this woman. He wondered what she was like. After all, he knew Henry, but he was a guy. The only image he could conjure up of a female version of Henry was some sort of spy out of the movies.

Before Peter knew it, they were at the Embassy of Switzerland. A beautiful building, ringing out with the flair and style that was the "Heyday" of Cuba. It was pure art deco. It reminded him of the newly renovated area of South Miami Beach. *Boy*, he thought to himself, *this must have been what the whole place looked like when Ricky Ricardo was singing "Ba Ba Loo."*

Peter was actually quite excited at that moment. He wasn't thinking about danger; he was only feeling intrigued and the exhilaration of being on foreign soil, about to enter into a dangerous mission. The thought of what he was doing in Cuba had completely left him for the moment.

He got out of the car and walked around to the back to meet the driver and get his bags. The driver said, "No need, senor, I will take it in for you, just follow me."

They walked inside, the coolness of the stucco building immediately changed his whole feeling. It was dark inside, with only the light of a few windows peering through. The lobby was grand and sort of reminded him of a hotel. At a desk in front was a handsome gentleman of Swiss descent. He had a full head of blonde hair and he stood about six feet, two inches tall. He obviously recognized Peter and was expecting him. The only difference was that from this moment forward all who met Peter would know him now only as Peter Riley, his new alias given to him by Henry St. John.

"Welcome, Mr. Riley, we've been expecting you. I'm Eric Von Zoest, special attaché to the ambassador of Switzerland. Miss Feher had given me instructions to meet you and show you to her." Eric turned to the driver and said, "Please leave Mr. Riley's bags here. We shall take care of them later when Miss Feher takes the senor to his hotel." The driver turned and as he went off, he looked at Peter and said, "Not to worry, senor, you are in good hands. I see you again, *buenos dias senor*," and he left.

As they walked down the hall, Peter said to Eric, "Quite a place."

"Yes, it is, Mr. Riley. After your countrymen left, with some internal negotiations, we reached a very amicable arrangement with your government to stay here. You could say, so to speak, we're babysitting your home until you return one day."

"Pretty bold of us to believe we'd be back, wouldn't you say, Mr. Von Zoest?"

"Not really," Eric said. "In the world of politics, life is sort of like a garment, lapels get thinner and then they get wide again. Things go around and come around. Being in the diplomatic corps, I see the world as ever turning. Eventually things always seem to come full circle."

Peter sort of liked Eric. He gave off that aristocratic charm. Ever so positive, proper, and polite, all in one fell swoop.

Ah, Diplomats, Peter thought, *they're all so smooth. They make you feel like everything can be resolved, given the time and space to warm you up.* They walked past a huge staircase and appeared to be headed to the rear of the embassy. They came upon a beautiful atrium, with huge palm trees and plants all about. In the center of the atrium was a fountain, with Spanish mosaic tile abounding all sides. There, sitting shaded by the sun in a wicker rattan chair, was a lovely woman sunning herself.

As Peter and Eric approached, the sounds of their footsteps caused the woman to turn. She saw them and rose to greet them with all the grace and charm that Peter would have expected were he arriving at an afternoon luncheon at a great mansion in New Orleans. She moved with a flowing air that captivated

Peter's gaze. She was beautiful. Dark hair, tall, a figure that could only be described as full yet slender.

She said upon their approach, "Welcome, Mr. Riley, or may I call you Peter?"

Peter just stared. He was almost speechless, which for Peter was most unusual. Her eyes caught him. They were like the dark pools of an oasis, like nothing he'd seen before. He was captivated and thought to himself, *If this is whom I'm going to be risking my life with, and never make it back, it will have been worth it.* She was truly beautiful, and Peter was having a tough time getting back down to earth.

Eric hadn't missed any of this. He knew that Peter would be stunned by her looks and when he got to know her, he'd really be hooked.

Theresa was a woman to be reckoned with. A Hungarian blue blood, she came from aristocracy. Her father had been in the Hungarian diplomatic corps during World War II and emigrated to the US shortly after the war had ended. There was breeding all about her and it didn't escape you when she spoke. She had looks, personality, and charm and when she walked into a room, like a fresh breeze, all heads turned. Surprisingly enough, unlike other beautiful women, she was not despised by their jealousy; they too were mesmerized by her zeal for life and they often befriended her for her charisma.

When Peter finally regained his composure, he said, "So you must be La Senora Feher."

"Yes, I am, Peter. And of you I have heard many wonderful things. You must be tired from your trip, please sit down and let me get you something to cool the heat of the day. What may I get for you?"

"Is cold beer out of the question?" Peter asked.

"Certainly not, we do have all the electricity we need. After all, we are of the diplomatic corps," and she laughed. "We truly have everything we need, while the country may be poor, we are not."

Peter tried not to stare, and said, "This I can see."

Eric did not sit down. He looked at Peter and said, "You are now most definitely in capable hands, Mr. Riley, so I shall be leaving you. I'm sure I will be seeing you soon."

After Eric left, Theresa began by saying welcome again.

"So how do you like your new name, Mr. Riley? We thought it was a good match for Kennedy, after all they're quite close if we were to keep with Irish tradition. Henry picked it, you know."

She continued the conversation by explaining to Peter that she'd been in contact with Henry on a safe satellite line and that she was completely briefed on everything. She asked Peter to call her Tess, that she liked being informal.

Peter could sense that while Tess was totally at ease and comfortable with all the details, she was nevertheless a woman on a mission. She had definitely been briefed by Henry as to Peter's novice stature and she moved through all conversations with an eye towards making Peter feel secure and safe about what they were going to do.

Peter could sense it all, and most importantly, he could sense that Tess was safe, and he was in capable hands.

After some small talk about Cuba and what was going on in the country, she explained her role at the American Special Interests Section. She told Peter that she would settle him in at the hotel and this evening they would meet with a contact of Castro to get on with the business at hand.

Peter questioned her as to how rapid this whole thing was happening. Tess explained that Henry's plans were less than two weeks away and that we had to get Castro involved in the idea of the missile trade for the biotechnology as quickly as possible.

When they finished discussing business, she smiled at him and said, "And now I will take you to the pride of Havana, The Tropicana Hotel."

Peter saw her smile and felt himself melt; he didn't know if he was going to be able to keep his feet on the floor. This was not the way he began his clandestine initiation into black work in Argentina, nor was this the Falklands War, and this was definitely not Henry St. John at a Christmas party at the American Embassy.

As Peter stood, he instinctively took Tess's hand to help her as she rose, and said, "May I?"

She answered, "With pleasure, Senor Riley."

While walking down the hall to the front to get Peter's bags, he asked if they'd kept up the Tropicana Hotel. Tess answered, "But of course, it is Fidel's pride. Never let it be said that our friend Fidel doesn't have an ego. The rest of the country might be starving, but our friend makes sure he has at least a show place."

When they got outside, there was an embassy staff car waiting for them. Peter's bags were already inside. It was a classic 1955 black Cadillac Limousine. In Cuba, there were many older, beautiful vintage American cars. They were status symbols, and Theresa made sure that she always travelled in style, even if it were just a ride around the corner. They got inside the car and rode off to the hotel.

When they arrived outside of the Tropicana, Peter could see it looked beautiful from far but was far from beautiful. The paint was not holding well, but the grounds out front were truly magnificent. The flora and fauna of the Caribbean made you feel like it was out of a James Michener novel. The bellmen and other attendants were dressed to a tee, despite the heat of the afternoon.

As they walked into the lobby of the hotel, everything was as it should have been. It seemed almost like a turn back of time. They approached the front desk and Peter began to speak in Spanish, but as he opened his mouth to utter the first words, Tess broke in and said, "You have a reservation for Senor Riley, he is the guest of the Swiss Ambassador."

"*Como no*, Senora Feher," he answered. "The suite has been reserved and Senor Riley's room should be all in order, Senora."

"Gracias, Manuel," Tess said.

Manuel handed the key to Peter and wished him *Bienvenidos* and asked that he have a good stay with them. Manuel then asked for Peter's passport. Peter remembered immediately what Henry had said about keeping the passport with him at all times.

Peter asked why this was necessary, but before Manuel could answer, Tess broke in and said, "That will not be necessary, Manuel, Senor Riley is our guest, and he has been cleared through the embassy."

"*Lo siento, Senora*, I am sorry, but as you know it is the policy of the government that we must hold all passports of foreign visitors to our country. I could lose my job over this. Please, *por favor*, Senora Feher, do not make problems where there need not be any," Manuel said.

Tess was infuriated over the idea that Peter would have to give up his passport. She knew from her contact with Henry that it was no ordinary passport, but for the moment, she would let them have it. They turned away from the front desk and Peter asked, "Should I be concerned?"

"It is nothing to worry about. Everyone is required to surrender their passport until they are ready to leave the country." Tess smiled to instill confidence in Peter and said, "It's one of the ways they've got you and they make sure that you'll leave on their terms. The way they calculate it, unless you can swim ninety miles off shore, they'd like to see you before you leave."

Tess said, "Go with the bellman upstairs to your suite. I will wait for you in the bar. Drop your bags and change if you like, it's much too hot for even a tropical suit."

Peter went up the elevator with the bellman. He spoke in Spanish and asked if the hotel was full. The bellman was surprised at Peter's Spanish. There was barely a foreign accent. He thought Peter's Spanish was Castilian, from Spain, it was that perfect. Peter knew he was surprised by his perfect language. Peter wondered what he thought the bellman imagined he was doing in Cuba. After all, Peter looked quite American, arrived with someone from the Swiss Embassy, and yet spoke perfect Spanish.

Peter stopped wondering what the bellman thought. He said to himself he needed to save his paranoia for his mission, not waste it on a hotel employee. When he arrived at the door to his room, the bellman opened the double doors and waved his arms before Peter, ushering him in. He put the bags on the bed, stood erect, facing Peter, and asked if there would be anything he would need immediately.

Peter was most impressed with the room. While it was old, everything was clean and looked to be in mint condition. It appeared that what the country lacked in new veneer, it made up for in its grandeur and the pristine condition of all the period furniture. Peter leaned over to feel the bed. It was soft and he expected as much. He didn't think for a minute that Fidel was importing Sealy Posturepedic mattresses.

The bellman asked if he might show Peter the bathroom. It was then that Peter finally realized the bellman was waiting for his tip.

Peter reached into his pocket and pulled out what paper money he had. He was about to give the bellman ten pesos when it occurred to him that dollars were probably preferred. He handed him three US dollars and the bellman smiled profusely and bowed his head as he said, "Senor, if there is anything I can do for you, my name is Pedro, and please call for me."

After the bellman left, Peter thought, *There goes one happy guy. He probably has a stash of US currency at home and is either saving it for his departure from Cuba or uses it on the black market to get those things that others can't get.* Working at a hotel where foreigners stay is probably one of the most privileged jobs you can get in Cuba. *Well,* Peter thought, *better change and get downstairs, I mean, how often does a guy like him get to have drinks with a babe like Tess.*

Peter went into the bathroom. It was large and spacious, not like what you'd find at a Hyatt these days in America. The sink was old with two spigots, one for hot and one for cold. He looked in the mirror, rubbed his face, and decided a shave was in order. He put his shaving kit on the counter next to the sink and put the plug in the basin, turned the water on, and waited for it to fill. He finished shaving, changed into a polo shirt and some khakis, and left to meet his lovely Tess.

He was alone on the way down in the elevator. It was the first time since his magical tour in Cuba had started that his thoughts turned back to the job at hand. He found himself to be in a sleepwalk. He knew what he was told had to be done, but it all seemed like he was on a vacation. Something inside, however, told him that he wasn't just going to meet a lovely lady in a bar. Whatever it was, it was all sinking in. The excitement was there, but so was reality.

He kept on thinking about the passport. He recalled that Henry was emphatic about the fact that he was to keep it on him at all times. Was it because in case of an emergency that certain people had his name, and were he to be in trouble, someone inside would know via the passport to get in touch with Henry? Whatever, he was feeling nervous about this passport thing. He had travelled to many countries in Latin America, and none had ever required that he surrender his passport. Even had Henry not said to keep it with him at all times, he always felt nervous about his passport. It was your key to who you were when you travelled. With an American passport, you always felt that no matter what happened to you, you could always get to an American Embassy and yell, "Hey, I'm an American, protect me." The problem was here in Cuba that didn't do much for you.

He reached the ground floor and exited the elevator and headed for the bar to the side of the lobby. The bar had a grand mahogany countertop with a stripped canopy. Half the bar was indoors, while half straddled the outside adjacent to the pool.

He couldn't get over how much it all looked like the newly renovated South Miami Beach. As he looked around, he saw Tess sitting over in the corner. She waved, signaling that she saw him.

"Hello again," Peter said, "long time no see."

"Not so long that I couldn't work my magic," and she handed Peter his passport.

"You are connected, aren't you?" Peter said. "I can't believe that in the short time I was upstairs, you were able to do this."

"Obviously, a mistake was made and the man at the front desk was not who was to be on this afternoon. It was no great problem, just a short phone call and all was corrected," Tess said. She smiled at Peter with a serene look that said all will be okay, and she tried to send him that message via her gaze. She didn't want to alarm Peter, but she knew he needed to have that passport with him at all times. While Tess was confident at what she did, she knew, unlike Peter, that in this business, things often went awry, like their experience at the front desk today.

"You look quite handsome, Senor Riley, may I buy you a Cuba Libre?"

"Why, yes, I'd love that, Tess."

Tess began to speak and stopped when the waiter came over to bring Peter his drink. After the waiter left, Tess started again, "Peter, you are really quite handsome and I wish that you and I were perhaps on a little holiday together, but unfortunately we're not, so while it's fun to pretend, our time is short and I really must fill you in on what's going on and where we begin."

Peter looked at her and knew she was right. He was not here on a holiday but on a covert US government mission which was way over his head, and if it weren't for Tess's beauty, he'd be scared shit right now. He knew all this and yet her eyes, those dark pools, kept him totally captivated. He said okay, let's get started but on the condition that before he left Cuba, he'd get to dance with her once under the stars, gaze into her dark pools, and kiss her before he left. She laughed and reached out to run her hand along the lines of his cheek. She leaned over and kissed him lightly and said, "I would love it, Peter, and we will dance under the stars, just be who you are, and we'll drink and toast to our success together when this is done."

It was Peter's turn to laugh, he said, "Okay, now that I've made a fool of myself and have gotten that out of the way, let's get down to business."

"Tonight, we will have dinner with a man named Fernando. He is the cousin of Fidel and will be our contact during the trade."

"I have met with him already and he understands the political dilemma that we are in at home."

"Although he is an ideological dreamer, he appears to be sincere. I actually believe, unlike Fidel, he truly cares about the revolution and more importantly, the welfare of the Cuban people. It is because of him and his wish to turn this deal for biotechnology to the benefit of his countrymen, that I believe we will be successful in diverting Castro from whatever his fallback plan is," Tess said. "You must remember that Fidel is looking for not only monetary benefit but also for the humiliation of the US. He has never really forgotten 'Operation Mongoose' and Kennedy's attempt to assassinate him."

Peter continued to listen and when Tess was finished explaining the evening ahead, he asked, "But what will I offer him?"

"It will only be a dialogue for the time being. You will tell him what you can do for their country. You'll explain how their technology will be transferred. You do know about biotechnology, don't you?"

"Of course, I do, it's my business."

"Well, then that's what you'll tell him. Explain about plasmids and how with a laboratory setup, one clone can be turned into millions of clones. He has some brief understanding of science and it's your job to break it down to layman's terms."

"Okay, so where do we start?"

Tess handed Peter a folder with about ten pages inside it. "Here, read this evening before we dine. It's a bio on Fernando and it will give you all the background you'll need in order to have a sense of him for when we meet tonight. We'll be meeting him here for dinner at 10:00 p.m. I'll introduce you. He knows what you're here for, and you need to only follow my lead and act confident about what you know and our ability to deliver all it will take to get them started. If he asks about assets, I'll be the one to explain how we'll be using a dummy CIA company through Canada to bring in the laboratory equipment."

"Okay, so what now?"

"Now," Tess said, "we sit, talk, and enjoy the afternoon."

Peter picked up his glass and toasted Tess with a nervous smile and said, "It's your game; you lead and I'll follow. Just don't forget that dance in the moonlight, I'll be keeping you to that one."

Chapter 7

The Accident

It was hot in the storage area, actually unseasonably hot for the late autumn in Miami. The air-conditioning was in repair as was usually the case this time of the year. Miami's summers were so hot that autumn was the typical time for the servicing of the air-conditioning systems. More to the point, the federal government had special servicing programs for all of its facilities on regular scheduled maintenance dates. So, it wasn't unusual that the deep storage area air-conditioning system for Miami customs was undergoing its servicing.

The guards were inside the storage area, sitting in the lunchroom, reading the morning papers. With the morning waning, the heat inside the building was becoming unbearable. It was approximately 10:30 a.m. when one of the guards, Tony, turned to Jorge and asked, "So what in the hell are we supposed to do for two days without the air-conditioning?" Jorge responded by saying they needed to get out of the room as it was starting to become a regular humidor, good enough for hanging cigar leaves.

It was at that moment that Tony said, “Hey, why don’t we go out front and open up the garage door and at least sit with a breeze.”

Jorge said, “Sounds good, let’s go.”

When they got out front from the back of the warehouse, they pressed the button for the electric door and with that, the door rose and they felt the breeze as it opened and crept under the large overhang door. The sun was hot, but the breeze was still able to evaporate the sweat from their brows.

Jorge said to Tony, “Good idea, at least we’ve got some air movement.”

“Yeah, but we don’t exactly have anywhere to sit, do we?”

“Well, why don’t you run to the back and get a couple of those folding chairs in the closet so we can sit on them?”

“Why don’t you go and get the chairs yourself?”

Tony turned and said, “Hey, it was my idea, the least you could do for my brilliance would be to get a seat for me to rest my weary mind.”

Jorge laughed and said, “You’re right on with that one. I always thought you had shit for brains and now you’re admitting your brains are where you sit.”

They laughed at one another the way good friends often do. The two of them had been working together in the civil service for almost twelve years. After they flipped a coin as to who was going to get the chairs, they spent the next hour sitting and talking just far enough inside the large door to be in the shade and yet catch the breeze as it blew into the storage area. It was getting near lunchtime when a truck pulled up in front of the door, filled with what looked like large oil drums. The driver got out with a clipboard and walked over to Tony.

Tony got up from the chair and walked towards the driver with an air of officiality. "So what do we have here?" Tony asked.

The driver explained that these drums contained liquid I-125, radioactive iodine, coming in from Venezuela in transit on its way to a medical facility in New York.

While Tony looked at the papers, Jorge went to get one of the forklifts in anticipation of the unloading that was sure to follow. When Tony finished with the documents, he told the driver to turn the truck around to make it easier for the forklift to grab the drums off of the truck. When Jorge pulled to the rear of the truck, he stopped the forklift and went over to Tony and asked which zone they were going to put the drums in.

Tony looked at the documents and said to Jorge that it seemed that this stuff wouldn't be here too long and that it was probably going to be cleared as soon as the customs broker got here. Tony could tell from the papers that this shipment was labeled for clearance by Miami Interbroke Inc., a company that Tony was familiar with from the years of working in Miami customs.

Jorge looked at Tony and said, "Shit, why do these guys send transit items to deep storage when it's going to be in and out in less than a couple of days?"

Tony answered, "Hey, what do I know, they probably didn't want to put it in short storage since it was radioactive. I guess it was too close to the general population, and they thought it would be safer at a far end of the airport."

"Oh great," Jorge said, "better, we should be glowing back here."

The driver interrupted and said, "Hey, guys, relax, and this stuff is mild enough to swallow. They use this for radioactive diagnostic testing on people. I can only guess that the boys up front routed these drums back here because they're not familiar with Miami Interbroke; they're always shipping it up here from Venezuela."

"Usually, the guys from Interbroke are here the same day the shipment arrives. I suppose there's some foul-up and until the papers are cleared, because it says radioactive, they wanted to move it out of the way. Believe me, there's nothing to worry about."

Jorge and Tony just stared at him and said at the same time, "So you say!"

The driver went on, "Seriously, I've been working around this I-125 material for ten years now, and there's really nothing to worry about. I even wear this dosimetry badge so they can see how much radioactivity I get exposed to on the job. Believe me, it barely ever registers."

Jorge said, "Okay, but if I glow in the dark, my wife's going to start asking questions, and when I tell her you said it was cool, she'll be looking for you, and if you knew my wife, I pity your ass if she gets to you."

Tony told Jorge to cut the crap, just start unloading the drums, and to put it in the rear near that wooden crate they stored last week. "You mean that large wooden crate we nearly smashed a week or so ago."

At Jorge's comment, Tony recalled when they received that wooden crate and how Jorge was clowning around, racing with the forklift. He also recalled how strange the two customs agents were as they were unloading it and moving it to the back of the warehouse. He didn't recognize their faces, buy they seemed almost to put on an air of a casual demeanor. He hadn't thought too much about it then, but one of the agents looked familiar. He wasn't able to put the face with where he'd seen it before and that bothered him.

It was the same with that attorney who showed up a few days before, making a stink about his client's rights and how he wanted to inspect the crate being held in a case against his client. He was carrying on about people tampering with the property and that his client's case depended on his proving that the goods had been switched once before and that he wanted to make sure that no Feds were pulling another switch again.

Tony was just a civil service worker, but he did have a college education. He chose this type of job versus something in the real world, especially because he wanted to escape the world of interfacing with people. But nevertheless, Tony wasn't stupid and in the kind of work he did here, it was rare that they interfaced with outside people. Even this truck driver today was a rarity. Guys like him never came back to deep storage; they usually were in and out in the transit area. In the past twelve years, Tony could count on both hands the number of times he'd seen people back by deep storage whom he hadn't seen before. He knew just about all of the faces around the customs area and strange faces stuck out; it was as simple as that.

Jorge engaged the forklift and brought down the first barrel. He drove it to a nearby wood pallet where he figured he could stack all eight drums and then move the entire load to the rear at one time. After he finished loading the drums on the pallet, he shut the forklift off to walk around the pallet and size up the move. By now the pallet was stacked high, and to move all eight drums, he thought, he ought to inspect the lay of the land before he attempted to move it.

"Well," Jorge said, "since this is only going to be here for a couple of days, where do you want me to put it?"

Jorge's question juggled Tony from his thoughts, and since he had been thinking about that wooden crate, he responded quickly with that which was on his mind, the wooden crate.

Tony said, "Put it on the back wall near the large wooden crate you stored the other week."

Tony was watching, and, while Jorge was walking around the pallet, he said to Jorge, "You better be careful, I don't feel like having to clean up a mess with you just because you didn't feel like making two trips."

As Jorge lifted the load, he was saying to himself, *Easy does it now.* Jorge had been working a forklift like this now for years, and he was pretty comfortable with the idea that if you took your time and sized things up right, you could do amazing things with the right stack job. As he made the lift, he turned the forklift and headed to the rear of the warehouse to set the pallet down near the large wooden crate they put at the far aisle near the back wall. As Jorge neared the wooden crate, he began to lower the pallet. It was at that time that one of the top barrels wobbled and crashed onto the floor. He winced as he saw it hit and the liquid spilt out.

Tony yelled, "Shit, you asshole. I knew this was going to happen the way you had it stacked. God, damn it, why do I have to deal with this?"

The driver and Tony ran to the back and the three of them just stood there with a look of pain at the thought that this all could have been avoided had Jorge not tried to move it all on one pallet.

Jorge said, "Well, I guess I'm not the greatest forklift driver after all."

Tony answered by saying, "Hey, my kid drives better than you."

The two of them stood there yelling at each other as to whose fault it was, when Jorge knew it was clearly his. Tony said again, "God, damn it. Now we're going to have to clean up this mess and God knows what kind of OSHA paperwork I'm going to have to fill out."

"Damn it," he said again, "I ought to kill you for screwing up on this, better yet, I ought to make you fill out all the papers." But Tony knew better, he was the supervisor and he was the one who would bear the responsibility for all of the papers that would have to be filled out.

The driver interrupted and said, "Listen, you guys, I deal with this stuff all the time, and these spills with I-125 are not all that hard to clean up. This stuff only has a half-life of about sixty days and you should be able to neutralize it with bleach."

Tony listened up real quick on the driver's every word. All he could think about was the hassle he would have to go through if he reported any kind of radioactive spill. The federal regulations and paperwork on this stuff were enough to choke a horse, and if Tony could squeak by on this one, all the better. He knew Jorge wouldn't say anything as he was the jerk that caused this in the first place.

Tony sent Jorge back to the cleaning closet to get a gallon of bleach. When Jorge returned, the driver said, "Just splash it all around and then just mop it up; the place will be clean as a whistle, and no one will ever know." Tony sensed the guy was really sympathetic, and in light of the regs and the questions about how the spill occurred, he preferred to try and skate out on this one.

Tony cursed to himself again as he knew that there were annual inspections from the OSHA and that when they came through, they would scan the warehouse, however short, with a Geiger counter. It was part of the procedure. In all government facilities, the OSHA boys looked for everything from bacterial contamination to radioactive waste.

In between Tony and Jorge's arguing, the driver could tell from the discussion that his presence was no longer needed, if anything, he just wanted to leave.

When Jorge returned with the bleach, they splashed the liquid on the floor and spread it around to make sure it mixed thoroughly with the spill. Tony stood there and watched with a smile as Jorge mopped up. It was of little consequence, but Tony at least thought he's making Jorge work for his cock-up. After Jorge finished, they walked back to the front with the truck driver and Jorge said, "It's all your fault for bringing that crap back here."

The driver said, "Listen, I'm sorry but I just brought to where they told me to bring it."

Tony jumped in, as he could see that Jorge was just pissed off about his screwup with the pallet, and he was looking for someone to blame for his mistake.

After the driver left, Tony said, "I hope you've now realized you're not the great Wallenda doing balancing acts in here. You really need to stop picking on other people just because you're pissed off at yourself."

It was now 2:00 p.m. and hotter than a God damned oven by this time. Now that Jorge was finished, Tony told Jorge to go and get the Geiger counter and make a sweep of the area to make sure that it was totally clean. He emphasized that since this whole mess was Jorge's fault for loading too much on the pallet, he should be the one to do the final check.

Jorge told Tony that he wasn't sure where the equipment was and he needed Tony to show him. They walked back to the front office where Tony grabbed the Geiger counter, handed it to Jorge, and said, "Here, go finish the job you started."

Tony remained at the front office and grabbed a cold soda out of the refrigerator and tried to relax from the heat with the fan in the front office. Jorge went to the back with the Geiger counter and turned on the switch. He set it down on top of the large wooden crate for a moment while he unzipped his fly and pulled his pants down to re-tuck his shirt. He was a total mess from mopping up the floor. While he was pushing in his shirttails, he could hear the Geiger counter ticking off in a rapid sound. He looked up and saw that the needle was reading off the scale. He switched it off and on again, and it still was spitting like crazy. He banged his hand against it once just in case it was out of whack or something, but nothing affected the high pitch of the ticking. He looked around to see if Tony was there and saw no one. *Maybe it's broken, who knows*, he thought.

About ten minutes later, Jorge returned to the office and said, "I don't know whether that guy was pulling our leg or what, but when I went back there and did a scan, the Geiger counter was reading off the wall."

Tony said, "Are you sure?"

"Sure, I'm sure, I can read you know. You don't have to be a jet pilot to read the directions, turn switch to on, and scan in lateral movements slowly."

At this point, Tony was tired, and he couldn't believe that they hadn't done a good job. He turned to Jorge and said, "Forget it, I saw you mop it up. Maybe that God damned machine isn't calibrated properly, after all it's probably not been used in a dog's age. When they come around for the next scheduled equipment check, I'll be sure to mention it."

In Tony's mind, this still didn't set right. Tony got up from his chair and went over to the file cabinet and pulled out the equipment maintenance log. He looked for the last check. It looked kind of like an elevator log sheet you'd see on the wall, very official. It listed the date it was checked last, and it was signed at the bottom by Inspector Gonzales. Well, whatever the story was, it could wait until the next inspection. He sure wasn't going to call anyone about today, about the spill. *The driver seemed too sure about the whole thing; it's got to be a problem with the Geiger counter*, he thought.

By this time, they were both bushed from cleaning and sweating in what must have been 110-degree heat inside the warehouse. Tony again said, "Relax, get something cold to drink and let's just rest for a while. This has been entirely too much work for one morning, and it was after all your fault."

Jorge looked at Tony with his feet up on the desk and said to himself, *What the heck, if he's not worried, why should I?* Jorge picked up the *Miami Herald,* stretched out on the stitchy leather couch, covered his face with the newspaper, and closed his eyes to catch forty winks.

Chapter 8

The Meeting

It was 8:30 p.m. when Peter met Tess again in the lounge on the ground floor. They had spent a lovely afternoon together. Peter learned a lot about Tess. He couldn't understand why such a beautiful woman with so much to offer would be spending her life in a situation of such danger, working as an operative for the US government.

Peter learned that Tess had been married once, and it hadn't worked out. Her husband had been a very wealthy industrialist, and after the divorce, she was left without much money and not much of a professional career. Since she had lived in a suburb of Washington, DC, she had made a lot of friends and contacts with people who had worked in the government. Given the flair and panache with which she entreated everyone she met, it wasn't long until one of her friends who was inside the intelligence business realized her predicament and what she could offer. In light of the fact that she was used to the good life and there was an obvious shortage of funds for that, she was easily recruited. It didn't take much of a presentation from her friend as she described what the remuneration would be and what the work would be like for Tess to become enchanted by the idea.

So it was with her desire to escape and run away from her failed marriage that she ended up being recruited by the government. It had been five years now since Tess was pulled in and remarkably, she found that she was a regular Mata Hari. The demands of her job kept her constantly involved in the diverse games that the government liked to play and what once began as a diversion or preoccupation from the distressed life she ran away from, she now considered herself to be good at what she did and the pride that evolved from those feelings made her even better.

Peter was so enthralled with her charm that conversation with her was at times difficult. He realized what was going on this night, but in light of her beauty, it was a constant struggle to remember what he was here for. He'd been so lonely over the years and now that he'd found what he thought was the woman of his dreams, he couldn't even get to her because for her, this was an assignment and nothing more. He wondered as they spoke if her time down here working undercover for the government had stripped her of her ability to see another life. As she told him her story, he could feel the aloofness that she exhibited about not having the opportunity to really have any relationships with anyone. Peter supposed that in this line of work, it probably was quite difficult to have a real relationship; after all, your life was undercover.

"You look quite handsome, Senor Riley," Tess said.

"And you look even more radiant in the light of the evening than you did this afternoon, if that were possible," replied Peter.

"Well," Tess began, "Fernando will be here by nine o'clock. We need to drop this mutual admiration love chat, although I must admit you have, for the first time since I can remember, gotten my attention. I too really did enjoy our time this afternoon, but now we must prepare for this evening. When Fernando arrives, we will meet here in the lounge for a while. Half an hour to an hour or so. He will want to size you up. He's going to ask you a lot of questions. Some will be in the same direction and others will be coming completely out of left field. He's going to want to see your reaction. They obviously don't trust us and gee, I wonder why," Tess smirked.

"You must remember this guy is a strange mix. On one hand, he's the cousin of Fidel and he does his bidding. On the other hand, he truly feels for the people of Cuba. He is a true patriot, unlike Fidel, who really only cares for his power and his ego. I kind of like Fernando. When I met him the first time, he appeared to care, at least that's the feeling I got, and I think I'm pretty good at that stuff, you know woman's intuition if you will.

"Anyway, he's been told that you're not with the CIA. He's been told that Langley recruited you to do their bidding because you were a true expert in not only biotech science but also in the commercial field, and that means your ability to deliver not only the technology but the assets it's going to take to set their labs up."

"Well, that's not far from what the truth is. They did recruit me for those reasons, only blackmail is the interchangeable word for recruited," Peter said.

Tess heard Peter's comment about the blackmail and said, "Whatever it's about, doesn't matter, Peter, now because he's going to be here shortly, and you're here and we've got this job no matter how they brought you in." Tess said, "Listen, he'll be here any moment and I want to cover a few more things. When he asks you about timing, you defer to me. I'll talk about the trade. If he asks you details about the biotechnology part, shoot straight. This guy's university educated and while he might not be a scientist, he's not stupid."

Peter interrupted, "Not to worry, I'm going to tell him about the hydroponically grown and genetically engineered tomatoes in the US and how the technology is accomplished."

"This should be very interesting for me too," Tess answered. "While I'm not the scientist type, I mean, I only had Biology 101 and 102 in college, I am fascinated by this whole decoy plot that Henry has come up with. It's much more believable than anything I could have fabricated."

As Tess finished, Fernando was walking into the lounge. She saw him over Peter's shoulder and waved to him to walk over. He was a slight man, about five feet, ten inches, narrow of frame with broad shoulders. He wore round wire rim glasses that tended to be low on the bridge of his nose. He was wearing a white traditional Cuban shirt jacket called a guayabera.

As he neared, both Peter and Tess rose. "*Buenas noches*, Senora Feher, it is a pleasure to see you again."

"And it is wonderful to see you, Fernando. Please allow me to introduce to you Senor Riley.

"Senor Riley, it is a pleasure. How do you like our Tropicana Hotel? Is it not like out of the movies you still show in America?"

Peter answered Fernando by saying that the hotel was indeed charming but was paled by the charm of La Senora Feher. Tess kicked Peter under the table as if to say, enough already, this is serious business. Peter knew when he said that, he would get a reaction out of her, but even in light of what was going on, he was still mesmerized by those eyes of hers. Those dark pools.

As the small chatter of getting warm continued, Fernando looked at Peter and began, "So, my friend, tell me of yourself and why you are here."

Peter began by telling Fernando of his history, how he'd started out in the university, left for the commercial world, and what he'd been doing in the world of biotechnology over the past five or ten years or so. Fernando asked some questions about Peter's family too. Peter found this curious even though he knew Latinos' had a very special feeling about family. Latins in general always kept the family, one's parents and children, in high regard. It was more than just the Catholic thing; it was part of their culture. It was for them the representation of how good a man you were. For a Cuban, it was not just the support but the love for your children and the respect for your parents. Fernando liked Peter and it was clear in his tone and interest. It was probably the fact that Peter had raised two sons without a wife. For Fernando, he saw this as a macho the thing, the man who could be a man and raise two sons at the same time. After all, in the Latin culture, to have sons in and of itself was macho.

After Fernando finished his personal interrogation into Peter's life, he moved on to the questions regarding what exactly Cuba would receive in trade for the missiles. Peter noted interestingly enough that Fernando rarely talked in the possessive form of Fidel; he spoke always of Cuba and its people and their needs.

Again and again, Peter was struck by Fernando's obvious sincerity. He felt that, like Tess, he really liked Fernando. He found himself almost wishing this wasn't a charade and that he could help the people of Cuba. It seemed such a contradiction that this should be the man of Fidel's bidding. But as Fernando continued with more questions about the trade, he was reminded what this whole thing was about, deadly missiles that Castro ostensibly could use against the US or worse that he might sell for cash to some radical group in the Middle East.

Fernando stopped his general conversation and moved quickly to a direct question, which he had obviously been primed with by one of their scientists. "Tell me specifically, Peter, how do you genetically engineer vegetables?" Fernando asked.

Peter sensed that this was a test, that Fernando had been given this question and the answer too. Peter knew that the way he answered this for Fernando would be the telling step as to whether the deal went forward or not. Tess was watching and listening with what appeared to be almost amusement. Peter had no way of knowing, but she too had truly fallen for him. Unfortunately, she'd been in this game so long now that she had almost forgotten what it was like to feel your heart race again, but Peter did that to her and even though she tried to ignore it, she knew inside it was there. She knew Peter was in his element in answering the question, so for Tess it was a newfound admiration she felt as she watched him, a novice at this game, perform so magnificently.

Peter answered Fernando with the confidence of a professor and the ease of a kid on the street. Tess really liked the kid about Peter. There was a youth there that she could see lives inside him every day and it was there for keeps; it was him.

Peter went on, "You see, Fernando, it's all very simple. We take the DNA from the vegetable or fruit we wish to genetically accelerate, and in a special solution, we separate the two strands of DNA. After we do that, we use commercially available restriction enzymes, we cut the chain at the part that we wish to affect. Whether it's the part of the chain that controls the size of the item or the rate at which it grows, it doesn't matter. What we do is insert the change we want, we reconnect the DNA helix and shazam, we have a new DNA, and it does what we want. The concept is very simple and I'm sure your scientists understand it. What's not so simple is what we have and that's the ability to know how to cut the DNA strand and where. That's what we're offering; how does it sound?"

Peter knew he handled it perfectly and he wondered whether Tess knew just how well he did it. After all, it was public knowledge how to clone and genetically engineer plants. What wasn't public knowledge was the recipe.

The pH or which restriction enzyme to use or where to cut the chain to create the effect you wanted, that's what the American companies had and that's what Cuba didn't have, that was the secret.

By the time Peter was finished, Fernando was a believer. They had been sitting and talking for almost an hour and a half. Fernando told Peter he was most impressed and that he had answered the question right. He explained that he had been prompted before the visit on the key issues that he needed to know. And it was true that what the scientists lacked was the recipe. Their people had been experimenting for years now, but with the antiquated systems they had and without the computer software mapping, the enzymes and cleaving the zones was near impossible.

When Fernando finished, Tess broke in at the appropriate time and asked, "Where do we go from here?"

Fernando told her that he believed that we were on the level about the trade. He explained that Castro didn't believe or trust the Americans unless it was done in the open, and by that,

Castro meant through the media. Fernando told them how he tried to explain to Fidel that the Americans would never deal in the open on this one, because of the ideological difference between the way he felt about his socialistic system and the way you Americans felt about communism, especially in light of your Cold War victories around the world.

Fernando continued, "So it was I who convinced him that we had to at least attempt this route. I told him you would never deal in public on this one. He ranted and carried on that if you wouldn't, he'd sell the warheads on the market to the highest bidder. I told him that while he could surely do that, what we didn't need was more negative world press making us out to be a renegade nation. I pleaded with him for our people's sake: try this, if they are plotting, I told him, I would know.

"So, I am most grateful that you are who you are. Many things have changed recently in my life that I can't explain to you but suffice it to say I am disillusioned by much recently. Because of Fidel, I've lost a very close friend, and this is difficult for me to rectify. There once was a time I would have done anything for Fidel, but now I do what I do for my people. I have thought much about my past, and I find recently little redeeming about who I am. If this plan were to work, I truly believe the Cuba I once knew could be again.

"I tell you this, we must make it work because Fidel is a pigheaded man, and if we fail, he will do something desperate. Of this I am sure because up until now, I too did something desperate about which I deeply regret but that is past. Fidel is a man who knows no conscience, of this I have truly come to learn recently."

After Fernando finished, he rose and said, "I must go now. You can be sure that even though I am Fidel's cousin, no one is trusted. He truly trusts no one, of this I am sure."

As he rose, Tess put out her hand and Peter rose with Fernando. Fernando kissed Tess's hand and said, "Senora, as always, it has been a pleasure, I hope that what we plan together will come to pass." He turned to Peter and said, "Of you, my new friend, I believe you are honest, you are not like the type I know your government to send were this a charade. A man who has two sons has much to be proud of and has much to show his sons yet. I hope that one day, your sons will know how you changed the world."

Before Fernando left, Tess asked when we will meet again to put things in a final form. Fernando told them both he must first meet with Fidel and convey that what they can offer is far more than dollars from the sale of warheads could bring. "I hope," Fernando said, "that we will meet again within two days. I will be in contact with you through Eric Von Zoest. He will tell you of our next meeting. The next time, we will have to meet in private, for it will be then, if all goes well, that the details of the trade will be worked out." Fernando bowed towards Senora Feher and nodded towards Peter and then left.

After Fernando had left, Tess leaned over and kissed Peter quickly and said, "You were wonderful; you almost made me believe this were a real deal."

"Yeah, I know. I actually feel rotten about the whole thing. This guy's for real and we're not. I mean, we're really in a charade and he really believes we're going to help him and his people. You know if we could bump off Castro, I think this guy could be a great leader."

"I know, Peter, but that's not what this is about. This is about a maniac who has six nuclear warheads, and if we don't get control of this situation, he's going to sell those things out on the open market."

"Well, it's a shame, I really did like him."

"I understand, but you need to understand that this bio-technology trade can't happen either, not as long as Castro's in power. The last thing we want to do is make him stronger. Remember we're the good guys, democracy; we're trying to unseat the bad guys, communism."

"It just seems a shame, a guy like this in his mid-forties, why isn't he leading the country? I mean, why don't we bump off Castro, like I said before?"

"Listen, if it were that easy to bump the guy off, don't you think the boys at Langley would have done it a long time ago. No, Peter, this is the plan and while I feel the way you do and sympathize with your thoughts, what we're doing is the way it's going to go down."

Tess was truly touched by Peter's altruism, for the way he felt made her feel warmer towards him. She was having her own conflict right now, that is to not fall for him? She was fighting the feelings, but she sensed she was losing. Peter was what she'd been looking for since her escape, only she didn't want it now. It wasn't the time. *Why*, she thought, *do all the good things always come to you at the wrong time in the wrong place?*

Peter interrupted her thoughts when he said, "Hey, dark pools, too soon for that dance."

Tess answered, "Too soon, Senor Riley, but I do believe your starlit night is not far from the horizon."

Peter smiled at her; he lifted his glass for a toast and said, "To that night." Tess lifted her glass in return and their glasses touched. As they did, Tess thought to herself, *You shall have that dance, that kiss, and more.*

Chapter 9

The Ready

Henry walked into Willie's office at NSA headquarters in Fort Meade. It was now only a day away from the assault. Henry had contacted everyone on team SIREN as soon as he had word from Theresa Feher in Cuba. Her coded message said all went well, the contact is now in the process of selling our story to Castro. They were now at the juncture where Castro would truly be involved in determining if the offer was real or not.

Henry had little doubt that Castro would listen to the proposal. He knew that ultimately whatever Castro got from us would not be enough, since what he really wanted was to bring the US to its knees. The money or biotechnology or any of it meant nothing for Fidel as far as Henry saw it. But he knew that Castro would have to put up a front for his junta or he'd start having problems keeping the lambs in a row. After all, they really believed the play with the missiles was for the betterment of Cuba. Only Castro knew better: he wanted retribution for all the humiliation, the blockades, and most important, a fair turnabout for Operation Mongoose, when Kennedy tried to assassinate him.

When Henry sat down in Major William O'Connor's office, Willie looked up from his desk and, in a definitively marine corps manner, said, "So I assume all must be go if you're here this morning."

Henry answered, "Yes, contacts have been made. We've got confirmation that it's proceeding as planned and Castro will have his attention diverted for two days at the most. Our contact says they've been told that if Castro accepts, they'll be meeting at the latest tomorrow or the next day."

"Well," Willie asked, "are we on target and are your men ready?"

"Yes, they are. We've encountered a few concerns, but they are by all calculation minimal."

"Explain," Willie asked.

Henry went into an explanation of some of the information that he had read in some preliminary notes that Spencer Briggs left with him after their meeting in Quantico a few days before. He began, "You see, Major, we've gotten some information based on a report Spencer looked into that the Congress received in 1988. It's a classified navy report about missiles undergoing an accidental chain reaction in certain abnormal conditions. The likelihood of that the right combinations of these circumstances occurring was very low."

Willie interrupted, "Wait a minute, Henry, I didn't think we had anything to worry about. I thought your man was the absolute definitive expert on the subject."

"He is," answered Henry, "but based on his research on the Soviet missiles of that era, he's found, believe or not, that they used certain techniques that we just started using in the mid-eighties."

"Okay, let's hear the details."

"Well, as I understand it, a fundamental rule of nuclear warhead design is that the enriched uranium and other nuclear fuels in it need to be 'subcritical' at all times before a committed firing. That is, the materials must be in a physical state that keeps them from undergoing a sustained nuclear chain reaction which could lead to a nuclear detonation."

"Henry, you're going to have to be a little more basic for me if you will. I'm neither a nuclear physicist nor a mind reader."

"This weapons report from the navy indicated the existence of a potential hazard. Sandia Laboratories designed a fusing and firing assembly that's very similar to what my man has discovered about the Soviet missiles. In light of the time these things have been sitting and the likelihood that there's been no maintenance or servicing, some of the nuclear fuels and the uranium may have been decaying in such a manner that they could be near critical. The likelihood of 'abnormal circumstances' as described by the report is not clear. My man feels it's highly unlikely that the right combination of adverse conditions would occur, but he said it could not be dismissed."

"If the worst-case scenario did occur, what are we looking at here in damage?"

Henry answered, "Worst case? Well, it would probably cause radioactive contamination and possibly an explosion but not a bomb like detonation."

"Well," Willie asked, "will it happen or not?"

"We don't believe so, but I had to tell you so you could let General Anderson know; after all, he is the deputy chief here and this is his operation."

"Henry," the major winced, "I'd appreciate it if you wouldn't speak so freely in my office."

"What, are you worried about being wired?"

"Henry, nobody knows who's wired, you know that. Just look at Ollie, who would have thought they had that one pinned? Willie ran his hand over his smooth military cut hair. He looked down and then around the office. There was silence for at least ten seconds and then he spoke.

"I don't see we have much choice, Henry. As I see it, you're telling me you've got the best man on your team in nuclear weapons and the time is short. If you and your team feel confident, then it's a go. Forget the body count, if something goes wrong on this one, the boys at the White House are going to have a hotter one than they've ever known, and in more ways than one."

"Sorry about the General Anderson comment," Henry said.

"That's okay, Henry, I'm just edgy on this one. I don't believe my office is wired, but we can't be too careful. This one is definitely out of bounds and if the Joint Chiefs of Staff knew what we were preparing to do, they'd have us all, including General Anderson, in the brig before we could wink. The reality is the politics of this situation are soft. Our government thinks they can pull off a diplomatic one on this. Now we know better, and we also know that Castro could easily turn on us without even an announcement and sell one of these babies on the open market. They don't believe it, but we're the ones on the inside and we're not going to be the ones to wait and see what he does, we're going in there and disarming those babies before he even gets the chance to sell one."

After Willie finished, Henry leaned across the desk and said, "We leave tonight."

"How are you going in?"

"We leave on a C-130, unmarked, loaned to us by the boys at Langley. It's parked at BWI Airport and it's registry belongs to a bogus freight company. We will be coming in east of Guantanamo, near the Sierra Maestra Mountain range. That's where our source tells us the missiles are. The C-130 will open up its cargo door aft and we will parasail in from about 100 feet. The plane will be down to about 60 mph and the ride should be a smooth one. Coming in from the east we've got clearance with the boys at Gitmo, it's all been set up. After we pass west of the base, we jump. At this altitude, no one should be detecting even our shadows. The plane will take a slow bank and land at the base for support. If anything goes wrong, we've found an open field with the help of our birds, where we believe the C-130 could land and extricate us in a fast pinch. I believe we're as ready as we're ever going to be.

"Well, you've got my best riding with you, and if you go up in a puff of smoke and you happen to have the time to think of me, don't worry, we'll be going up in smoke here too."

Henry got up and before he could salute the major, Willie stuck out his hand. At this point with the kind of mission they were going on, Willie felt he wanted to shake Henry's hand.

As Henry left NSA headquarters, he headed back to his place in Alexandria. He had a few hours left before they would meet at the airport, and he thought he'd go home and take care of a few personal items. He wasn't nervous or superstitious, but prudence always told him to be prepared.

It was 3:00 p.m. when Henry left for BWI Airport. He had given everyone instructions that they were to rendezvous at 5:00 p.m. When he arrived at the airport, they were all there and waiting. The C-130 was already loaded by the boys from Langley based on a little shopping list Henry had passed on to them.

All of the team SIREN group were ready and waiting. They met in the corner of an empty work hangar. They were all dressed in civilian clothes. They would change their clothes on the plane after they took off. There was no reason to cast any suspicions by arriving in military gear at a commercial airport.

Barry Henson laid a map on the table as they all gathered around to review their landing area. The hangar was completely empty. This hangar was rented by the same bogus CIA company that had the lease on the C-130 they'd be flying in on. With the late afternoon light streaming in from the skylights, they all focused on Barry's instructions.

"We'll be dropping in approximately twenty miles to the west of the missile storage area. We're coming in from the west as they'll likely only be watching to the east, towards Gitmo," Barry said. Barry was well familiar with this area, as he'd done some hiking and climbing in the Sierra Maestras back in the days before Fidel's arrival, when Americans were welcome and abounded as vacationers throughout the island.

Joel, the electronics man, said they'd be covered from detection with a low altitude approach of the C-130. What he was concerned about once on the ground would be the motion detectors. Since Eliot was the recon expert, Joel said he and Eliot would have to be maneuvering about fifty yards ahead of Henry, Spencer, and Barry. He'd be with Eliot in the forward point, identifying any motion sensors as they approached the missile storage area. All evidence pointed to the fact that they had such devices from the Soviets; the question was, was everything still in working order now that his military machine was running on empty?

Joel indicated that the chances were good that the sensors were still operable, since they were solid state and needed next to no maintenance. They were after all developed for outside use in all weather and all terrain situations.

Joel had developed a device for just this type of situation. It was an electronic source reflector which used some of the same simple technology that state troopers used to determine if truckers had radar detectors. The device he developed could have been worth quite a bit of money, but since Joel developed it on government time and government money, it now belonged to Uncle Sam.

With Eliot at his side on point, they would not only do well in traversing the terrain but could set up a solid trail with markers which the rest of team SIREN could follow easily. While they would be setting down in a low-lying wooded area at the foot of the mountains, there would be a certain amount of climbing they'd be doing before they reached ground zero. In any areas requiring a vertical climb, Eliot would be setting in the pitons with lines, so the group would follow smoothly. Henry said they would all catch up with one another every fifteen minutes as they moved towards ground zero.

Spencer was silent as each of them reviewed their various jobs and how it would all go. He knew his work would be beginning once they reached the warhead storage site. He really had no major concerns at this point. If the warheads were in stable condition, he would know it the minute he examined them. About the only thing he needed from team SIREN was to get him there.

It was now 7:00 p.m. and it was time to get on board. They all walked out of the hangar together. It was dark out and they could make out the outline of the C-130 as they walked towards it. The aft cargo door was open, and they walked into the plane as if they were walking into the belly of the beast. Although everyone was casual and calm as they sat down and buckled up for the takeoff, Henry knew that they each shared the same thoughts at that moment, focusing on what their task was, getting it done, and then getting the hell out of there and returning home safely.

As the plane lifted off the runway, Henry leaned his head back against the bulkhead, closed his eyes, and tried to let it all go blank. They had six hours until zero hour and shut-eye right now was the best thing he could hope for at the moment. Henry had learned a long time ago in this business, "Ain't no reason to worry about it until you're in it."

Chapter 10

The Sell

Fidel was sitting in his office behind a huge ornate wooden desk. There were carved corners and beveled legs. He was, as usual, wearing his fatigues. It was traditional that he should be dressed in his revolutionary garb whenever he was meeting with his junta. For him, it was as if he needed to be in fatigues as compared to a uniform in order to remind everyone in a subtle manner that he was still a leader of the revolution and not some military figurehead who ruled from on high. Across the room was a huge conference table made of beautiful mahogany. Fernando was standing in between Fidel and the rest of the generals sitting around the huge table.

Fernando began, "I have met with the CIA contacts. Their story is good, at least what I was able to learn from our time together. What they propose is to give us the power to control our future, not through a short-term gain by aid or trade benefits, but by allowing us the possibility to do it on our own.

One of the generals spoke first. He said, "What we need now is the lifting of the blockades, we need food for the people. What we don't need is promises for the future."

Fernando looked at him with a plea of passion in his eyes. He said, "General, this is more than we could have hoped for; this is a real future. Fernando proceeded to tell them all the benefits of what the US was offering. He explained that even with his meager understanding from the briefing he received from their scientists, what they were about to receive would mean more than any blockade relief or aid could ever bring to the people of Cuba. "Be it their way of avoiding a confrontation or not, what they give us now will truly spell freedom for our nation and our people."

As Fernando spoke, Fidel looked on. He was keeping silent, so as not to act too hastily in either direction. Actually, Fidel had no desire to accept any proposal from the Americans but only to play his part. He has allowed the charade to live alongside that of the Americans. His feeling was that nothing would satisfy him until he had his revenge on those pigs who have kept him in the cold so long. During the days of his partnership with the Soviet Union, he was much less affected by the US Sanctions. They had almost become a joke with Russia at his back for support. During those years, he had almost forgotten what Kennedy and the others had tried to do. His country prospered and he was their hero.

But that was then, and this was now. With the Soviets gone, his country rapidly slid downhill economically without their support. In only a matter of three years, his nation had become starved for fuel, food, and other necessities to keep their economy going. He knew that their future would not be linked to any kind of under the table trade with America. The US no more wanted his nation and regime to flourish than they wanted the massive immigration of all those Haitians. With his warheads, he would bring America to make a deal in the open.

It was as his conversation was with Fernando before, the only safety he could truly count on was if the deal for the warheads was done in the open, with the world looking on. Fidel understood with what was going on in the Middle East, that the rest of the world would force the trade by coercion on the US. After all, what if a radical group from the Middle East did get the warheads. The rest of the world cringed at the idea and he knew it. Whatever happened, Fidel had no intention of ever doing a trade with the US; this charade would only allow him to get his junta to believe that he was seriously considering the idea. He looked at Fernando and thought, *What a fool! He truly thinks we can win by doing it this way. He is too idealistic, a fool. He is no longer the one I can count on; he is lost.*

After their last meeting, when Fernando talked of what he did in Miami, Fidel saw there was a change. He knew Fernando was no longer gullible to follow the party line. Fernando now almost thought of himself as a savior of his nation. Fidel had taken note of that during their meeting and made up his mind then, at that moment, that when all had passed and he had gotten what he wanted in the end, Los Hombres de Los Muertos (the men of death) would have to visit Fernando. His usefulness was long since passed. He believed too much in the cause and not enough in Fidel.

While Fidel was listening and pondering Fernando's fate, Fernando went on with all the zeal of a man who had just discovered the new world.

Fernando was pacing the floor. His hands were ablaze in an animated fashion that exclaimed his excitement. "Think of it," he continued, "with this technology we would truly become a leader nation."

Another general spoke from the rear, "But we do not have the time to wait, our people are starving today."

"I know," said Fernando, "but just try and follow with me. If we were to get aid and the sanctions and blockades were dropped, what do you think would happen?" He paused. "I'll tell you what would happen, we'd become the very pawns of the very nations that freed us. We would be given aid, but always just enough to mold us in the way those countries wanted."

"I realize we go hungry every day in the streets of Havana, but if we were to get this technology, while we may go hungry a little while longer, when we do rise from our ashes, we will be truly independent, as we once wanted, a free nation with equal shares for all. We will have triumphed over all who said our way of life could never be."

The generals mumbled amongst themselves, creating a dull hum in the room and still Fidel said nothing. Finally one of the generals turned to Fidel and asked, "What do you think, you've sat there and said nothing."

Fidel smiled to himself, dissention was amongst them now and they turned to him for his word. "What do I think you ask; I believe we must listen to Fernando's counsel and hear him out. After all, it is for our nation that we think now, not of ourselves." Fidel stood and walked around the desk. He leaned back against it with his arms folded and his feet angled to the floor. "I believe," Fidel continued, "that the Americans are pigs and that they wish to starve us. I further believe we should not consider doing anything with them under the table, as they will deceive us, but I also believe in Fernando, and we must not be blinded by the past or our hatred for what the Americans have done to us over the years. What we decide here today cannot be one man's decision. Let us hear Fernando out completely before we as a group reach our final decision."

Fidel had now planted his seeds. His anger was heard by everyone, yet he ended on a note of an impassioned plea that we should at least hear out the American proposal. He knew he had them. Fidel turned and walked to the window, where he could stare out at his lovely city with his back to the room, giving everyone the appearance that he put his complete trust in theirs and Fernando's decision. He knew with this posture that when they were finished, he could appear impartial and it would not take much for him to persuade them all that the only deal was the one he wanted, in front of the world press, with the threat of selling the warheads in the open market.

Fernando was oblivious to Fidel's whole charade. After Fidel turned his back to the room and stared quietly out the window, Fernando continued, only to be interrupted again by another question. This general asked, "You say we would not go hungry very long with this technology, but how long is this time you speak of?"

"*Mi amigos, escucha me* (my friends, listen to me)," Fernando spoke from the heart now, with as deep a passion as anyone could and all those in the room with the exception of Fidel sensed this. "I come before you all with one and only one desire to see my people and yours live well and free from the tyranny and inequities of capitalism, where only the rich live well and all others struggle to survive.

"Let me explain to you with a simple story what this technology could do for our people, and when I've finished, I will let you here today decide, and I will speak no more.

"I will give you all just one good example of how our future would prosper with this technology. Please bear with me a little longer and follow my story.

"Years ago when our leader, Fidel, first led us in our revolution and we became free, he had a dream of growing and exporting strawberries. We cleared many fields and grew what we could, only to find our goods competed in a world market where we failed to be able to deliver. Why, many have asked, had we failed in growing and exporting our agricultural products to generate the trade we needed an island nation to be able to prosper? We failed because we offered nothing to the world that they could not get in greater supply at a lower price from somewhere else. With this technology, we could change the genetics of a simple strawberry, so that we could pick it at its most ripe moment and ship it, so that it would arrive at its point of destination as ripe as when it was picked. It would be as hard and firm as the day we picked it. That's what would make our crops more desirable than others in the world and that's what would generate the money and trade that would sustain us in our growth to financial freedom and true independence.

"The world today is an economic one. Wars are not won by weapons; they are won by financial power. Look around you at the rest of the world. Can any one of you tell me of a nation who is powerful now because it invaded another country and took its wealth by force. Did Iraq succeed in its endeavors? No. Success today is economic; war and might no longer win the day. The world is too small, and it has consolidated. Why do you think we are alone now because the Soviets won the Cold War? It was just their loss which should tell us all that where we need to succeed is economically. This is what we would get from this trade with the Americans."

Fernando looked around the room and he knew he was way over their heads. He thought he was reaching them, but the look in their eyes told him they were Fidel's and they feared anything that was not as Fidel wanted it.

They looked at him with their thoughts on their faces; his story was preposterous to them. He too, he thought, would have probably felt the same with Fidel at their backs and hearing what he was telling them today. He became angry and frustrated. He turned to Fidel and asked, "Why aren't the scientists explaining this all to them, where are the ministers of finance who understand so much of what makes an economy tick?"

The room was silent, and Fernando finally understood he was truly alone. He searched their faces for something, anything, but all he saw was a blank wall staring back at him. Why wasn't Fidel standing behind him? After all, Fidel was with him when the scientists were explaining what the Americans were offering. Was Fidel even interested in this or was he, Fernando, just Fidel's stooge? "Fidel," Fernando turned, "tell them what we were told of this technology."

Fidel had it all now, just the way he wanted it. No one believed anything Fernando had said. With his zeal and desire to sell the trade, he had gone too far. It was truly beyond them and Fernando was not capable of realizing that this group of morons could never have grasped the meaning of all this. Fidel knew that anything above grade school science was far beyond them. This was truly the way Fidel had wanted it; he was delighted and hid it well from everyone. The group not only didn't understand what was at stake but their ignorance only enhanced the situation and made it easier to show this as an American trick.

When Fidel did speak, he did so with great deference to Fernando.

"What Fernando says may be true, my friends. This is what the scientists have told us, but after all, it too was hard for me to understand. If this is true that they can give us this science, then surely the rest of the world must have it too. If this is so, then what is it that we will have that others won't I ask myself? The answer I get is nothing. So, I see this as another American plot to lure us into giving up the one thing that we have to bring them to us, the warheads.

"No, I cannot see making a trade under the table for this biotechnology. I know that Fernando believes this will set us free, but I've lived more years as a foe of the Americans to know better."

Fernando was listening in disbelief. He now knew that Fidel really never had any interest in this biotechnology. His anger and bitterness towards the Americans even outweighed what this trade would do for the people. As he had felt when he left Castro upon returning from his mission in Miami, he had again felt the same. Castro truly cared more for his own power and force than he did for the people of his nation.

As Fidel spoke on, Fernando had slowly moved towards the corner of the room, out of line from Castro's speaking direction. He was sitting down in a large high back chair, lowering his head into the palms of his hands without being noticed. He could not believe what he was hearing. That all his hopes for what this biotechnology trade was going to bring to the people of Cuba was now nothing but a dream.

Fidel continued, "We must tell them no. We must insist that this all be handled by their precious United Nations. The same pigs who have allowed the US to starve us with their blockades.

Is there anyone here in this room who believes I am wrong?" Fidel asked. There was only silence until the general closest to Fidel turned to the others at the table and said, "Fidel has been our leader and has saved us before, we must believe in him now. The Americans cannot be trusted and this trade must not take place as Fidel has said."

The general turned to Fernando and said, "We know your heart speaks for the people but it's by the head that we must be led, be with us on this, Fernando."

Fernando knew it was of no use. Fidel had masterfully led them all this way and he had just been a pawn, being used to present the ridiculous.

"Yes, of course," Fernando said, not believing his own words as he heard them. "We are all together on this. I would no more think of not following the cause of our people than I would to leave our wonderful land and go to America."

Fidel stood away from his desk and said, "Good, we are all decided as it should be. There will be no trade under the table with the Americans. Tomorrow, Fernando will meet with these CIA pigs and tell them so."

As they all got up to adjourn, Fidel asked Fernando to stay. After the generals were gone, Fidel called Fernando to his side and put his arm around him. "Listen," he said, "I know you are disappointed at how this all worked out, but you must not be, it is for the best. These Americans must be brought to their knees for how they have treated us and humiliated us before the world. It is the only way."

Fernando did not argue; he too played his part well for Fidel. He realized now that it was all becoming a game of cat and mouse. He left Fidel even more disillusioned than he had thought possible.

When he was outside the Capitol Building, he was too disturbed and decided not to go home just yet. After what he had witnessed this afternoon, he no longer felt sure where he stood with Fidel. If he could have been a pawn for today's show, then perhaps he was a pawn for more yet to come.

He drove down to the Havana Harbor and parked his jeep. He sat for hours before he came to the decision that with what he had done in Miami and how Fidel had played him today, it would not be long before he would disappear. Surely Fidel knew how much he wanted this trade and how dedicated he was to the nation, that Fidel would have to remove him as an obstacle to his power.

It was with these final thoughts that he called Tess at the embassy and told her they needed to meet somewhere as soon as possible. She had asked him over the phone about the decision.

Fernando hesitated and then said that he preferred to wait and speak to Peter and her in person. Tess suggested that they meet at the hotel in two hours. She looked at her watch, it was 8:45 p.m. She said to give her an hour to contact Peter and set up the meet.

Fernando interrupted and said, “I’m afraid this time it needs to be really private, how can we do this?”

Tess asked if something was wrong. Fernando only answered again saying, “We need to speak in private, and the hotel salon will not do.”

Tess said, “Okay, where are you calling from?”

Fernando answered, “A public phone.”

Tess replied quickly, “Give me the number and stay there. I’ll be back to you within ten minutes or so.”

“Okay,” Fernando answered and gave her the number. He said he would wait for twenty minutes but no more. He feared it might be dangerous at this moment. He’d been sitting here too long already and for all he knew, he was being watched right now.

“Hang on, Fernando, don’t panic. I’ll be back to you in twenty minutes or less.”

Fernando hesitated and said, “Okay but be careful who you call and that your phone is safe.”

“Not to worry, Fernando, this is what I do but you knew that already. Hang in there, I’ll be with you soon.”

When Tess hung up the phone, she got a secure line and called to a location near the Tropicana Hotel. She had a safe messenger go and give Peter the message to take a cab to the corner of Cabo Rojo and Avenita de Revolucion. He was to wait there and within ten minutes, a car would come by. He was to get in and let the driver take him. Tess told Peter in the message not to worry, he would be okay, as he would recognize her driver who had picked him up at the airport when he first arrived in Cuba.

After she took care of securing Peter for the meet, she called Fernando back and gave him the directions to a safe house she had out in the country.

Fernando was a little concerned about the location, but Tess assured him it was far enough out into the country that if he were being followed, the car would never be able to stay out of his sight without losing him.

She told him that in case he thought he was being followed, he was to call this other number and just return home. That the number he called would get a message to her that the meet was called off, and they would have to try again the next day.

Tess knew something had gone wrong or Fernando wouldn't be doing what he was doing. Even more, Fernando wouldn't be worried about being watched. The question was what had happened, and the answer was what worried Tess right now. Tess was a pro and, in the years, since she'd arrived in Havana, she'd learned that being calm and in control was all you could do until things unfolded. The key was always to arrange yourself and the game at such a distance that if things came apart, they weren't happening in front of your face.

In a matter of hours from now, Tess would know if the fallout was their problem or Fernando's. Tess couldn't fathom what possibly could have gone wrong. After all, as far as anyone knew, other than Henry, Peter, and herself, this deal was for real. Whatever the case, if the worst scenario revealed itself and the charade had been compromised, she would get Peter out of Cuba tonight. The game, based on the fear she sensed in Fernando's voice, was beyond Peter's realm and she knew it.

Chapter 11

The Incursion

The C-130 circled low at about 150 feet just west of the Sierra Maestra Mountain range. It was now 1:00 a.m. and they'd been in the air for six hours, right on plan. It was a clear night, what they hadn't wanted, but with Joel's Magellan Navigators and the low altitude, it was highly unlikely that they'd get lost or anyone would pick them up. The yellow light came on signaling two minutes until jump. At that moment, a second lieutenant came out from the cockpit, cupped his hands so as to be heard above the noise of the engines, and yelled, "Stand by on the green." They checked each other's equipment and made ready. The noise was deafening from the sound of the engines and only became worse as the aft cargo door opened slowly for their departure.

Everyone was calm and moved about in mechanical precision. The tension was in the air and everyone felt it but the one thing they all focused on was the task at hand, never about making it back. For each one of them had learned a long time ago that if you didn't focus and visualize the mission's success, you didn't have to worry about making it back, there'd be no return. No one spoke, only hand signals were used. It was understood that upon landing if anyone was off on the landing coordinates, they were to use their Magellan's to get to LZ1 (landing zone 1) to rendezvous with Eliot.

They were dressed in complete black, with grease paint on their faces so as to camouflage their skin as much as possible. They all had on terrorist-type ski masks, exposing only a small six-inch circle about the front of their faces. They each wore lightweight fiberglass headsets for instant communication with each other. Their equipment was the best that Uncle Sam had and unless someone was hurt or killed on the jump, there was very little chance that any of them would become disconnected from one another.

The green light illuminated, and they each checked their equipment and chutes one last time. Henry was standing forward in the cargo bay. He too cupped his hands as the second lieutenant had done and yelled at a slow count, five, four, three, two, one, go, and with each downward swing of his arm, each man of team SIREN exited through the cargo door. They each sailed gently down towards their target, moving like black swans soaring through the night against the backdrop of a clear moonlit night.

When they touched down, they each quickly grabbed the silks and pulled them in. Eliot crouched low to the ground and began to verify that all of the team had made it. Eliot flipped open his Magellan first to verify they were on the right coordinates. The Magellan Navigator was about the size of a pack of cigarettes and looked like a small Motorola flip phone. It sent its signal up to satcom satellite, and in an instant, the coordinates were directed back to the pocket navigator. *Perfect*, he thought, *we're right where we should be, on target.*

God, Eliot thought to himself, *those C-130s may be old but boy can they do the job.* Eliot spoke into his headset and said, "Verify," and they each answered him in succession, SIREN one, check, SIREN two, check, and so forth until each man was accounted for. Henry was team leader, and as such he gave the command for each one to check their Magellan to verify everyone was reading the same coordinates and then he gave the command for everyone to move out to LZ1. While each of them was at some distance from the other, they were basically in an open area which Barry had selected based on his knowledge of the terrain. When Eliot stood erect for just a moment, he was able to see all of them, from all sides, as they moved together towards the rendezvous.

They jogged slowly in a semi-crouch like stealth ninjas through waist-high grass. The field was surrounded by gnarly trees with some palms intermingled. As they moved through the field, Barry could feel the dry earth of Cuba's autumn crumple as he stepped on it. At the edge of the field, they first came upon thick bushy plants about six feet high with pointy serrated leaves. The forest ahead at the foot of the mountains was filled with scrub brush, palm trees, and thin wiry scrub oaks that looked like cherry trees. There were no thick oaks, and the forest offered no canopy. Barry had explained to them, when going over the terrain, that the mountains here were more like those of northern New Mexico than any Caribbean rain forest they were familiar with. As a consequence, there would be a lot of zigzagging from one covered zone to another until they reached ground zero.

The first problem they had to be aware of was Loma Picota, which was the highest point in the mountain range. It was from there that the Cubans were ever vigilant at their observation post high above Guantanamo Bay, forever keeping their eyes on the Americans. When Henry's informant, the DIA's paid asset, had given Henry the information on the location of the warheads, he again found himself admiring Fidel in an odd way for being smart enough to hide the warheads right under the noses of the Americans all these years. And on top of that, keeping them protected from any possible search by traitors amongst his own by hiding them right under his own soldiers at the near base of Loma Picota in the Sierra Maestra's. It was as slick a trick as could be conceived; he had his own military protecting his hidden warheads, and they didn't even know it.

At LZ1, the group set up for the march to ground zero. As planned, Eliot and Joel moved out first, since Eliot was recon, and Joel carried the motion sensor detectors. Henry, Spencer, and Barry trailed back at about 300 yards to the rear. The idea again was if anything went wrong with Eliot and Joel on the point, at least Henry would have Barry, who was familiar enough with Cuba to enable them to make it back to Gitmo.

Henry estimated, based on Barry's calculations, they would arrive at ground zero, moving at a steady pace, within ninety minutes. That would put them at approximately 3:00 a.m. With one hour for Spencer to disarm the warheads, they would be back to the extraction point by 5:30 a.m., just before sunrise, with enough time before their cover was compromised.

Eliot and Joel moved out first towards the first cover ahead. With Barry's help, Eliot was able to map out incremental positions for each point where they would reconnoiter. When they reached their first point, ALPHA, Eliot signaled back to the rest of team SIREN to move up. As they connected at each point, the point team would again move out first and again signal back for the rest of the team to follow. The points of contact went from ALPHA through TANGO, twenty points in all. If Henry had been given the right information and Barry and Eliot hadn't made miscalculations, the trip wasn't going to be much more than a walk in the park.

It was at point MARY that they first heard the sound of a jeep coming down a dirt road. At that point, Eliot and Joel were waiting for the rest of team SIREN to come up from the rear. At the sound of the jeep, Eliot gave the command through his headset, "Papa Bear says lay down." At the command, Henry, at Eliot's side, dropped immediately to the ground, and when he turned back, he saw Spencer and Barry were already frozen, lying face down and flat, as two men in the jeep passed by them.

As the jeep passed, Eliot signaled all clear and they once again resumed their connect to point MARY. When they were all together, Henry said, "Jesus, I didn't think they'd have movement at one forty-five in the morning."

Barry responded by saying this wasn't a change of the guard. He continued, "Something must have happened and for some reason, they're going back down to the bottom."

Henry spoke next. "Well, there isn't much we can do about what's going on, except be as quick as we can, get the job done, and get the hell out of here. Okay, we've only got seven more points to cover until we reach the cave."

"How'd your asset know about this site anyway?" Spencer asked.

"My asset saw a lot before he left Cuba in 1962," Henry said.

"He was directly involved in the dismantling of the war-heads, and he served closely to Fidel. He was working in the war room just before the big showdown between Kennedy and Khrushchev. He was the one who led the secret team that dis-mantled the warheads. Needless to say, after he was given the order to execute all of the men involved in the operation, he knew it wouldn't be long before Castro removed him too. So one day, not too long after he finished Castro's dirty work, he arranged for an accident, only the explosion in his jeep burned another man and his driver. After that, he sneaked out of Cuba as quietly as he could and then just showed up on the doorstep of the boys at Langley one day. And so it goes, gentlemen, he's been in deep cover with us ever since."

"So why didn't he ever give us the info on these warheads before?" Spencer asked.

"Would you ever give up the biggest trump card you ever had, if you didn't have to?" Henry asked.

Spencer responded, "Yeah, but."

Henry interrupted, "Look, the bottom line was this guy was an old hand at espionage and we guessed he was smart enough to realize his gravy train would end one day. The guy liked to live good and that was the signal that told everyone we'd only be getting things out of him whenever he saw his good life dwindling. So, the boys at Langley kept him on all these years because he beautifully doled out just enough, every so often. Anyway, he was near the end of his trail over these past years, and for all we know, he'd been doing some double work and he knew about this coming down and came to us for his big last handout."

"I still don't get it," Joel said, "why wouldn't he have come to us before with this info and gotten back on the gravy train when we were slowing down his lifestyle?"

"Hey, would you have believed him if he came and told you that Castro had six nuclear warheads hidden just above Guantanamo Bay?" Henry asked. "No way. Basically, the guy held his cards close to the vest until he could use them. Anyway, enough about the story, if we keep this up, we'll never get to ground zero and what's worse, we'll miss our extraction time. Let's move out."

Eliot and Joel moved out again, on to point NANCY. It was quiet and they didn't hear anything else as they made their way, point to point, until they reached point TANGO. At point TANGO, Eliot and Joel waited for Henry, Barry, and Spencer to catch up. When they were finally all together, Henry checked his Magellan against the coordinates he had been given by his man. When the numbers checked out, he looked up and searched for the sloped area as it was described by the asset.

He'd said there'd be an overhang in the rock formation and due west he'd find the opening to the cave. Henry guessed by the way the shrubs were growing that the opening was covered by the heavy brush growth. Henry pointed off to the right by about 45 degrees and said, "That's it, boys, we're here." The terrain at this point was fairly steep and the entrance to the cave would take a few minutes to clear.

It was Henry's estimate based on the way things looked that no one had been to this area in years. Henry couldn't figure it, why would Castro not check on his goods unless he really didn't care if they went off right on top of the Americans in Guantanamo. *Well, whatever,* he thought, *at this moment, being here, it was too late to try and second-guess our boy Fidel, and this wasn't the time to try and figure him out.*

Henry turned to Joel and asked him to move out first and scan the area for any motion detectors. Joel crawled out on his stomach and moved along the slope ever so carefully, moving his motion sensors in long, wide sweeping patterns. When Joel returned, he indicated that nothing was showing. Once again Henry was perplexed at how lax it all seemed. It was an eerie feeling that something wasn't right; it seemed too good to be true. It all felt weird; why was there nothing, he thought. It was almost a certainty that there would be booby trap, somewhere. In his caution, if not paranoia, he asked Joel to crawl out from under the brush and sweep the area one more time. Henry just couldn't accept the possibility that it was going to be this easy.

When Joel returned again, he said, "Hey, like I said before, it's still all clear. I can't pick up a thing."

Henry said quietly to himself but loud enough for the others to hear, "Shit, I just don't like it. Castro would never be this loose; something's wrong here and we're just not seeing it."

Eliot looked down at his watch and said, "Hey, whatever's bugging you, we're already behind schedule, and if we're going to do it, now's the time or forever hold your peace."

"Okay, okay," Henry said. "It's just not right and I can feel it."

Henry looked at his watch and knew Eliot was right. Between his diatribe about his asset and the few minutes they lost when the jeep passed, they were now fifteen minutes behind schedule. If they were to allow themselves close to an hour for Spencer to do his handy work, they needed to move now.

"Okay, Barry, you and Eliot go up there and clear the brush, we'll wait here for your signal."

It was pitch black, as the moon was now covered by the clouds that were hovering near the peak of Loma Picota. They no longer had the moonlight to assist them. While Eliot and Barry were clearing the brush, Henry put on his night vision glasses in order to be able to better see Eliot's signal that the area was clear.

While Henry was waiting, the minutes seemed like an eternity. He kept on thinking, what's wrong here but nothing registered. It persisted in his mind how could Castro leave this so unprotected. Amidst his thoughts, he looked up and saw with his night glasses Eliot's signal. He turned to Joel and Spencer and signaled with a hand movement to them to come closer. He pointed his index finger to the dirt and indicated by scratches in the ground that they should move out one at a time. His last movement was to point to himself, signaling that he would go last.

When Henry arrived at the entrance, he knelt down and pointed for them to all move inward. In the dark, Henry pulled out glow sticks, like the kind kids got at the amusement parks, only these were military issue and they glowed a whole hell of a lot brighter. It was still and quiet and yet with the slight echo you find in hollow areas; every body movement seemed to emit an amplified sound. Henry signaled for no one to speak until Eliot had a chance to move out ahead and see what surprises awaited them.

Eliot moved stealthily in a crouch from one side of the cave to the other every ten feet, for about seventy feet, until he reached what appeared to be a cement wall with a door in the center. He immediately signaled to Henry through his headset that he wasn't going to believe what he'd found.

"Hey, Henry, you're never going to believe this, but what we've got here is one strong, mean, and solid cement wall."

"You've got to be kidding me," Henry responded.

"Well, if you think I am, just wait until you get up here and see this baby. This babe has got to be several feet thick. If you ask me, I'd say we've hit a dead end."

When the group arrived and gathered at the site of the cement wall, Henry stared in amazement. "Jesus H. Christ," Henry said. "How in the hell are we supposed to deal with this?"

Joel turned to Henry and asked if his asset had told the boys at Langley about this.

"If they did, do you think I'd be acting like I was at a surprise party?"

"Now, now, gentlemen, bombs are what I know best, and a good man comes prepared for every eventuality," Spencer said. "What I have here, boys, is what we call C4, plastic explosives, what every proper assault man travels with."

"Well, I'll be dammed, you son of a bitch, you truly are a prepared demolition expert," Eliot said.

Barry chimed in and said, "This all may sound good to the rest of you, boys, but when and if we blow this door, we're going to have the whole God damned Cuban army down on us like flies on shit in less than five minutes, unless our demolition man here has invented silent explosives."

Henry entered the dialogue. "Well, this presents a whole new set of circumstances."

Henry pondered for a moment. He had been in this business for over twenty years now, and this wasn't the first time a set of circumstances presented themselves as an obvious obstacle. Accessing the obvious that the Cubans were no more than a half a mile away and that the explosion would obviously be heard, Henry's next thought was the neutralization of the entire observation post at the top of the peak.

They were all crouched in a circle in front of the cement wall when Henry spoke, "We're going to have to neutralize our friends at the top if we're going to pull this off. The way I understand it, there shouldn't be more than a squad of twelve at the most. If we synchronize our watches, we should be able to be in position when Spencer detonates the C4. When they hear it, all hell is going to break loose. By that moment, we should be in position to begin the neutralization." Henry turned to Barry, who was the expert on the Cubans as well as their strategies and asked what he thought their strength and setup would be like.

Barry agreed; he too estimated that there wouldn't be more than the twelve, a full squad. He was confident based on his time in Guantanamo Bay that these boys had long since become bored watching our boys at Gitmo, and since the Bay of Pigs Invasion, not much had taken place, except the routine vigil that we each kept upon one another. Barry continued, "The only thing we can't really be sure of is, has the Ops site layout changed?"

"I thought our big birds kept an eye on these boys, and we had pictures," Henry said.

Joel, the communications expert, responded to Henry, "We do, but things can change. The problem as I see it is where the Comm Ops center is located."

"Okay, enough speculation," Henry said. "What we've got to do is get up there and do it. If we keep up this dialogue, we're just going to lose more time."

"Every minute we waste here having a discussion is another minute we lose on our timetable. We've just got to deal with what we've got." Henry looked at his watch and saw that it was now 3:00 a.m. and they should have been already started with the disarming of the warheads. He turned to Spencer and asked if with the time now cut, could he still get the job done.

"I would guess that with Joel's help, it might be possible for us to get it done in under forty-five minutes."

"Joel, can you assist?" Henry asked.

Before Joel answered, he turned to Barry and asked, "How much time do you figure it'll take to get to the top?"

Barry turned to Henry and said, "I make it at no more than fifteen minutes to the summit and possibly another ten for setting up. I've seen pictures from the birds before, and if things are the same as I saw them at Quantico, we'll only need to confirm which one of the Quonset huts is the communications center and that shouldn't be hard based on the hardware we'll see on top of the structure."

When Barry finished, Joel turned back to Henry and said, "Listen, this isn't exactly my field, but in the time we'll have before you guys get to the top, I'm sure Spencer could bring me up to speed on what I've got to do. I mean, I am an electronics whiz, I've just never applied those skills to disarming a nuclear warhead. If Spencer feels confident, then I'm game! After all, it appears our options seem to be evaporating with every tick of the clock, if you get my drift," as Joel looked at his watch and then at Henry.

Henry again turned and looked at his watch for a moment. It couldn't have been more than five seconds when Henry looked up and said, "Okay, time's a ticking and we've got no choice; it's now 3:05 and we've got to move."

"Everyone, synchronize your watches. At my mark, it will be exactly 3:06. Mark," Henry called out quietly at the exact moment.

Henry looked at them all and said, "I'm going to give us twenty-five minutes to get there and get in place. When we hear the plastics blow, we'll begin the assault. Joel, you'll be here with Spencer. Barry, Eliot, and me will hit them when they've heard the explosion and all hell breaks loose. Spencer, your time will begin at that moment. I estimate, if we're successful, completion in only a matter of minutes. You're to begin your work the minute that concrete wall is blown. You're not to wait a minute longer."

Joel asked, "And what if you guys aren't successful?"

"At that point, it won't make a bit of difference," Henry said.

"Once you guys have blown the wall and they've heard the explosion, if we're not successful, they'll be on you anyway. We've got to proceed as if everything is go. Alright, everybody got it. It's now 3:08, at exactly 3:33, you hit it, we'll be ready and in place. If we're not, nothing's going to matter anyway, because we're going to be way outside any possibility of making our extraction time, and as far as the American government knows, this operation doesn't exist and neither do we, so I don't see a lot of choice here. Let's go."

After Henry, Barry, and Eliot left the cave, Spencer began setting the C4 explosive. He considered this the most delicate part of the job and didn't really feel comfortable with Joel handling this stuff anyway. Spencer figured this was all dead time anyway because he and Joel still had to wait until the rest of the team made it to the top. After Spencer pressed the C4 in the outer frame of the steel door in the center of the wall, he proceeded to tell Joel about the disarming of the warheads.

Henry, Barry, and Eliot moved at a rapid pace up the side of Loma Picota. It wasn't until they were within fifty yards of the encampment that they stopped to reconnoiter their positions relative to the camp. Henry looked at his watch and smiled; they'd made it up the hill in exactly fifteen minutes. He thought to himself, *well, at least they were on the clock on this one, everything else so far had gone to the shitter as far as their time was concerned.*

Under Barry's direction, they had made it easily up to the backside of the camp. As expected, there were only a couple of guards standing by what looked like a boardwalk perched out over the edge of a ridge. One of them seemed to be looking through wide-angled mounted telescope, but he was only glancing through it occasionally. As Barry had thought, they seemed to be moving about and talking in a pretty lax manner. Barry put on the night vision glasses and didn't see any others outside. He still guessed there weren't more than twelve, a full squad, as Henry had been told by his asset. He saw the small barracks and a Quonset hut where the Comm Ops center should be located.

They were lying amongst some brush, clearly out of sight of anyone. Barry took the night vision glasses off and turned to Eliot with a thumbs-up motion. Eliot acknowledged the signal and then sized up the area to give Henry what he thought their best positions would be for the assault. Henry looked at his watch and turned to Barry and Eliot and said, "Three minutes till *hell night,* boys, let's move out to our positions."

Henry stayed where he was and Eliot moved to the west, near the communications shack (OPS), while Barry moved to the east side of the encampment.

Eliot had decided, since he was the recon man, that he was best suited for the assault on the radio room. Eliot was the youngest and in the best shape, and if anyone was up to the rapid-fire situation that would unfold in the radio room, Eliot was the best man for CQB (close-quarters battle). While Henry was the team leader, he couldn't argue about the fact that Eliot was the best man suited for the CQB.

The waiting seemed like an eternity, although it had not been much more than a minute since they had assumed their positions. Henry looked at his watch and counted down the last ten seconds. Like clockwork, the explosion came and gave off a distant glow of light like watching a Fourth of July show in downtown Alexandria from his backyard. It was only half mile away and yet it sounded like it was next door. Henry tensed at what he knew was coming next. For Henry, this was somewhat above and beyond him too, he thought. At that moment, he remembered what Peter had said to him about this mission being way over his head, and he found himself smirking at the thought of his current predicament as he got near the side of the barracks and released his safety.

When the explosion came, the two men on watch turned and charged towards the Ops shack. Simultaneously, Henry could hear others jumping up in the barracks as they headed for the door. On the west side of the camp, Barry stood up erect and opened fire on the two running from the observation point and watched them drop as his automatic weapon fire cut them down at their stride. Eliot was waiting just under the porch before the explosion, thinking of how he wished he had a hand grenade to just lob into the Ops room. Unfortunately, they hadn't been planning on a confrontation or an armed assault, so there were no grenades. He was however grateful that at least Spencer was the man for all seasons and had that C4 with him. In light of all their obstacles, they were at least a step closer to completion of their mission.

When Eliot heard the explosion, he slid out from under the porch and jumped over the rail to enter the Ops room. The door was open, and when he stepped in, there were three Cubans. The one at the radio didn't even bother to turn around. He was already in the process of trying to get out on the radio for help. One of the Cubans was going for an AK-47 leaning against a chair when Eliot opened up on him first. Simultaneously, at that same moment, a second man had reached his weapon and turned to fire on Eliot just as Eliot turned on him. Eliot was hit first, clipped in the shoulder. Hit, he fell to the floor in a roll, firing as he went down at the second soldier. The Cuban dropped and Eliot continued firing, taking out the last man on the radio in one clean sweep.

Henry, with his back against the side wall of the barracks, waited as they all ran outside. The sweat was running down the side of his face and his back was pressed so hard against the wall, it almost felt as if he had become part of it. With fear as his guardian angel, he patiently waited until he was sure that they were all outside. They had all come out in a cluster, one right after another, no more than a few feet apart, when Henry stepped from the side of the barracks and opened fire, taking them all down in one motion. When the noise from the weapon fire had stopped, Henry figured it was all over and walked over to view the damage.

While Henry knew what his business was about, he was not a professional soldier and killing of this scale was not something he was used to. Henry stepped out into the open and approached the fallen bodies, to view the carnage of which he was now a part. Eliot was still standing in the doorway of the radio shack. His shoulder bleeding but he felt no pain. He just stood there looking at Henry standing over the dead soldiers and thinking how it reminded him of Vietnam at the end of a fire fight, total silence. At that very instant, he saw a last Cuban come running out onto the steps of the barracks and take aim at Henry as he stood over the four men he'd cut down. With the cool cunning of a marine recon, Eliot picked up his weapon and popped off a quick single round, hitting the man square in the chest before Henry had even realized how close he was to being one of the body counts lying before him.

Henry, with a look of surprise as the last Cuban fell at the steps of the barracks, turned to Eliot and said, "I guess, it's a good thing I picked you for this trip, like American Express. I'm glad I didn't leave home without you."

Eliot laughed and said, "You've been away from the field way too long, my friend, carelessness like that leads to fatal endings."

"Well, thanks anyway," Henry said. "Hey, Rambo, is that blood we see on your shirt?"

"Yeah, just a nick. It's the kind of thing you need every now and then to feel real, otherwise it all just seems like you're in a shooting gallery."

When the three of them regrouped in the center of the camp, Barry said, "Like clockwork, I like it, and speaking of clocks, I make it at 3:40. I'd say we did well for a bunch of out of shape covert ops boys."

Henry turned to Barry and said, "It seemed a little light on the body count. I make only ten, there should have been twelve based on what you said about the head count."

"You can be sure the two we saw going downhill, when we were on our way up, are the two that are missing from this squad," Barry said.

"You're probably dead right and that means that they'll either be coming up here or they're gone for the night. Either way, if they head back up here, we're going to have to stop them on their way back, if they come back."

"Okay," Eliot said, "I'd say we kicked enough ass for the night, especially considering this wasn't part of the planned program, and in light of the fact that we're missing two of these boys, I don't suppose it's going to be too long before we encounter them again. Let's get moving on the double, we definitely don't have much time now."

It was now 3:45 a.m., and Henry had hoped that the blast they heard had actually led to a hole in the wall. They got started down the hill and Henry expected that when they reached Spencer and Joel, they had actually gotten at least half-way through the job and Joel hadn't been more of a hindrance than a help.

The door blew on and cement wall looked like a paper bag with a hole in the middle after you've popped it, massive. Spencer knew just what he was doing and after the explosion, there was a beautiful, neat hole about five-foot high and four-foot wide for them to step through. The cement wall was about eighteen inches thick and didn't offer much resistance to Spencer's technique. Spencer had squeezed the C4 all around the seams, not just on the hinges. His handy work was something to be admired. In many ways, he was like a physicist, honing in and locating the least paths of resistance. He knew that to just doing the hinges would not give him the opening he wanted. *Even distribution*, Spencer thought, *that's the key to the right-size hole.*

When they stepped inside, sitting upright on wooden cradles were six canvas-covered conical-shaped nuclear warheads, about twenty-four inches in diameter and stretching four feet high from the floor. Spencer pulled the canvas cover off the first one and there stood a beautifully solid, cobalt, jet black, vintage ala 1962 nuclear warhead.

The first thing Spencer had Joel help him with was turning each warhead onto its side. He had already given Joel instructions on what to do in order to disarm the warheads.

Spencer had explained to Joel the details he needed to know in order to assist in disarming the warheads. He explained that they weren't triggerable in the configuration under which they were working. He continued explaining that at the rear of the warheads was the guidance system and that in order to neutralize them, they needed to destroy the connecting cables and break the pins.

Next, they would need to decode the triggering mechanisms with the alphanumeric thumbwheel switches. But first Spencer continued to remind him they had to get to the connector cables. These were like a serial computer cable; they were never symmetrical and had a certain pattern. They went from the guidance system to the coding vault, only one way, and once they were removed from the outside collar, they would have access to the code box of the warhead. Once these had disconnected, they would then finally be able to disconnect the ignition devices.

Joel asked, "You mean when we're done, these bombs will be of no use?"

"I never said they'd be of no use; we're just making sure that these babes will never fly again. Unless of course, the Cubans have somehow gained the technology to build guidance systems and that my man takes microchips and silicon, and without the support of their big brothers over in Russia, I don't believe we've got anything to worry about."

"But these puppies could be removed and detonated?"

"Well, maybe if they could plant them somewhere. But even if they could, their kill power as a nuclear device is reduced by at least 90 percent."

"But even if they could plant them somewhere, we're only talking about the possibility of an explosion with a quarter-mile radius. In order to really do what you want with one of these, you'd need an air burst at about 2000 feet," Spencer said.

"Incredulously," Joel said, "so in essence, we really haven't done much."

"No," answered Spencer, "we've done a lot. With what we're doing here, these babies won't fly again, not under Fidel's flag. And what's more, their value on the open market to a terrorist group is now going to be severely depressed. Listen, guy, this ain't a perfect world and we're doing what we can. Remember short of an invasion, how would you suppose we could remove these from Cuban soil?"

"So, in the end, we've really just disabled these puppies."

"Yes, that's exactly what you could say. But what's really important is that Fidel won't have functioning weapons to trade, and by the time this guy gets help, which I doubt he can get, he'll be too far gone for help anyway. So in the long run, what we've done here is to minimize this maniac's ability to utilize these weapons for his own threats. Just remember, our job is to keep Fidel on the short string. He's going to fall, one way or another; it's all only just a matter of time and he will fall."

As Spencer and Joel were working, the rest of the team returned and marveled at what a beautiful job Spencer had done in blasting through the wall. They climbed through and saw for themselves the awesome sight of Fidel's private nuclear war chest.

"So how are we doing, boys, it's 4:05 and counting," Henry said.

"Just great, boss man," said Spencer.

"How did it go up there?" Joel asked.

"Not bad," answered Henry, "but time's a wasting. In case none of you have looked at your watches lately, it's now just after four and if my memory serves me right, we need to be leaving just about now. Not to mention that we're missing two Cuban soldiers, and they could be showing up here any moment. So, what do you say, Spencer, are we almost there?"

"Fifteen minutes at the most and we'll be done."

"Okay, Eliot's out at the entrance keeping watch, is there anything we can do?"

"No, shut your mouths and wait out front till it's done, Chief!"

Henry and Barry left the two of them to work and returned to stand watch with Eliot. They didn't know what had become of the two missing from up top, but they knew it wasn't going to be over until they were at the extraction point and saw that beautiful C-130 circle and come in to get them. In about ten minutes, Spencer and Joel emerged from the cave and Spencer said, "High five, boys, let's get the hell out of here, mission accomplished."

They headed down the hill at a faster pace than Eliot wanted to. In the dark, with a steep grade, the terrain was not easygoing; however, Eliot knew that they were short on their extraction time and chances had to be taken.

As they approached a leveling on the terrain, both Eliot and Barry knew they were nearing the extraction point. Henry glanced at his watch and saw that it was now 5:20 with only ten minutes until the pickup. With all that had taken place, he couldn't believe that they were actually going to make it. When they came upon the waist-high grass, Eliot signaled for a stop as he knelt and checked his Magellan Navigator to see if they were on target for the extraction area. The coordinates bounced back, and Eliot gave a thumbs-up to everyone and said, "Five minutes to pick up, boys, all we've got to do now is hang tight and wait until our beautiful boys from Langley come to deliver us unto salvation. They all chuckled together at Eliot's little imitation of the good Baptist, and then they fell silent while they waited.

They were huddled together, each alone with their thoughts. Despite all of the obstacles which they had encountered, they all sensed the moment was near. Their anxiety levels peaked, each one of them the same, a jumble of emotions, one side exaltation at having completed their mission and the other side fear, knowing each that they were so close and yet so far.

Henry, the former aspiring actor before he had been sucked into the DIA, kept hearing Robert Frost running through his head, "The woods are lovely dark and deep and I've promises to keep and miles to go before I sleep and miles to go before I sleep . . ." Henry remembered that reading from when he was nineteen and the director asked him to read those lines for a part he so desperately wanted and failed to get. They'd stayed with him all these years and perhaps it was now with safety so near and yet so far away, that they came back to him now, waiting in some field, as Eliot had put it, for deliverance.

Within moments, they heard the C-130 engines as the plane approached and Eliot gave off two flashes with his signal beacon. As they saw the plane come into view, they all rose to run and meet the plane at its landing point.

At the very instant, they rose from the tall grass; from out of nowhere, Barry heard the command, "Alto!" Henry turned and looked at Barry and they both knew the moment they looked at one another, that there'd be no going home today; it was over. Barry knew in an instant what had happened, and Henry did too. The two Cubans whom they had seen earlier going down the hill in the jeep were part of the observation post squad as they had suspected and, on their return, heard the explosion and then headed back to the local garrison to report what had happened and to get reinforcements.

Eliot, ever the marine recon man, lifted his weapon, crouched down low and signaled immediately for everybody to spread out and form a perimeter. Weapon fire seemed to erupt from everywhere, and each of them, while lying on their stomachs, returned fire, not really knowing which direction the assault was coming from. After a few moments, Henry realized it was futile. The C-130, while coming in for the final approach, had obviously seen the automatic weapon fire. The Cubans must have been using tracers, with tenth round or so giving off a flash of light. It was at that moment that Henry's heart sank, and he knew it was over.

Henry cupped his hands and called to everyone to cease fire. Within seconds, the field fell silent. The next thing they heard was a command in accented English for them to drop your weapons and stand with their hands in the air. Henry nodded and said, "Let's do as the man says, boys. Just remember, this may turn out to be an embarrassment for our government, but if we choose to stand and fight, there's not going to be any going home, except in a body bag."

As they stood with their hands in the air, they backed up towards one another until they were in a small circle. As they did so, at least a platoon of soldiers began to encroach, their weapons pointed, in a complete circle all around them.

A lieutenant, Barry judged by the bars on his shoulder, stepped forward from behind the men closest to Eliot and said, "Who is in charge here?"

Henry stepped forward and announced, "I am."

"Your men are guilty of spying and sabotage, and as such, so will you be treated. You are not soldiers, you are criminals, who have invaded our country," the lieutenant said. At that he took his pistol and smacked it across Henry's face so hard, that even in the moonlight you could see the blood fly from his mouth. Henry fell to the ground holding his face but said nothing. This was not the time for heroics.

Henry knew that if they could just get to Havana, the politicos would know what to do with them and what they'd be worth in a trade to the Americans. Henry's biggest fear at the moment was that these guys might just do four of them in here and save only one to bring back to Fidel as a trophy. He knew that silence, while painful now, was the way to play it and he just hoped that the others would take his lead. Guys like these, Henry thought, with their Latin machismo, would not take pride in shooting them without a fight. It was Henry's hope that while they might get punched around, alive, these boys had something to bang around with and dead, they didn't. Spencer was watching intently as Henry went down. It must have been the fear on his face that gave the soldier to his left the incentive to shove the butt of his rifle right into Spencer's gut. Spencer doubled over, and he too went down.

The lieutenant then said in Spanish, "*lleva los* (take them)."

Two soldiers grabbed each of them and they were led off to some military transports nearby. Henry, as he was being led away first, whispered back to Eliot and said, "Whatever you do, don't resist, we need to hold out until they've gotten us to someone who realizes who we are and our value. Pass it along." And as they were dragged towards the troop carrier, each one managed to pass the word along.

As they were thrown onto the floor of the truck, Henry's lips hit the floor and he spat the dirt out of his mouth. He closed his eyes in pain and thought, *God be with me now, I've never asked before.*

Chapter 12

The Safe House

Fernando made it to the safe house as instructed, and he felt confident that he hadn't been followed. As he parked his jeep, he thought about the irony of the day's events and how they had unfolded. He, the revolutionary, who had believed in this leader Fidel for so long. The idea that he had even killed for him in the name of the revolution was now beyond Fernando's belief. He was nauseous with disgust from having finally seen the true Fidel. His stomach ached, so he could no longer stand the recriminations and he mentally forced himself to redirect his thoughts to the immediate situation at hand, the fact that he hadn't been followed. "Perhaps since no one followed me, Fidel has not yet decided to dispose of me." At that thought, Fernando laughed and said out loud to himself, "Fidel probably hasn't yet finished using me as his toy."

Fernando's departure from Havana had been mentally arduous. After he had spoken to Tess, based on their shared concerns for secrecy, he decided to make several stops before he left the city in order to give himself the opportunity to see who, if anyone, was stopping with him.

When he first left the harbor, he drove for about a mile, zigzagging with a series lefts and rights until he reached a little bodega (grocery store) to stop for a beer. He got out of his jeep slowly, stretching his body and arching his back as if he had been driving for a long while before going inside. He did this so as to allow himself time to observe all the cars parked in front and near the bodega. When he came out of the store, he paused and drank his beer slowly while leaning against the jeep, taking his time to observe if these were same cars which he saw when he first arrived. He painstakingly noted all the cars and after five minutes when he had finished his beer, he got back into the jeep, looked in the rear mirror, and drove to his next stop.

When he arrived at his next stop, a little cafe about six blocks from where he'd had his beer, he once again got out of the jeep, but this time he stooped over to tie his bootlace. As he did so, he was not able to observe any cars similar to those he had seen at the bodega. He went inside the cafe and looked around, pretending as if he were looking for someone. After a few minutes he walked out, giving the impression to the owner near the door that whoever he was looking for was obviously not there.

As he departed the cafe, he again looked in the rear mirror a few times and still he saw nothing. As he approached the outskirts of the city, he was starting to feel more secure.

He knew that with the gas shortage in Havana, there weren't many cars on the road during the day, let alone at night. So if there were any cars following him, he knew they would stand out like an oasis in the desert.

At this point, despite his paranoia from the events of the day, his confidence was building, and he was truly sure that no one had followed him. Once out of the city, he continued to grow more secure. He had not seen any headlights on the sparsely travelled roads, nor had he recognized any of the same vehicles from his two side stops.

While Tess and Peter had been waiting for Fernando's arrival, Tess had tried to fill Peter in on Fernando's phone call. She told Peter the truth at first that when he called, he seemed sure that his confidence with Fidel had been broken. She emphasized that he was very suspicious, that even as they spoke, he was afraid perhaps he was being watched. Tess then switched back to the charade of the mission and explained to Peter, not knowing that it was in fact the truth, that she didn't believe Fernando had been successful in convincing Fidel and the others about the biotechnology trade for the missiles.

It was during this part of the conversation that Tess looked at her watch and realized how late Fernando had been. She started to become concerned about where he could be. If he had been followed, she'd told him to call, yet the phone hadn't rung. He was long overdue and she worried. It must have been the time element that made her decide then and there that she had to end the charade with Peter. She wasn't sure, but something was telling her everything was starting to get out of hand and for Peter's safety, she needed to stop the act and bring him in.

She had been pensive as to whether or not this was the time to tell Peter that the mission to disarm the warheads was about to happen. More to the point that our team would be landing near Loma Picota in just over one hour. In light of her distressed conversation with Fernando and the fact that she wouldn't have confirmation of the mission's success or failure until the team was extracted, she finally decided it was time to prepare Peter. After all, she thought, Henry St. John carefully selected Peter because he was an amateur. While he had once done some intelligence work before, none of it was as perilous as this might become in the near future.

She took a deep breath and said, "Peter, within just over one hour from now, our boys, of the good old US of A, led by your pal Henry St. John will be landing for the real mission here."

"I thought that they weren't even going to consider that maneuver until we had Fidel on the hook," Peter said.

"Unfortunately, Peter, they never intended to wait that long. They only led you to believe that so you would remain calmer and thereby be more believable in your negotiations. Henry knew from the start and so did the others in operations that Fidel would never bite on this. It was just that we needed him to be preoccupied for a day or two. We knew that while he was busy trying to figure out what we were really up to, we'd have just enough time to pull off the raid."

"From the beginning, everyone but you knew Castro would never believe this. There's just been too much bad blood between us and him. We knew all along that our window of opportunity would be short. That Castro would be puzzled only briefly as to why the Americans would be so stupid to think he would fall for such a ploy. About the only people who really ever believed this trade was ever possible were you and Fernando. I'm really sorry, Peter," she said sincerely, "it's how it had to be. I've only told you what I have this evening because Fernando is now very late and something has gone wrong. I'm not sure if it's on our side, with the incursion, or if it's something on their side, with Fernando."

"Whatever it is," Tess continued, "we need to be ready for the worst possible scenario, that the plan has been compromised somehow. If that's the case, we're potential hostages and we'll need to get out as quickly as possible."

Peter stood, rubbed his brow, smiled, and said, "I guess, I'm the altruistic fool here, but I can't say I'll have regretted having met you no matter what the outcome."

Tess had felt the same sense of attraction that Peter had obviously developed for her. For whatever the reason, she too felt the same romantic bond for him. "Hey, I'm just responding to you negatively because I don't know what we're going to get hit with when Fernando gets here. He didn't give me much on the phone, except an extreme sense of urgency. Knowing Henry and the plan, I'm still confident we're going to pull it off," Tess said.

Tess knew the appointed time for things to fall apart was supposed to be tomorrow and not now, on the eve of the incursion. She looked at her watch again and realized that in the midst of her preoccupation with where Fernando was, she hadn't yet coached Peter on the party line, for when and if Fernando ever arrived. Tess proceeded and continued to explain that no matter what Fernando unfolded to them, he, Peter, was not to betray what he had just been told. Obviously, Tess felt confident that Fernando still thought they were on the level about the trade.

Tess ironically thought it odd from the beginning, Fernando was the one who had trusted them while Fidel never did. It was not because Fidel had seen the charade but rather it was his desire for retribution with the United States that no matter what it cost Cuba, he would refuse to make the deal.

There was silence for a few seconds and then Peter said, "So all this means that if the mission is successful, I'll be on my way back pretty quick."

"Yes, Peter. You'll be out of here by tomorrow at midnight."

"Answer me one thing, Tess. If the mission is successful, then what would they or Fidel have thought about the trade?"

"Nothing, Peter. First, the mission will be a success. Second, like I said, Fidel never would have agreed to the trade anyway and we knew that. He will merely remain guessing as to what we were up to until he decides to check his little hideaway. The success of this mission, however, will have left the warheads just where they were, only neutralized. By the time Fidel even realizes what's been done, he'll be fuming, because there won't be any trail to us or anyone. For all he'll know, he could have been sabotaged from within. So you see, Peter, in the end you truly were, as Henry first described this scenario to you, just a decoy. We, our team, will have come and gone so fast that Castro will never have believed that his secret warheads had been compromised. I'm sorry that you couldn't have known we were moving this fast, but it was best to have kept you in the dark. You played your role so handsomely that for a while I too almost became a believer in the trade and you."

Sad at the thought that he'd be leaving Tess so soon, he responded with the question, "And our dance in the moonlight together?"

"Yes. No matter what you think now, you need to believe that I have become quite filled with you also." Tess laughed, reached over to him, and put both of her hands on Peter's chin and with a smile said, "We shall dance together tomorrow and we will kiss like I haven't kissed since the last time I loved anyone. You know, Mr. Peter Kennedy, since your arrival, I've been caught by you too." At that point without realizing what she was doing, Tess found herself moved by Peter and she reached for him and kissed him deeply.

At the sound of a jeep outside, Tess released herself from Peter and went to a window to see if it was Fernando. At the sight of his jeep, she relaxed a bit, and a sense of resilience came over her, as if she still had the control of the situation.

Over the years, her skills had grown as she had also. Once Tess was like a lost little girl who had been naively sucked into a world, she knew nothing about. Now, with time and experience as her teacher, she'd grown up and had become the consummate artist. With the skills she had acquired and been taught, Tess had gained the ability to manipulate adverse events and still keep things on track. At the sight of Fernando, she again felt like she was in control again.

Tonight, however, things were not going the way she liked them—this clandestine meeting and revealing to Peter earlier than planned what was going on. She was now straining and reaching deep to orchestrate and keep things under control. Tess didn't like things out of control and for her controlling the dance meant safety. But on this night, she particularly didn't care for the beat of the dance.

As Fernando walked up the steps to the front door, Tess turned to Peter and said, "Let's not forget who we are and who Fernando is. We still need to assess what's going on. Don't interrupt while I handle this, but for God's sake don't be too stiff either. He'll see that too."

"Hey, I'm the novice here, remember," Peter said.

She was now addressing him in a very professional manner which Peter thought was unusual in light of the relationship he felt they had developed. At the sight of Fernando from the window, her tone seemed to become more tense as she prepared for his entrance. At observing this, Peter thought to himself perhaps he needed to be a little less calm and a little more nervous about things too. It was finally occurring to him that there was much more going on here than he had first perceived. While Peter might have been calmed by Tess's charm before, now for the first time since his arrival, his nerves were on edge as he sensed Tess's anxiety. He had no doubt, with what she'd told him tonight, that there was cause to be concerned and he was.

As Fernando approached the front door, he found himself transported back to another time and another day when he had been here before. He had always been awed by the size of this hacienda. It was seventy kilometers outside of Havana, and as a man of twenty-one, he remembered visiting this ranch after it had been taken over by one of Fidel's comrades after the revolution. At that time, if his memory served him right, it had belonged to an American writer.

It was a large, sprawling ranch, built in white stucco with large Vegas (beams), cornering and offering support for the roof structures. At each point along the roof, every five feet, the Vegas extended out like huge battering rams. As Tess opened the door, Fernando entered a huge atrium hallway, filled with small palms and crotons, of all colors. Ahead in the living room, he recalled the beautiful red brick floors. The room was filled with magnificent furniture, all of leather and wood. The room was filled with beautiful paintings and obviously had been decorated by someone to whom money was no object.

As Tess led Fernando to a seat, Fernando was still agog as he continued to look about at such luxury. It struck him odd that an American no less was able to own a place such as this in Cuba, once again confronting his new reality that for a price, Fidel would offer such comfort and grandeur to anyone who would pay. The beauty of it all only served to remind him of the irony that when it was all said and done, Fidel had really become no better than what he had replaced during the revolution, a self-serving capitalistic pig. The only thing different now was that Fidel was the supreme ruler instead of Batista.

As he was seated, Peter walked over with a drink from the bar and handed it to Fernando. "Here's something to wet your throat, *mi amigo*," Peter said as he handed it over to Fernando.

"Where have you been?" Tess demanded like a mother scolding her child, "it's 11:50 and I had expected you no later than 10:00 or 10:30."

"Well, I was most scared by what I saw and heard today, so I decided to drive around a little before I left the city, at least until I was sure I hadn't been followed," Fernando said.

Fernando began by telling Peter and Tess all about his day in Havana with Fidel and the generals. He explained about his impassioned pleas and about how the whole thing had been staged by Fidel to give everyone there the impression that they were partaking in a decision regarding Cuba's future. But never, Fernando emphasized, had the truth been further away. He continued to tell them how by the end of the day, it was quite clear that Castro had never had any intention of participating in this trade.

Fernando clenched his fists and banged them on his knees and said, "Fidel's only goal has always been and will continue to be to shake the world and bring the Americans to their knees." As his words spewed out, he was again sick to his stomach at his newfound reality. It all hurt and he was so filled with disgust that he was again finding it difficult to even think coherently.

As Fernando continued to explain the day, he thought about the bomb in Miami and whether or not he should be saying anything at this time. His thoughts were confused. He was no longer sure what side he was on and who was to be trusted. After all, these were the Americans. These were the same people who'd kept the embargo on Cuba all these years. But it wasn't the Cuban people, it was Castro and his regime that the Americans had been fighting. His mind was a whirl. *God*, he thought to himself, *but I was part of that regime and the revolution*. It was all running together. Right from wrong didn't seem to have the clarity it once did. Everything was becoming so confusing that he wasn't sure he could even think anymore.

As Fernando sat there and continued to rant about the events day, Tess became more frightened. She wasn't sure why, but there was something that Fernando had inside that seemed to be more upsetting than just the events of the day. Whatever it was, she knew she needed to bring him into a calmer state. She lowered her voice and said to Fernando, "I see your frustration and can only start to imagine how it must feel to have been so disillusioned by a man who had been your hero and mentor for so many years, but you must gain control and we must decide what we're going to do. Where are we now, Fernando?"

Fernando answered that he wasn't sure. At this point, his head hurt and he wasn't any less confused than he had been before he called Tess from the harbor. "Frankly, La Senora, I don't know. I'm at a point where everything I've ever believed in has all crumbled in one short day. I realize now that Fidel cares not for the people of Cuba but only himself and his stubborn pride."

Fernando hesitated and then said, "I realize now that as long as he is in power, my dreams of helping and changing Cuba are just that, dreams. I regret to tell you both there are things I have done for which I am very ashamed, and I did them all in the name of the revolution."

Peter broke in, "Listen, Fernando, we're all dreamers, that's why we do what we do, because we each believe we can make a difference. But sometimes we clash with reality, and we realize we're not omnipotent. It's not your fault. As a matter of fact, it happens to be a trapping that a lot of great men," Peter paused, "and women too" as he looked at Tess.

Tess interrupted Peter, "I'm sorry, Peter, but we're getting off track here, let's get back to where do we go from here."

Peter looked at Tess in amazement, she was keeping up the game. It finally hit him that she needed to stay on this track in order to continue the charade and leave the impression that the trade was what this had all been about. Peter, on the other hand, had felt so bad about Fernando, that he had almost forgotten that the trade was a ploy.

"Listen," Tess said, "do you want out? I mean, would you like us to get you out of Cuba?"

Fernando looked up in amazement. He had never given thought to that idea before. He pondered for a moment and said, "I don't know, I truly don't know."

"Well, perhaps you haven't given it much thought in light of the events of today, but we believe in you, Fernando," Tess said ever so sincerely. "We know that if you could have your way, you would have done the trade for the people of Cuba, something your ex-mentor obviously never intended on doing." Tess just couldn't help from putting in that little jab.

"I just don't know, as I said before. I would have to give much thought to that. After all, I've got my family to think about. In the meantime, what's really important is what Fidel is going to do next. I'm afraid that if the Americans don't trade economically in front of the world, Fidel will sell one of these warheads on the black market. He is driven with a hatred for you Americans that I only now truly understand. I once thought it was the welfare of our people, but now I know it is not; it is only his passion for revenge with the Americans that drives him."

Peter heard and could sense, while listening to Fernando, all his pain and disillusionment. He wanted so badly to tell him that he need not worry, that the warheads had been disarmed, but seeing Tess was a constant reminder that this was a covert operation and he needed to stop being so emotionally moved and he needed to stay in touch with reality.

"Okay, Fernando, so where do we go from here?" Tess repeated.

"Tomorrow morning, I will be with him, and he will undoubtedly give me instructions to tell you that the answer is no to the trade."

Tess listened and thought. When she spoke, she said, "Tomorrow, Fernando, we will meet as if we never saw you tonight. I have no doubt based on what you told me today that you'll be watched. At our meeting tomorrow, we will look very dejected. There will be pleas of reconsideration on our side, and you will have to act quite stern, to the point of eventually getting up from the table, as if you don't care to hear anymore. We will sit after you leave and look very disappointed. After a while, we will get up. Peter and I will then leave for the Swiss Embassy. The reality is, Fernando, there's not much more any of us can do. If you wish to get out, you'll need to contact me at the embassy before 3:00 p.m. tomorrow, and if the answer is yes, we'll get you out and it will have to be quick," Tess said.

"But what about the missiles and your government, what will they do?"

"They'll do what all politicians do, negotiate, compromise, and yes, Fidel may have his day of political revenge with the US government, it's not for me to predict."

"After today I fear that if it's that simple, Fidel may not be satisfied and he may just go ahead and complicate things in order to maintain a constant threat against you."

"Whatever, Fernando, that's not our task," Tess said. "We tried what was asked of us and we weren't successful, and you've just got to accept that. It's now going to be in the hands of the politicians, as I said before."

Fernando, realizing that there was nothing more to be said, just stared first at the floor and then at each of them for a moment. He then rose and said, "My friends, I wish it had been different. This all could have meant so much for the people of Cuba. I am sorry we are parting as we are. I wish it could have been more."

Peter rose and held out his hand, "I feel the same, Fernando. I too wish things were different, but our futures are in the hands of those more powerful than us." Peter felt guilty at his petty words, knowing this meant so much to Fernando and was only an act for him.

Tess got up and walked with Fernando to the door, and as he walked out the door, she watched him as he climbed into his jeep and said, "*buenos suerte, mi amigo* (good luck, my friend)."

As Fernando drove off, Tess and Peters looked at each other with a joint sense of guilt at having just betrayed a man who truly cared and believed in helping the people of Cuba. Tess turned and stood at the door for a while and just stared out into the night after he drove away. Peter came up from behind her and put his hand on her shoulder. Tess just stood there motionless and whispered almost inaudibly, “God, it’s a shitty world and this is a shitty business.”

Chapter 13

The Catastrophe

It was 5:10 a.m. and General Anderson hadn't been able to sleep all night. He found himself tossing and turning at almost the very hour that team SIREN was preparing to land. He tried to sleep, but the thought of how deep this operation had gone was just more than anything he'd been involved with before. He'd just been appointed this year under the new incoming Democratic administration, and he knew that a failure at what his group was trying to pull off would mean tens of careers down the drain, not to mention his own.

The phone rang and as he looked at it, he hoped that it was word from Willie over at NSA that the mission had been a success and that all of the team were safe and accounted for. When he picked up the receiver and heard Major Willie O'Connor's voice, he knew something was wrong.

"General," Willie asked.

"Yes, Major, you have news."

"Yes sir, and it's not good." Willie paused and, in the silence, the general said, "Go ahead, Willie, give it to me."

"Well, sir, we've just received the transmission from the extraction team via our safe network that as they were going in for pickup, a firefight erupted, and the extraction had to be aborted. They've not yet landed and they're flying direct into Andrews AFB. We expect them to touch down within the next two hours, and we'll be receiving the details at that time. We felt it was better to wait until they got in for interrogation rather than transmit any lengthy messages over our code networks. We believe the networks are secure, but in light of the fact that they're heading directly back, I gave the order to discontinue any transmission until we had them directly in front of us for a better understanding of the situation. I felt that the team was either on the run or they were already under detention, in which case timing was not of the essence right now. If they have them, they have them and what we'll need to do now will only be determinable once we've gotten the full lowdown on what took place."

"Okay," Anderson said, "I'll meet you over at Fort Meade within an hour."

"Right, sir, see you at my office. I believe we'll be less conspicuous there than at yours."

After Willie hung up the phone, his mind was racing with thoughts of his boys. The message they got was as short as the one he gave to General Anderson, simply that a firefight erupted just as they were coming in for the final approach and that they were forced to abort the extraction. Other than that. Willie was still hoping that the team had somehow evaded capture. He knew in his heart that the latter was not likely and that his boys were now probably in the hands of some pretty rough characters who were waiting for the word from their boss, Fidel, before they did anything.

Willie threw on his jacket, locked his door, and proceeded to get into his car for the ride to NSA headquarters. It was still dark out and as he drove to Fort Meade, he kept on running over in his mind what could have gone wrong. They had everything planned down to the last detail and he just couldn't see how this whole thing could have fallen apart. In a moment of clarity, he tried to settle in his mind whether or not they had been successful. He concluded that they must have been, in light of the fact that they were on target for their extraction and that it was only in the last minute during the final approach that the firefight erupted.

As the general entered Willie's office, the major stood up at attention and saluted. The general waved his hand and said, "Not necessary, Willie. From this point on, we may be sharing a cell together and if that's the case, who's counting rank here?"

"General, we've gotten word that the C-130 is within less than an hour's range from Andrews and I made the request that the pilot and navigator were to be flown by chopper directly here once they've landed."

"What do you think happened, Willie?"

"I don't know, sir. I can only say that they were in fact on time for their extraction, that the pilot had made a visual and he was circling for his final approach when the firefight erupted. I do believe, sir, that they were successful in neutralizing the warheads. I just believe something, or someone spotted them on their return to the extraction point."

"But how did they get pinned down so quickly by so many soldiers? Could they have been spotted and perhaps have not achieved the objective?" the general asked.

"I don't know, sir, and we won't know much more of anything until the pilots are brought here to enhance more of what we already do know, which is very little."

"Jesus, this is going to go down hard once the press get wind of this. Not to mention that we're going to be right up there with our friend Ollie North when this whole thing is through."

"Sir, has this whole thing remained clandestine as it was in the beginning?"

"Yes. It was my hope that we could have kept it that way even after completing the mission. You see, Willie, we didn't want the White House to have even known of this unless we were forced to expose what had taken place. The way we figured it, after we neutralized the warheads, we thought we'd just let Castro continue to threaten, since he'd have no way of knowing that his trump card was no longer viable. Next, we'd just let the powers that be come to a tentative agreement, showing the rest of the world that we were going to negotiate in good faith like poor souls who had no choice but to agree to Castro's terms. The group felt this would have put the White House in the best possible position in light of the intense world focus that's already taken place. This agreement would surely have to include some sort of onsite verification. We knew that once our government had the site inspection and received the surprising evidence that Castro didn't have anything to threaten us with, that US would have then been able to walk away from all this without having been accused of anything, except having shown good faith during the negotiating period. Of course, now there won't be any site inspections because Fidel now has our boys to parade before the world press. I'm quite confident that when our friend Fidel gets to the press, he'll be carrying on about how their sovereignty has been impugned and how the US illegally invaded their country, etc., etc. The general paused for a few seconds and then said, "Willie, if these boys aren't in hiding and they haven't evaded capture, I'm afraid all of us are in for a rough one."

"Sir, you can count on me to be there at your side."

Thanks," the general said, "but I'm the one who organized this party and if I can keep as many of you clean as possible, I intend to. There's no reason for all of us to go down. The first thing I've got to do is notify the White House of what's taken place and to prepare them for the Cuban ambassador, who I'm sure will be launching a protest at the United Nations as soon as he can get someone on the phone to lodge his complaint."

The general picked up the phone in Willie's office and dialed the special code number to reach the White House situation room. He knew no one would be in at this hour, but he also knew there would be an aide to answer the phone and he would get the chief of staff for the president immediately.

When the chief of staff got on the phone and General Anderson explained what had taken place, the response was as hostile as he'd expected.

"What do you mean you authorized a covert operation to disarm those nuclear warheads?" "Jesus H. Christ," with a note of exasperation in his voice, "I'll get the president immediately and we'll be back to you. Stay where you are, I'm sure he's going to want to talk with you directly."

The general just hung up the phone and stared at Willie.

"Well, how bad was it?" Willie asked.

"Bad enough," the general answered. "The president should be ringing back here at any moment."

The phone rang within three minutes and the general answered it, "General Anderson here."

"General," the president said, "I've just been informed by my chief of staff that the US government launched a covert operation against the nation of Cuba for the purpose of disarming those nuclear warheads we've been threatened with, is that a correct statement, General?"

"Yes, sir."

"Well, I don't need to tell you that before noon today, this is probably going to be all over the news and we're going to be looking pretty bad, John."

"I know, sir, and I accept full responsibility for the entire operation, sir."

At that comment, Willie took a pretty deep swallow and looked down at the floor. Willie knew that if Castro in fact had the team, General Anderson would have to be singled out as the fall guy in order for the American government to save face. He hoped beyond hope that Henry and the rest of the team had evaded their captures, but he knew it wasn't so. Willie listened as the general explained to the president what the operation had been and who had been involved. He avowed that everyone operated under his orders and that he must bear the full responsibility for this action. Willie could tell by the way the general was listening after that admission that the president assured him, he would be held responsible.

When the general got off the phone, he explained that the president's aides were in the process of contacting the Cuban Mission as they spoke to try and get control of this whole thing.

Willie said, "Hey, we don't even know yet whether or not they've been captured."

"They have," the general said, "I'm sure of it. I mean, it's a small island. Where could they go or hide? You know and I know, the Cubans have got them."

"Maybe, sir, but maybe they were able to make their way to Gitmo."

"Not likely, Willie, so let's stop kidding ourselves. What time are we expecting the pilots to be here?" the general asked.

"We should have them here in less than forty-five minutes, sir. Let's get some coffee, sir, and relax. As you said to the president, there isn't much more that can be said or done until we speak with the inbound pilots."

When the pilots arrived, they were escorted directly to the major's office. When they came in, Willie immediately pulled up two chairs and asked them to take a seat and get started on what took place and what they saw.

The navigator spoke first. He was young, maybe twenty-eight or twenty-nine at most. He appeared a little nervous, which was to be expected from someone so green to the world of covert operations. This was probably not his first covert assignment; however, it surely was the first one where he personally witnessed a catastrophe unfold before his eyes. "Sir, when we approached the site, we picked up their signal right on the money. I gave the captain the coordinates for the approach, and he executed them and that's about all I can tell you personally. Obviously, the rest of what I know comes from the captain's visuals. I was down below and was strictly operating on the instruments, sir."

Willie then turned to the captain. The captain was in his mid-forties and Willie was sure that he was no babe in the woods as far as covert operations went. The boys at Langley don't usually run an amateur hour operation. When they select someone to captain an aircraft for a covert rescue operation, they know a cool head and steady hand are primary in their manpower assessment. Willie first asked what were his visuals. He then asked the pilot to be careful and slowly go over in his mind for each and every detail up until they were out of visual range.

When the captain spoke, he did so extremely articulately and addressed each step of their engagement up until they were out of range. "Sir, as we approached the landing zone, I requested that the navigator, on our first flyby, turn on our instruments to scan for our prearranged signal. After receiving confirmation from navigation, I set our instruments to head directly for our target. As we approached our target at five hundred feet, we got our first visual of the team. They were closely clustered, forming a perimeter of no more than ten or twelve feet. We had sparse light from the moon; however, it was enough to confirm our sighting. I then turned the equipment and proceeded at a 55-degree turn and descended for a final approach into the field.

"At about three hundred feet and a mile from our touchdown point, I observed the flash of tracer rounds coming from all directions surrounding the team's perimeter. I would estimate that the tracers were coming from a larger perimeter of perhaps one hundred and fifty yards and no more.

I leveled off my altitude at a closing height of three hundred feet and flew directly overhead of the team to get the best possible sighting of the firefight. Our equipment did not take on any hostile fire and I can only assume, the hostiles were preoccupied with containing our team, sir."

"Were you able to determine the number of hostiles on site as you made your pass-by?" Willie asked.

"Not accurately, sir. I can say that by the time we were losing visual range on the team, it appeared that the hostile fire had ceased. I considered making another pass, sir, but I was under orders from Langley that if anything went wrong, we were to pull out immediately. I did take a wide sweep, sir, in order to maintain as much visual time as possible; however, again, sir, my orders were to exit immediately if there was any deviation from the prearranged extraction."

"If you had to make an estimate, captain, how many hostiles would you say they encountered?" the general asked.

"Sir, if I had to make a guess and it would be just that, I would have said there were between thirty and forty hostiles."

The general looked at Willie, paused, and said, "What do you think, Willie?"

"My guess, General, is that they are now in the hands of the Cuban military and that they were taken back to Havana. It's now 0820 hours and I'd say that the US ambassador should be hearing something from the United Nations or the Cuban Mission very soon."

The general turned back to the two officers and thanked them for their effort and their time. He reminded them again that this was all a covert operation as they previously knew and that they weren't to speak with anyone about what took place this morning. He further asked them to remain available for the rest of the morning as they may need to speak with them again. The general told them to stay on base at Meade and that he would clear it with their superiors at Langley." "Gentlemen, thank you and dismissed," the general said.

After the two officers left the major's office, the general asked Willie to call over to Langley and clear the detention of the two officers until they were sure they wouldn't need to talk with them anymore.

The general walked over to Willie's window and stood there staring out at the morning sky, wondering just where this whole thing would be going from here. As General Anderson pondered what was coming next, Willie picked up the phone and contacted Langley to clear the hold on the captain and his navigator.

General Anderson and Major Willie O'Connor spent the next two and a half hours waiting in the major's office for a call from the White House. General Anderson knew things were bad, but the waiting as with all things was always the worst part. It was now 1050 hours and still there was no word.

"I just don't get it, Willie. Why would Fidel be waiting to contact us about the capture of our boys?"

"Perhaps our boys did escape capture," Willie said.

"Come on, Major, you can't really believe that, can you? I mean, we've gotten definitive statements from the pilot and the navigator that they were surrounded by at least thirty and maybe as many as forty soldiers. You know Castro's got them; it's just why is he waiting to make his announcement."

Just then the phone rang. The major picked it up and answered, "Major O'Connor here."

The major heard the voice at the other end request for the general. He passed the phone over to him and said, "For you, sir."

It was the White House's chief of staff and when the general got on the line, he was thrown the same identical question that the general had been asking Willie, "Why are they waiting?"

The chief of staff asked, "Why do you think we haven't heard anything, General? Is it possible that our team evaded capture?"

The general answered, "I can't believe they did, sir. Based on the information we received from the pilots, they were completely surrounded and only God knows what Fidel is up to."

The chief of staff continued and told the general that whatever was going on, it's now obvious that for whatever reason, Castro was not playing this trump card. He then asked the general if we had any other current operatives in Havana that could perhaps make inquiries so we could get some solid information to help us get a handle on what Castro is doing. "Obviously, they have our boys, but what is not obvious is that Castro hasn't told us or anyone else so far, and if he intended to exploit this, he surely would have done it by now."

The general answered, "Sir, we've got some operatives down there and we're going to make every effort to try and find out what we can. I'll be back to you within the next thirty minutes. I'll need time to get through on a safe network before we can put the inquiry in motion."

After the general hung up the phone, he told Willie about his conversation with the president's chief of staff and how the rest of our people and certain members of diplomatic corps are all holding tight, wondering just what's going on and why has Fidel not done anything yet. The general and Willie pondered back and forth about the possibilities, but none of them included the idea that the team had evaded capture.

General Anderson asked, "Willie, can you get to the agent who was with the decoy immediately?"

"Yes, sir, I believe we can get through to the woman right away. As you know or don't know, sir, she is the American delegate in charge of the Special Interests Section, working out of the Swiss Embassy. We'll need to get the message to her via our setup at Quantico. I'll place the call immediately, sir."

Willie picked up the phone and dialed over to the marine corps base at Quantico and got directly into the team's Comm Ops room. They had no idea what was going on and Willie wasn't about to start a dialogue with them. When the officer on duty asked the major about the team and if they were back yet, Willie just snapped and said, "Soldier, I need immediate contact with our operative in Cuba, how long will it take, son?"

The soldier responded by saying, "Stay with me, sir, and I'll have you online via our satellite within ninety seconds, sir."

While Willie was waiting for the connection, he covered the mouthpiece to the phone and told General Anderson that he expected contact immediately. When the soldier spoke again, he said, "You're on, sir." Willie then proceeded to speak, "Who am I speaking with please?" He said with a sense of urgency, "This is William O'Connor, on staff with the US state department, and I need to speak with Theresa Feher, in the US Special Interests Section immediately."

"This is Peter Von Zoest, sir, special consul for the Embassy of Switzerland. I'm sorry to say but La Senora Feher has just left for a meeting with Mr. Peter Riley and a special representative of the Cuban government at a hotel here in Havana."

"Is there any way that you can reach her before she arrives at the meeting?"

"I don't believe so. It's now 11:00 a.m. and I believe the meeting was slated to begin right now."

Willie paused on the phone as his mind raced and he tried to figure out where to go from here. The major was well aware of the fact that what this meeting was about was the biotechnology trade proposal, and if Fidel already had our boys, then he's figured out our little game and this meeting was going to end up to be nothing more than the Cubans arresting the two of them and holding them along with the rest of their hostages.

"Eric," Willie said, "if there is any way you can reach the hotel, do it. Their lives may be endangered and I can only hope that the Cubans are late and you can still get to them. If you are unable to reach them by phone then go there immediately, and if they're gone, you're to call this number I'm about to give you as soon as you know something. If you do reach her, get her out of there and back to the embassy as quickly as you can. Whatever the result, call me at this telephone number as soon as you've been able to locate her, thanks."

Eric played it safe and when he responded back to the major, he answered by saying he wasn't sure whether or not he could get to her, but that he would phone them back with whatever he was able to find out. Eric knew what was going on and had been involved in this operation with Tess for quite a while. Tess's counterparts were aware of him; however, he himself was not sure whether or not they knew exactly what he knew. As a consequence, Eric played it close to the vest on the phone just in case the line wasn't safe or this was some kind of setup. He knew by the tone of the caller's voice that something was wrong, and he moved with as much speed as possible to try and get to the hotel and reach Tess.

When the major hung up the phone, he turned to the general and said, "I'm sorry, sir, not only was I not able to reach our operative but if Castro's got our boys, then our operative and our decoy will surely be picked up and arrested at a meeting they're attending right now. Her assistant is going to try and get to her but based on what he said, it appears they're already at this meeting and my hunch is when he goes to the hotel to try and get her, she'll be gone."

"Well," the general said, "like everything else, I guess we just wait."

Their wait wasn't long—no more than thirty minutes when they received the call from Eric Von Zoest. "I'm sorry, sir, but what you feared I believe has taken place. They were not at the hotel and the man at the desk told me that the gentleman who was meeting them arrived with six soldiers and that they all immediately left together."

"Did the man at the desk say whether there was a struggle or anything?" Willie asked.

"No," Eric responded. He told them that the man at the desk said they all left quite quietly and that he didn't think anything was wrong. Willie thanked Eric and told him that if he heard anything, he was to get a message to this number right away. Eric assured Willie that he would do everything he could to try and find out where they were and what was going on. They hung up and Willie just stared at the general and said, "We're too late and I guess now we wait for their move."

The general turned again to the window, looked out, and said, "God, what have we created now? I guess now it's my turn to use the phone. I've got to tell them at the White House."

After the conversation with the White House chief of staff and the phone was hung up, Willie turned to General Anderson and asked, "So where do they want us to go from here?"

"Nowhere," the general said, "the chief of staff says we're to hold on everything and just sit still, unless we hear something."

Chapter 14

Castro's Retribution

Fernando received the call from Fidel at seven o'clock in the morning, earlier than Fidel's usual wake-up but not unusual based on the command that Fidel made, "Be at my office at the Capitol within thirty minutes." On his drive over, Fernando wasn't sure what Fidel had on his mind. He only knew that the tone in his voice was of irritation, and something was up. He hoped that what was up wasn't him. The thought occurred to him to flee, but where would he go? Unwittingly, Fernando thought, Fidel might be pushing him to take up Tess and Peter's offer to leave. At any rate as of this moment, he didn't have much choice but to show up as commanded by his former mentor.

When he arrived at Fidel's office, Fidel was standing there in his typical garb of green fatigues with his cigar in hand. When he walked in, Fidel responded immediately by saying, "So you thought these wonderful Americans wanted to trade biotechnology for our missiles." Fernando responded with a puzzled look and said, "Yes, that is what I believed, is there something you know now about this that I don't?" At this comment, Fernando tried to size up Fidel's question as to whether this was some sort of trap or was he setting him up with this question because he had learned of his clandestine meeting with Tess and Peter the night before. He wasn't sure, but whatever Fidel's game was, he was bracing himself for what might be coming next.

"Last night, my friend," Fidel said, "while you and I were sleeping, it seems our American friends had had some plans other than trading for our missiles. It seems a group of US commandos invaded our sovereign country around midnight to try and sabotage our bargaining chips. We are not yet sure what damage they may have caused, but soon we will know."

"But how could they have known where they were? I mean, no one but you knew the location," Fernando asked.

"Well, that is a question which has yet to be answered. However, what we do know is that they killed ten of our comrades in arms and we captured them shortly afterwards."

"And where are these American commandos right now?"

"They are here," Fidel said in a leering manner. "We have them right here in this very building. I wanted you, my loyalist of friends who was losing his way by these American fantasies, to see these criminals."

Fidel had obviously not yet finished playing his games and Fernando still feared he was not to be trusted. Fidel himself wasn't sure what his final disposition was going to be with

Fernando. However, he felt he would at least take pleasure in showing Fernando what a fool he had been. As to whether or not Fernando would meet with "Los Hombres de Muerto," he still wasn't sure but this he would decide later.

Fidel continued, "I wanted you to see this, Fernando, especially because I wanted to bring you back to the truth." Fidel waved his hand to pull Fernando by his side and said, "Come, *mi* amigo."

Fernando, however startled, tried to act naturally as he walked towards his former mentor. He was taken by surprise with Fidel's attitude. It immediately signaled to him that possibly Fidel didn't know about his meeting last night and at least in the near future he believed he was safe. Fidel obviously, Fernando thought, hadn't yet realized that he no longer belonged to his spell.

"Well, what do you plan to do with these Americans?" Fernando asked.

"There are many things we will do with them; however, first we must learn how they knew where the missiles were. That will be among one of the first things we are going to do. Then we will get hold of those two American agents we have in our midst, La Senora Feher and this impostor of an actor these CIA spies have sent to us. Then we will parade them to the world. In the meantime, we take pleasure in keeping these Americans wondering as to what we are doing. But first, my friend, I recall you have a meeting to attend this morning with these two former friends of yours. You will take with you a squad of soldiers and arrest them immediately. Be nice to them. I do not want to see any marks on these people; they are not like the American commandos whom we've caught in their uniforms, and we don't need the world press to see us as barbarians. But as far as these commandos go, perhaps we will kill them after we are through with them or perhaps not. After all, the Americans will never know whether they died during their little invasion or not."

Again Fidel spoke with bravado, "Treat these two spies well; bring them here first so we can show them these commandos of theirs and then you will take them back to their hotel and hold them there under house detention. We will let the Americans know of our intentions once we've gotten out of these soldiers what we need to know. I will enjoy seeing the panic on your friends' faces when they see their American compatriots here. It will be a pleasure." Fidel's words trailed off with almost a growl.

Fernando stood erect and said, "I will do what I should have done a long time ago, think for my people. Forgive me, Fidel, for being so blind; it was only for my country that I was so ardent."

Fidel smiled and said, "You are forgiven, *mi* amigo. Go, you do not have to see these criminals now; you may take your pleasure alongside the Americans when you bring them back. You too will enjoy seeing their panic as they realize their own fears before them," Fidel said.

As they walked to the door together, Fidel kept his arm around Fernando. It wasn't as if Fidel had been grooming him as a successor; it had been more that Fidel had to bring one of his children back to the fold. Despite whatever plans he had for Fernando; Fidel's ego could not bear the thought that someone did not ascribe to him as the great savior of the Cuban people. He had lived so long with his charismatic charm that he almost came to believe he was somewhat messianic. He truly couldn't comprehend why Fernando did not believe as all of the others did, but soon Fernando would learn where his allegiance should have been, even if it turned out to be one of his last lessons.

As Fernando went outside to his jeep, he saw six soldiers sitting in a jeep directly behind his. A lieutenant sitting in the passenger seat got out and saluted him. He then said, "Sir, we shall follow you to the hotel and will await your orders."

"Yes," Fernando said. "When we arrive, you will wait outside until I've called for you. I will go in first."

"But sir, do you not fear that they may try to run?"

Fernando responded, "To where, lieutenant? This is an island, where do you expect them to run to?" *What fools*, Fernando thought, *they are so anxious to capture the Americans that they couldn't even look around themselves to realize that their prospective captives have nowhere to go; unfortunately for them, they are trapped.*

As Fernando drove off with the soldiers behind him, his mind was racing with thoughts of Tess and Peter. While he had been somewhat shocked this morning by the fact that the trade had been a hoax, he also comprehended beyond that. He knew that he too was in danger and that Fidel was watching him. What he feared most now was that Fidel might use the warhead in Miami for revenge. Fernando's trust in Tess and Peter was surprisingly undaunted even in light of what he had just learned. The fact that the Americans were trying to disarm a madman could not really be seen as a betrayal, for as he had come to learn in the past month, Fidel was nothing more than a power-hungry maniac, who cared more for his power than for anything else. For after all, it was truly only Fidel who had isolated Cuba from the rest of the world, not the Cuban people or the Americans.

What Fernando feared most now was that Fidel for the sake of his own vanity would be willing to push the Cuban people further into a world of isolation just to have his retribution. At that thought, Fernando painfully recalled what he had done to his old friend Juan and the others, how he had killed and taken human lives all for the sake of this madman. It was clear to him once again that all that had taken place with Fidel was at the root of all of Cuba's isolation problems. But first, he needed to stop thinking about the past and get to the immediate problem at hand, the task of arresting Tess and Peter. He wasn't sure how he would protect them, but he knew he would.

When Fernando arrived at the hotel, he once again instructed the soldiers that they were to wait outside the entrance to the hotel until he either called them or came out with the Americans. As he left them, he could see that the lieutenant was not happy with the order, but that he had no choice was made obvious by the tone under which Fernando gave him the order.

"I will handle this and if I need you, you will be called. Is that understood, Lieutenant?"

The lieutenant with eyes straight ahead and in a begrudging tone said, "Yes sir."

As Fernando walked into the hotel, he went directly to the salon area near the bar. When he walked into the semi-open-air atrium, he saw Tess and Peter sitting near some large plants off to the side. "Hello, my friends," Fernando said. "I'm afraid this is not a morning to celebrate, for we have many problems." Fernando sat down and began to speak. He told them about his visit with Fidel this morning and about what he had learned and how the US commandos had been captured the night before. Their surprise was a look of pure shock, and they immediately tried to explain to Fernando why they had done what they had and what was at stake.

Fernando responded back with a plea for them not to apologize. He explained that after the past few days and the exposure to the idea of a biotechnology trade, that in a funny way, many things had changed for him. He told them that even though he learned that it had all been a hoax, it really didn't matter. What mattered now was how he had come to view Fidel and the situation of the Cuban people today.

"You see, my friends," Fernando said, "I have come to realize that even if this was a trick, had Fidel really been willing to help his people and not just preserve his power, this type of deal could have possibly taken place a long time ago. You see,

I now truly understand that Cuba's problems are not with the American people. We were once two close nations and the only thing that has kept us from

being close again has been Fidel. Had Fidel been willing to change as the rest of the world did, then my people would not be suffering today."

"You see," Fernando continued, "you've made me see the possibilities. What I mean to say is that even though this was a hoax, I've come to see the futility of Fidel's revenge and how it has hurt my people. When the Soviet Union decided to expand their political economy and integrate with the world, you Americans welcomed them with open arms. So it is difficult for me to see you as anything other than two sane people who were working to prevent a madman from possibly destroying your world and others at the same time."

"Fernando," Tess spoke, "after you left us last night, we both stood and watched you leave with a sadness inside, for as Peter has said many times since meeting you, had you been the one running Cuba, perhaps this trade would have been a wonderful prospect for your country. We, our country, only wanted to prevent the catastrophe that might have ensued had Castro lived up to his threats."

"Well," Fernando said, "that catastrophe may yet still occur."

"I am here right now at the orders of Fidel to put you both under arrest and bring you directly to him. He has your commandos down in a jail in the basement of the Capitol Building, and I fear the only reason they are still alive is that Fidel still does not know how they learned of the warhead storage site. It was a very guarded secret, which only he and I don't know who else knew of. I am now to bring you there first so that, as he put it, he might take pleasure in watching you see your comrades. I'm not sure what I'm going to do but I will help you and your friends somehow. I cannot allow this madman to continue on this path."

Nervously Fernando continued, "We will have to leave now and there are six soldiers waiting outside whom Fidel has instructed to come here with me to bring the two of you back to him. After that I am to bring you back here to the hotel to be kept under house arrest until he is finished with your friends and has made a decision on what he intends to do."

Peter jumped in and asked, "What do you think is he intending to do, Fernando?"

"I don't know," Fernando said. "I'm not even sure where I stand with him. I get the feeling he is playing with me, and this is all just a final show to humiliate me for my struggle to convince the junta about the trade. I'm not sure what he intends for me. But right now, we must leave for Fidel. By now I have spent too much time already in here with you. The soldiers will surely be cross-examined by Fidel or one of his captains as to what took place when I came to arrest you. Surely, they will tell him that I made them wait outside and how much time I spent in here.

The more time I take, the more he will be questioning me as to what I was doing in here with you two.

"Come, we must go now, but trust me, I will be back to you at the hotel, and we will figure some way out. I have been thinking of ways of how we could all, your comrades and yourselves, escape off the island but as yet I've not come up with any ideas, but somehow we'll get you out."

As they got up to leave, Fernando took both of their arms and said, "Not to worry, I am with you. When we walk outside, you're going to get the rough treatment but nothing more. Fidel has given instructions that for the meantime nothing is to happen to you two."

When they came out to the entrance of the hotel, the soldiers came to attention as Fernando addressed them. "One of you will accompany me in my jeep and the rest of you are to follow behind me. Do not worry, I don't believe these American spies will give us any trouble."

Fernando was acting as formal as he possibly could. Both Peter and Tess understood this. They knew that their only hope was Fernando and that the game needed to be played to maintain Fernando's credibility. As they drove to the Capitol to meet with Fidel, Peter and Tess looked at each other with thoughts of what was awaiting them. The idea that the mission had failed, and that Castro was now holding them all as pawns struck its fear deeply within both of them.

As they entered the jeep, Peter could see how tensed Tess was and he squeezed her hand tightly as if to reassure her. Peter could now see that while Tess had been in this spy business for quite a while, nothing like this had ever happened before. She had, Peter realized, over the past years, obviously just been a go-between and albeit a good one as he had observed, still she had never faced a life-threatening situation like this. The situation was frightening to Peter; however, he still seemed able to retain his composure. Tess's persona of bravado from the night before, however, had now turned quickly to one of true fear. This concerned Peter as he knew that they needed to be calm and keep their wits about them.

Although Peter was admittedly a novice at this game, for some reason he knew inside that he wasn't going down without a fight. That someway or somehow, he was going to get them out of this. With his adrenaline pumping, Peter's flight or fight syndrome was emerging and it was ready to fight. He didn't know if it was the being on the edge or what, he only knew that he was prepared to do whatever it took to get out of this.

Peter hadn't ever considered himself a brave man per se, but nevertheless there was a newfound strength that seemed to come forth from within that he had never felt before. Despite all the events unfolding around him, there seemed to be this calm from within that he couldn't explain to himself, and for whatever the reason, he sensed its presence. The question now in his mind was, in an escape, could he physically deal with the rigors of perhaps a hand-to-hand confrontation with a guard or a soldier? He knew he was in good shape but to be tested like this was something he'd just have to bank on. Whatever it was, Peter knew he wouldn't go down without a fight.

His mind had been moving rapidly since Fernando's disclosure, and the only thought he was having at that moment was where did they go from here. He tried to focus his mental energy on developing his recall. He felt certain that whatever was to follow, by being alert, with his eyes on everything he sees or hears, that he just might end up with the greatest ally of all, himself.

With what he had learned over the past two days about Fidel's vengeful mindset, Peter tried to prepare mentally what would be Fidel's next logical move. Whatever it was going to be, he found himself making mental notes, as if preparing for what they needed to do next to plot their way out of this.

When they arrived at the Capitol, Fernando escorted them both up the stairs with the soldiers following close behind. As they walked into Fidel's office, he stood and said, "Welcome, I am so glad you could both be here." Fidel continued to taunt them both with his conversation about their comrades' capture and how he intended to make the Americans pay.

While Fidel went on, Fernando listened and tried to look the part he was supposed to be playing. When Castro finally finished with his ranting, he said, "And now to visit your friends, come." They were then all led by Castro to a staircase leading four flights down to the basement. They moved in a procession with Fidel continuing his verbal taunts as they continued down the stairs.

Once in the dark basement of the Capitol Building, the smell of urine and sweat overcame both Peter and Tess. For Fernando, it was not quite as much of a shock, as he had visited Fidel's private little hellhole before. They walked down a corridor until they came to a set of locked steel doors. There were six on one side of the hall and six on the others. At the very end of the hall, there was another room with its steel door wide open, from where they could hear screams of pain in the distance. Fidel turned to his guests and said, "Please do not disturb yourself at this noise, we are only trying to get to the truth, and we all know the truth shall set you free. Wasn't that a famous phrase of one of your great American writers?" Fidel asked.

Fidel then ordered two of the guards to grab the two Americans and bring them close to the door he was in front of. At that, both Peter and Tess saw four men lying on the floor amongst filth and dirt, each in torn fatigues with blood all around their faces, concluding that they too had had their turn in Fidel's little torture room. "Well, I hope you're not too disturbed by what you see. After all, these are criminals who've invaded our country, and as such, we must find out what their mission was. I mean, as you can see by their uniforms, this was a military invasion." Fidel smirked at his own comment and then laughed out loud.

Fidel then turned back to Fernando and told him to take them back to their hotel. "They have seen enough; it is now time that we finish with our friends here. When we are done, we will get back to these spies." He then turned to Peter and Tess and said, "In the meantime, my friends, until we see you again, not to worry we will eventually let your government know we have you. Although I am quite confident that they already know that we do." With anger in his voice, Fidel turned to them and said, "But I shall make them wait until I am ready to talk, waiting you know builds a better bargaining position." As they were led away by the soldiers, Fernando followed close behind. Peter again squeezed Tess's hand and whispered, "Hang in there, Tess. This is a long way from over and I'm not going down for the count, no matter what." Tess squeezed Peter's hand back in a thankful way, and he knew then that with a little time and Fernando's help, they'd get out.

As they left after Fidel's last taunts, Peter began to think to himself again, and all he continued to find was the same calm he had found before. A voice inside just kept saying the same thing, *stay cool, it's all going to be okay, you've got the advantage.* As these thoughts continued, he almost wanted to shake his head. His logical side kept thinking, who did he think he was, some sort of superhero? But again, for whatever strange reason, he seemed to be rising to the situation and he felt nothing but confidence and strength inside.

When they arrived back at the hotel, Fernando went inside and asked the lieutenant to wait outside with the prisoners. When Fernando went inside, he made arrangements for Tess's and Peter's belongings to be brought to a new room where they would be held together. Fernando reasoned that if he was able to help them escape, it was certainly going to be a lot easier if they were contained in the same room. After making the arrangements, he returned back outside and escorted Peter and Tess to their new room. Playing the part, he ordered two soldiers to remain at their door at all times. He then instructed the lieutenant to keep the other four posted, two at the front entrance and two at the rear of the hotel near the entrance to the parking lot. He knew that he was at least leaving the kitchen entrance unguarded. At the door to the suite with the lieutenant and two soldiers behind him, he turned to Peter and Tess and made a very direct eye contact with Peter so as to signal it's going to be okay and said, "You will remain here until Fidel is ready for you. I will look in on you later and may just want to have my own little interrogation with you later in return for the personal embarrassment you have caused me in front of Fidel."

After he finished his little charade, he turned to the lieutenant and said, "Are my orders clear, Lieutenant?"

"Yes, sir, we will keep the guards posted as ordered."

At that, Fernando left. Peter and Tess were then escorted into their room. Once in the room, Tess turned to Peter, with tears, like small rivulets coming down her face, and put her arms around him. While holding him tight, she whispered into his ear, "At least whatever happens, we're together." Peter couldn't believe what he was hearing from this once brave little agent, but however the roles had reversed, he knew now that all he could do was try and calm Tess down and wait until they heard from Fernando.

Peter took her head and put her ear close to his mouth and said softly, "Shhh," as he put his finger up to her lips. He then chuckled quietly and said, "Hey, you know if this is anything like the movies, we gotta be real careful what we say; after all, there might be some bugs here and I don't mean the insect type." At that, he pulled her face close to his. He looked deep into her eyes and said, "Don't worry, we're going to get out of here." They then embraced and kissed passionately for a long while, and when they finished, he looked at her again and said, "By the way, if you haven't realized it by now, I'm crazy about you and I couldn't think of anyone I'd rather be stuck here with you."

Chapter 15

The Jail

The sun was just coming up and the coolness of the morning had been quickly evaporating. As the daylight filtered through a small, barred basement window, the dark cell began to illuminate with only the barest amount of light. The early heat of the day had already begun to re-infest the cell with the stench of human waste and the overwhelming smell had quickly become a wake-up call for Henry and his team.

When Henry awoke, he looked around and saw all of his men lying about him, either against the wall or stretched out on the floor. He was still groggy from his beating the night before and he couldn't quite remember how or when they had arrived at wherever they were being held. His head was killing him and he could only guess that he must have passed out during the beating he took after he was thrown into the floor of the troop carrier, which took them away. Their ride back to wherever it was that they had been taken was now a near blank.

As his head started to clear, he again looked over at the rest of the team to take a head count. From what he could see in the dim light, everyone pretty much looked the way he felt, beat-up. He got up and hobbled over to check on Eliot since he was the one who took the bullet during the assault the night before.

When he reached Eliot, he was unconscious but at least it appeared that the Cubans had attended to his wound. After checking him, Henry turned around to the others and asked if everyone was okay. While it was still pretty dim, he was able to make everyone out and they all, in one way or another, mumbled back, okay and holding.

Barry spoke first, "Well, wherever we are, this certainly isn't the Hotel Ritz. Christ, it stinks in here."

"Well, I'm not sure where we are," Henry said, "but you can bet we aren't far away from our old pal Fidel."

Spencer then sat up and said, "What do you think really happened, Henry?"

"I'm confident that it was the two soldiers who we saw going down the mountain shortly after we first arrived.

"They must have been on their way back when they heard the explosion and must have gone for reinforcements. Whatever it was, the only thing that matters now is how we're going to get out of here."

Henry paused for a few moments deep in thought, deciding what he was going to say next to the team. He knew he needed to discuss with everyone the interrogation. He guessed it would be only a matter of an hour or two, at the most, before someone was going to show up and start working them over one at a time. He himself was not looking forward to what it was going to be like, but he knew as sure as the sun came up this morning, they were each destined to be put through some sort of roughing up at a minimum. Henry at this point really had no idea how bad it was about to become, but it was nevertheless better to prepare them for the worst.

When he finally spoke, he said, "Listen up, guys, I'm sure each of us is going to be put through an interrogation, and I want all of you to remember that you're to hold on for as long as you can. No one is going to look at you as if you're a traitor or a coward if you break, but we each us needs to hang in for as long as we can. We've obviously invaded a foreign country on a covert operation, and we can expect that they're going to be pretty rough, so I can only ask each man to stand as much as he can, for as long as he can."

"Do you think they've contacted our people yet?" Joel asked.

"I don't know," Henry answered. "There's a lot here, and I haven't really been thinking clear enough to even address that issue. If we try to examine the facts, this is what I would guess on the first round. Fact one is that they've caught us in an act of sabotage. Fact two, we were simultaneously involved in trying to keep Fidel diverted with a decoy proposal for an under-the-table biotechnology trade. We've got a US agent who was being used as the rue and another US agent who was working with him out of the US Special Interests Section at the Embassy of Switzerland here in Cuba. My first guess is that they'll be rounding them up this morning. My second guess is that they won't announce anything to our government until they're done interrogating all of us."

"Hey, I'm sure that's the game, but why wouldn't they contact our people simultaneously?" Spencer asked.

"Because Fidel needs something from us first," Henry answered.

"And what's that?" Barry asked.

"He needs to know how we knew where the missiles were and he's not going to do anything until he finds that out. Remember, guys, we were involved in a covert operation, the likes of which no one, I mean no one outside of a small cadre of people at the NSA, knows about. Castro's got that much figured out.

"He knows the United States government is not going to sanction a covert assault like this. He's got his own boys spying on our boys from Langley and McLean, and he's not going to do anything until he's gotten the answer to the question, how did we find out where the warheads were. In his mind, he's got a hole in his organization somewhere and he doesn't know where and that's scarier than anything else. He's been compromised and he doesn't know by who. So that's why I gave you guys that little speech about holding up as long as you can. We're stuck here, and he's not going to let up until he finds out how we knew where the warheads were."

Henry looked down at his watch and saw that it was 0645 hours. Eliot made some noise as if he was coming around, and Henry moved over to him to see how he was doing.

"So how's it going, buddy, welcome to the Hotel Ritz," Henry said.

Struggling as he spoke, Eliot asked, "Where the hell are we?"

Barry jumped in and said, "Hey, if you're gonna keep sleeping the morning away, pal, you're going to miss out on a lot around here. Don't you know, buddy, we're the personal guests of our friend Fidel Castro. We've just been discussing what we should be ordering for breakfast. Do you want your eggs over easy or scrambled?"

At that, they all kind of laughed and moved in to get closer around Eliot. As the morning hours started to pass, they sat there, each telling stories about other jams each had experienced before. Henry talked about the failed Iranian Hostage recluse attempt during the Carter administration and Barry talked about the cock-up during the Bay of Pigs Invasion.

At about 8:00 a.m., some food of rice and beans was brought to them, and Eliot looked at it and turned to Barry and said, "I thought I told you over easy."

Barry got up and went over to Eliot and said, "Let me see that plate, grunt," and after he grabbed it from Eliot, he passed it back and said, "God, damn them, I said over easy like you asked."

He then paused and with the southern accent of Strother Martin said, "Gentlemen, what we have here is a failure to communicate." At that, they all laughed and applauded. After the laughter trailed off, Henry told them all to just relax, that there wasn't much more to be done except to just sit and wait. "They'll be here for the questioning sooner or later. It's just a matter of time, boys."

It was about nine thirty when the cell door opened, and an officer walked with two soldiers standing beside him. In broken English he asked who the senior officer here was. Henry immediately volunteered that he was and the officer then commanded, "*Saca lo* (take him)."

Henry was taken down to the end of the hall to an empty room with a small table in the center, with a single chair placed in front of it. He was seated in the chair facing the table and the officer stood directly in front of him. Behind Henry there were four soldiers, the two who brought him and two who had been there already. Two of the soldiers from behind came forward and tied his hands behind the back of the chair. At the same time, someone in a sterile-looking white jacket came in from a side door, pushing what looked like a portable EKG machine. When Henry saw the box, he knew instantly that they were going to be using electric shock treatment on him. He immediately tried to brace himself mentally. He forced himself to try and recall all he had been taught about pain diversion. With as much fear as any man could have in his heart, he held fast and prepared for what was coming next. He knew it would be just a matter of how long he could outlast the pain before he would pass out.

When Henry awoke again in the cell, he was lying on the floor with all of the team leaning over him, while Eliot remained still propped up against the wall. As Henry came to, he started to remember the pain of each jolt, as they applied the electrodes to his body. He wasn't sure what he had said, he could only remember that he hadn't lasted long.

Barry, next most senior in experience, spoke first. "How you doing', big guy? It looks like you got a new wave permanent in your hair."

Henry chuckled at the thought and with that slight laugh, he grabbed his ribs. As he held his side, he said, "God, I must have passed out from the electric shock, and they must have tried to revive me by hitting me in the ribs. Hey, how long have I been gone?"

"About forty-five minutes," Barry said.

"Anybody else been taken yet?"

"No. The way I figure it, they're going to take us one at a time so that we each get a chance to see the others return nicely beaten up." Barry then turned to each of the others, smiled and turned back to Henry, and said, "But based on how you look, how bad could it be?"

Henry answered, "Very funny, very funny."

While they were all joking about, the door opened again and this time there were no questions as to who was senior. The officer just pointed to Joel and ordered the soldiers to take him. After Joel was returned, with the exception of Eliot who was still drifting in and out of consciousness, the others were taken in succession, one after another. It was at about eleven forty-five, while Spencer was at the end of the hall, that Henry and the others saw the two Americans. Even though the opening in the cell door was small, Henry recognized Peter immediately and when he caught a glimpse of Tess, he knew that she must have been the contact at the Swiss Embassy. In further dismay, Henry knew that they were now all captives. When Peter's and Henry's eyes met, Henry tried to convey through his returning gaze, "We're okay," although he knew their appearance gave anything but that impression. The look on Henry's face was one of apparent pain. Henry caught Peter's slight nod and also heard gasps from Tess as she saw them all in the cell. Henry was not surprised knowing Peter, that he seemed to be doing his best to appear calm for the benefit of Tess.

After Peter and Tess had been taken away, Barry turned to Henry and asked almost rhetorically if they had been the team's counterpart operation here in Havana. Henry told Barry and the others that they in fact were the two Americans who had been working the decoy side of the operation and that obviously Castro was now holding them too.

Just as Henry was finishing up, Spencer was brought back into the cell, the last of them to be interrogated with the exception of Eliot. Henry was hoping that in light of Eliot's wounds and his drifting in and out of consciousness, they'd hopefully be leaving him alone for the time being.

The interrogations had been a painful ordeal for each of them and afterwards they each sat in silence, alone with their thoughts. Henry, like the others, could only wonder how this would all play out and for how long they were going to be held until the American government was able to secure their release. None of them were sure if they had revealed anything, as each of them had held their own and passed out long before any information could have been extracted from them. In many ways, Castro's pressing techniques were overbearing and they defeated their own purpose of obtaining information. His henchmen had been so overzealous at finally having gotten their hands on the American captives, that they hadn't considered how to dose out their medicine. Their results were nothing short of poor. They had literally turned on the juice to the point where even if the team was capable of giving information, the electric shocks were so violently applied that none of them maintained consciousness for much more than five or ten minutes.

Henry had been sitting alone in a corner of the cell. It was the role he knew and had been trained in as the team leader. As the commander, he knew it was his job to keep the morale up and he needed, even in these confined quarters, to be somewhat apart from the others in order to think. He was certainly concerned about himself and the team, but now he pondered what would be happening next for Peter and Tess. He had hoped they would have gotten word of the mission's failure and would have had time to have fled to the safety of the Swiss Embassy. But obviously, time had not been their ally, and they hadn't gotten the word in time.

He knew Peter was in good shape and was mostly worried about the woman. Although he knew that neither Peter nor Tess could ever betray any information they didn't possess, he was still pained at the thought of what the two of them would be going through. He was confident however that Peter would fare up well. He knew he wasn't a trained expert, but he also knew that Peter possessed an inner strength that he was sure would see him through. As for the woman, Tess, he didn't share the same confidence for her that he did for Peter. For that, he truly regretted what was probably lying ahead for them.

It had been quite a while, perhaps an hour or so, before Henry finally spoke. When he did, he said, "Well, I guess they didn't get much out of any of us or else they would have proceeded with working each one of us over. My guess now is that they'll begin to work on our friends who were here before. Since neither of them know anything about who the mole was, I can only hope that they pass out from the pain quickly."

"Where are we going from here, Henry?" Joel asked.

"Nowhere, not until they've gotten what they're looking for. But based on the fact that they've got two more Americans to work over, I would guess they won't make any sort of contact until they're done with our counterparts, and they've taken the time to assess that they've got nothing. At that time, Castro's only move will be to make contact with our people and go the public humiliation route before the world press. Remember while we may have neutralized Fidel's threats, he's now got us and we're his new pawns. So, boys, we're here and until we hear anything else, we best just get some rest and save our strength for whatever is coming next."

While listening, Spencer sat up and said, "What about an escape?"

"I've been thinking about that," Henry answered, "but as of now all we can do is wait. I've sized up this area and I'm guessing that we're at some sort of government facility. I don't believe this is their standard prison compound."

"Based on what I've seen through our small window, we appear to be in the heart of a city, and I can only guess it's Havana. My count on the number of guards was only about ten, including the boys who worked us over. We'll wait until dark and see how many are left here in the evening. If there are no more than four or five, my guess is we might have a chance to pull something off and make it out. If we are able to somehow get out of here, our next problem is how do we get out of the city and make it to Gitmo."

"Whatever, it's now about 1300 hours and all we can do is wait until this evening, so let's just settle down and wait until we see what we can see."

With that, Henry turned away from the others and tried to get into some sort of position to catch forty winks.

Chapter 16

House Detention

After Fernando left, Peter and Tess figured there wasn't much more that could be done until they heard from Fernando again. It was one thirty and about all they could do now was to try to relax and wait. They'd lain down together on the bed and Tess rested her head upon Peter's chest as they waited until they would see what would be next.

Tess had eventually fallen asleep. Peter however couldn't find any sleep as he mulled over in his mind all of the events of the morning and tried to make some sense of it all, now realizing that with Henry's team held captive and them stuck in the hotel, surely now Fernando appeared to be their only chance for escape. He thought about the coming evening and decided that if there was ever going to be a time to get out, tonight was it.

He tried to think about the layout to the hotel and the guards at the door. He felt confident that he could find an excuse to get the two guards to come in the room. The next question was how he would overpower them. If he could do that then he would have accomplished the first leg. The second leg would be getting out of the hotel. In his mind, he knew that for that leg to move forward, Fernando would have to assist them. Obviously, they would need transportation and that was something from the inside they'd never be able to do.

Peter moved Tess's head and got up to look around the room. He saw a heavy ice bucket. After sizing it up for a moment, he figured that he could probably use it to take out one of the guards, but it would never provide him with enough time to get to the second one. At that thought, he realized the ice bucket alone wasn't going to work as a weapon. What he needed was some way to neutralize both of them at the same time. These guys had weapons and he didn't. He needed some way to stop them both briefly, allowing him enough time to then knock them out one after the other. He thought long and hard and remembered when he was a kid at camp, they used to use a match with a can of Right Guard deodorant spray to make a mini flamethrower. With that in mind, he figured if Tess were the decoy and he waited behind the front door, he could give both of them a frontal shot to the face, keeping them at bay just long enough for him to smack them both good and hard with the ice bucket.

After working out the setup in the room, he walked back over to one of the big chairs and sat down. While reclining in the chair, he thought to himself, *It'll work, Peter*, and then with an air of confidence he said to himself out loud, "Not bad, not bad at all."

With the first leg of their escape worked out in his mind, Peter then began to think about the rest of the trip and how they would accomplish it. He found himself at a loss on some of the details. He knew what they needed to do, but he couldn't figure out what would really be possible without Fernando supplying the transportation. While thinking about Fernando's role, Peter wondered if he were overstepping his confidence. Was Fernando really with them? Was he really going to be the one to get them out? It had all appeared that way from their conversation at the hotel. Peter knew, however, that there was nothing he could do about it but assume Fernando was going to be with them and would come through.

Tess awoke and walked from the bedroom into the salon. She saw Peter sitting in the large sofa chair and walked over to him.

She sat down on the arm of the chair and, in a sleepy tone, asked, "What time is it and how long have I been asleep?"

"Oh, it's about three thirty. You must have been pretty exhausted from our morning revelations because you've been out cold for about two hours."

"Well, beauty is as beauty does, and we do need our sleep," Tess said with a smile.

Peter laughed and then looked up at Tess in a provocative manner and paused. He then reached up to her and pulled her into his lap where upon he kissed her passionately. When they disengaged, he looked at her again and said, "You know, nobody knows what our future holds and I for one don't want to have said good-bye without having told you how in love I am with you."

Tess paused for only a second and then stroked Peter's face and said, "And I likewise have found that I too am in love with you."

"Well then," Peter said, "since neither of us know what tomorrow will bring," he paused, kissed her again, and got up with Tess in his arms and carried her into the bedroom. As they fell on the bed together, they quickly found each other wrapped in the other's embrace. Peter caressed Tess's hair and told her how much he adored her. Tess started to cry and said, "Why is it always that when you finally find the love you've longed for so long, that it's only there for a fleeting moment."

Peter answered with, "I don't know. I only know that I'm in love with you and I'm thankful for whatever time we're going to have together." He looked deep into her eyes, they were truly like dark pools, and continued, "I do know that no matter what tomorrow brings, at least we're together now." With that, they embraced again and made love in the face of the afternoon sun.

They had both fallen asleep after they'd made love and didn't awake until sometime around five thirty. Peter stirred first and then nudged Tess to wake her also. He reached over and put his arm around Tess and said, "I don't know about you but I'm ready for something to eat. If my memory serves me right, we never did get to eat this afternoon and I'm famished."

"Well, I would have to say after our wonderful lovemaking that I'm a trifle hungry too," Tess laughed and continued, "Shall we see if we can get room service?"

"I don't know but we can try and see what happens." Peter then reached over from his side of the bed and picked up the phone. He dialed the room service number, and lo and behold, they took his order. He ordered without asking Tess what she had wanted. For some reason, their closeness of the afternoon seemed to make him feel that whatever was okay with him was going to be okay.

They both got out of the bed and picked their clothes up off the floor. While they were dressing, Peter told her about his plan and explained what her part would be. He explained that she would start throwing things, such as a few lamps, about for some real sound effects. Then she would start screaming at the top of her lungs and if anything was going to draw the men outside the door into the room, surely the ire of a woman could. Peter went on with what he had thought up and explained that once the two guards were out cold, they'd have a chance to at least make it downstairs. From there he hoped that either with the help of Fernando or not, they could make it out of the hotel.

Tess asked about the commando team and if his plan included them in the escape. Peter told her that he was a long way from figuring anything else out other than getting out of the hotel. Obviously if Fernando is able to assist us then we can consider all sorts of options but until they heard from him, all he could do was plan for their escape. In the final analysis, he hoped that if they were able to get out of the hotel, they would hopefully be able to steal a car and try to make it to the Swiss Embassy.

At that, Tess said, "If we can make it there, Eric will be able to get us out of the country."

Peter asked, "I've never asked you this, but is Eric part of your clandestine operation?"

"Yes, even though he is paid by the government of Switzerland, he is in fact on our payroll, and I'm sure he's already made plans for our exit should we somehow make our way back to the embassy," Tess said.

In the midst of their conversation, Peter heard the door open in the other room. He heard Spanish being spoken and went inside to see who it was. When he walked in, to his surprise, it was the waiter with the room service. Peter walked over, thanked him, and put a nice US five-dollar bill in his hand. As he departed, the soldier at the door let him pass and said, "*Come, lo esta possible por que debe ser la ultima vez*," which meant eat, it may be your last time, and he laughed as he shut the door.

After the door was shut, Tess could see that Peter was fuming from the guard's comment. He turned to Tess and said, "Tonight when I'm done with that bastard, we'll see what side of his face is laughing then." Tess turned to Peter and said, "Please let's not let him change the moment, please." Peter realized that Tess was still not grasping the moment herself but felt there'd be plenty of time for her to grasp it later. He then calmed himself down and turned back to her and said, "If you please, my lady," and he pulled two chairs up to the small table and stood behind one chair, holding it out for Tess.

"Why, thank you, Senor Riley, or should I say, Senor Kennedy now that we are so familiar with one another."

While they were eating and enjoying each other's company, it almost seemed as if they were on holiday together and everything was right with the world. The day's events had certainly given them both ravenous appetites. When they finished, in a joking manner Peter leaned over the table, kissed Tess, and said, "I hope, my dear, everything was to your liking."

Tess answered in her most formal voice, "Yes, my love, thank you ever so much for asking."

They both got up laughing and walked over to the window together to look out on the early evening. While standing in front of the window, they heard the door open and turned around to see who it was. When they did, a smile came over both of their faces as Fernando entered the room. Before he shut the door, he told the guard he was not to be disturbed unless it was Fidel himself who was calling him. He finished by asking the guard if that was understood. The guard acknowledged Fernando's request and then closed the door.

After the door was shut, he went over to Peter and Tess and put one arm around each of them and said, "How are you doing, my friends, I came back as quickly as I thought it was safe to."

The three of them then walked over to the sitting area and Fernando began to tell them what was going on and what he had up his sleeve for all of them. He explained that after he left, he had to go back to Fidel to let the whole thing settle, as if he was truly now converted back and had seen the error of his ways. He explained that for the moment, perhaps this evening only, he felt he was still safe from suspicion. Fernando continued to explain what his plan was. He told them that later this evening, he was going to come back and get both of them out under the guise that he would be bringing both them back to Fidel for further interrogations. He'd then take them out of the hotel and to Fidel with only two guards to accompany him in his own jeep. Then while they were all traveling back to the Capitol, he would make an excuse to stop on a side road and then take out the two soldiers accompanying them.

After that, he had set it up so that they would be able to enter the jail from a side entrance and get to their comrades. He told Peter and Tess that there wouldn't be more than four guards at the jail at this time of night. He explained that where they were being held was not a high security area; it was just a convenient place where Fidel preferred to do his personal interrogations.

"What do you plan from there?" Peter asked.

"From there, I planned to put you all into a troop carrier that I got my hands on and have waiting for us not more than fifty yards from the Capitol Building. We must then make a run to pick up my family. You must understand that once I do this, anyone here related to me will surely face the wrath of Fidel. Fernando then hesitated and said, "Although I still wish to get out with you both, I could not leave without making sure my family got out also."

Peter jumped back in and said, "I've a possible adjustment to the plan which might give you more time to secure your family and our comrades." Fernando was surprised by Peter's bravado and thought he'd at least hear him out. After all, he had nothing to lose, as it was going to be all uphill from here anyway. Peter explained that based on how Fernando had sparsely placed the guards, if he could supply him with a weapon, he felt confident he'd be able to handle the guards and escape without any assistance. Peter emphasized that he preferred it that way, as he had a little personal note he wanted to give one of the guards before they left. That would then eliminate at least one stop for Fernando and give him more time to secure his family and then get to the team. He explained that with the five Americans and one of them injured, they probably wouldn't be able to move that fast. So it would be better for Fernando to get to the others first and then meet up with Peter and Tess afterwards.

Fernando came back at Peter and said, "The reason I wish to keep you all together is namely our manner of escape." He then proceeded to explain that he had a motor launch stashed away on which he planned to get everybody out to take them to Miami. Fernando continued by saying that he couldn't foresee any other way of getting all of them out at the same time.

Peter again came back with the problem of the team. "As I've said before, you've got to see that with one hurt, you're not going to be able to move fast enough. Put them together with your family and however good our chances are, you now diminish them by some percentage. It's just too many people." Peter continued to explain that the thing to do was to put his family on the boat first and then send them on their way before we even started any kind of escape. That was truly the only way to ensure that his family would be safely out of Cuba before they started their plan.

But Fernando asked what would happen to his family once they reached Miami. Peter answered by telling him not to worry. "We'll make sure that when they arrive in Miami, they'd be carrying a personal message from La Senora Feher to someone at the NSA; that from here, they'd just be held as political refugees until this whole thing is resolved." Peter then reached over and put his hand on Fernando's arm and said, "But what's really important here is that they'll be safe. Only with their safety assured can you really move ahead with helping us, and you know I'm right about that. It's just too much to expect that we'd all be able to make it out together. The group would just be too large and that could attract too much attention. Besides, with you risking all for us, the least we can do is to make sure that your family is safe before helping us escape," Peter said.

"So what's your plan to get out of Cuba?" Fernando asked.

"Well, I didn't have it exactly all worked out, but I was counting on you for the transportation. Now that I know you got that troop carrier, the rest is simple: we head for Guantanamo Bay where the Americans are. By now, the Americans know we're all captives. Even though Fidel hasn't announced it to the world, our government knows we're being held and they got to figure that one of the possible escape routes, if we were to get out, would be Gitmo. It's only logical."

Tess concurred with Peter's logic and said so. She couldn't believe that Peter was laying it all out so clearly but she knew he was right about everything and felt confident that he was sizing up the escape correctly. She too knew that with the team, his family, and them, it was going to be just too much. After all, that would have made it twelve people with Fernando's family. While Peter continued, Tess took a piece of hotel stationery from the desk to write out the letter that Peter had told Fernando would guarantee his family's safety once they landed in Miami.

Peter emphasized again that the first thing Fernando needed to do was to get his family out on the boat now while everyone was where they were supposed to be. That way no alarms could go off before his family had had time to reach the safety of the Florida coast.

Upon giving it more thought, whatever his reservations, Fernando did like parts of Peter's plan because it allowed his family to reach Miami before the fireworks went off.

The part of the plan where Peter wanted a weapon, however, caused some problems for Fernando. First, he explained, because he didn't have one on him and second because any gunshots would surely alert the other guards, and once the fireworks started, it might complicate the rescue of the Americans at the jail. Peter pondered the gun issue and told Fernando that even without the gun, he still felt confident that he could pull it off. He then explained what the first plan had been for the guards and how he was sure that with Tess's help, he'd still have no problem in pulling it off. Peter continued, "In this way, while you're taking care of our people at the detention jail, we'll already be out on our way to meet you at a predetermined point." After hearing this, Fernando had nothing but admiration at Peter's bravery. Fernando sensed that Peter's motivation was his anger, and whatever it was about, he felt confident that that would be enough to see him through.

Despite all the changes from the way he had first figured it all out, Fernando still liked it and was willing to go at it Peter's way. After all, it cut down on the roundup time by letting Peter and Tess get to a rendezvous point without him. With just a few more moments of thought, Fernando became quite satisfied that Peter's plan worked well for them all. It gave him more time to get to the American prisoners and it also guaranteed that his family will have made the ninety-mile journey offshore to Florida long before they even started their escape. They then synchronized their watches and set their rendezvous for no later than midnight. Tess knew the rendezvous site well and told Fernando not to worry; they'd be there.

Peter jumped in one last time and said, "Listen, my friend, if we're not there by twelve ten, something's gone wrong and don't wait. While we may end up being stuck here, there's no chance that we'll end up disappearing. However, if you don't get the team out, I'm afraid those guys just might end up dead. Remember, they covertly invaded your country and Castro doesn't ever have to let the world know they're here, but as for us, too many people know about us and somehow we'll eventually get out."

Fernando gripped them both firmly on their shoulders and just said, "*Buenos suerte*, my friends."

He then got up and went to the door. Before he left, he made some loud negative comments just so that the guards would have heard the taunts and not have suspected anything.

After Fernando left, Peter looked at his watch and said, "Okay, it's nine fifteen, let's rehearse this thing and get ready."

Chapter 17

Escape

It was eleven fifteen when Peter got behind the front door and Tess started in on her routine. First, she threw a lamp across the room and it smashed in a wonderfully loud noise that seemed to shake the night. She then began to scream obscenities in Spanish and did it with great panache. Peter was most impressed.

As expected, the guards heard the noise and rushed into the room as Peter had hoped, unprepared. He swung out from behind the door with a lit candle in one hand and the spray can of deodorant full blast, like a flamethrower, in the other hand. As the guards covered their faces and screamed in pain, Peter immediately dropped his makeshift weapon, picked the ice bucket off the floor, and proceeded to smack them both, one right after the other. They fell to the floor and Peter yelled quietly to Tess, "Quickly, help me drag them over here."

Peter pulled down some ropes from around the heavy drapes by the balcony window and tied both of their hands and legs together, while Tess stuffed some rags in their mouths. When he was satisfied that they were tied up nice and tight, he looked down at the guard who had made the wisecrack before and gave him a swift kick in his side. The guard moaned and Peter said, "Well, I guess that wasn't our last meal after all, amigo. Be seeing ya, pal." After that, he grabbed Tess by the hand, and they headed for the door. He opened it slowly and peeked out to look up and down the hall to see if anyone was coming. In light of how loud the guards had both screamed before he coldcocked them, he wasn't sure if anyone had heard anything.

When he was satisfied that the coast was clear, he signaled Tess it was now or never. They left the room and crossed the hall to the fire escape exit stairs.

They had been on the top floor and made their way down ten flights to the mezzanine level where the banquet halls were. Tess and Peter had discussed before that by Fernando's leaving the kitchen entrance unguarded, it was where they'd be making their exit. They both knew that they needed to use one of the service elevators from the banquet hall area to get to the hotel kitchen. From there, at this time of night, they figured there wasn't going to be any problem to then casually walk through the kitchen and exit to the service alleyway of the hotel.

It was eleven forty, and when they reached the kitchen, as expected, the place was already buttoned-down tight for the evening. They left the kitchen via the loading dock platform, and both easily made the four-foot jump to the pavement. From this point, Tess took over as she knew the streets of Havana and she would be the guide to get her and Peter to the rendezvous point to meet up with Fernando.

They arrived to the rendezvous area earlier than expected at eleven fifty, and as agreed with Fernando, Peter and Tess then slid into a dark hallway of an apartment building and prepared to wait until he got there.

After Fernando left Peter and Tess, he headed immediately for his home on the outskirts of Havana. When he got there, he rounded up his mother, his brothers, and his sister and brought them into the living room where he sat them all down. He began by saying that as they all knew, things here in Cuba had only gone from bad to worse and that the way Fidel was proceeding, he didn't see things getting any better.

His mother was most surprised by this turn of attitude and said, "But, Fernando, you've always believed that with Fidel, one day our nation would be mighty again."

"Yes, *mi madre*, I did always think that way, but in light of work I've been doing lately, it appears I've been wrong about many things and most importantly about Fidel."

"Fernando," his mother said with tears of joy streaming down her face, "I can't believe you are finally saying this. I had given up all hope of ever trying to get you to see what a pig Fidel had become, because you were always so dedicated to him and the revolution."

"*Mi madre*," Fernando returned, "there is no revolution now with Fidel, only his ego. But I had always thought you were the supporter of Fidel since he had been part of our family."

"Yes, I was, but that was years ago when your father was alive and young, we all were, but things were different then. However, in the past few years, my son, since Fidel's Russian friends have left, it has become clear to all of us who were young with him once that our great leader has let his pride and vanity come before our people. All of us have come to know that he cares now only for his power and has really never cared for the people of Cuba. Oh, perhaps when he was young, he truly cared, but that was then and this is now. He is a changed man. In recent years, as I have watched you with him, I feared ever telling you how I felt. I feared that you were under his spell and had I ever said anything to you, that you might turn on your own family as others had done."

"*Mi madre*, this is a most wonderful thing you could have ever told me, because now that I understand your true feelings, I can now tell you what we must do tonight, and we will all be of the same mind and heart." Fernando paused so as to let the anticipation build and then said, "*Mi madre*, tonight we all leave for America."

"What!" his mother exclaimed with a look of total shock. "But how and why?"

"There is much I could tell you but time does not permit us now to have that luxury. You and my sister and brothers will leave tonight on a boat for Miami. When you get there, you will be received well by the Americans and our lives will finally be right as they should be."

"But what about you, Fernando, you will be with us, *como no?*" his mother asked.

"No, no, *mi madre*, not tonight but I will be there by the next day. First, I must get you out. I then will follow, do not worry."

"But we will not leave without you, Fernando."

"You will and you must. Trust me, *mi madre*, I will be alright but for now you must move quickly, as I have a boat ready to take you. I promise, when I see you in Miami with all the rest of our cousins, I will explain it all to you then. Trust me now, we must go, hurry."

With that, Fernando helped his mother and the rest of his family get a few things together. They then quickly left their house and got into his jeep. On the way to the inlet where Fernando had the boat waiting, his mother kept asking him what had happened and why this was all happening so quickly. Fernando answered, "*Mi madre*, I told you there's no time for that now, in Miami I will tell you everything when I see you again."

When Fernando reached the boat, he helped everyone out and onto the boat. The captain, Raul, had been a close friend of his for many years. Raul had always wanted out of Cuba, as he had never been a fan of Fidel's, but he didn't have any close relatives in the US who could have helped him get permanent resident status. He had always had the boat to get to Miami, but how he'd be able to remain there was always the problem. So, when Fernando had approached him and explained that he would be rescuing Americans and that in exchange for this, the Americans would surely grant him resident status, his friend Raul welcomed the opportunity to finally escape to America.

Fernando kissed his mother good-bye and patted his oldest brother Pedro of twenty-six on his shoulder and said to him, "Remember Pedro, you are now the man here and you are to watch over our mother until I see you next. Is that understood, Pedro?"

"Si, Fernando, I will take care of them all."

"Good, I am counting on you as the man of the family now," and he shook his hand. He then turned to his friend Raul and handed him the letter in an envelope that Tess had written out before he left them. He then said, "When you are picked up by the American Coast Guard, and you will be, ask for the senior officer on the ship and give this to him. After that, all will be okay, and I will see you all in a day or two."

Fernando's mother began to cry again and said, "I can't believe it, my son. May the saints protect you and be with you until we see you again." She then hugged him as the rest of the family gathered around and held on to him too.

He then broke their embrace and said, "It is late, and you must go now. I have many things yet to do before I too can leave and be with you, go now, *vamos*." At that, they all got on board and Fernando watched them leave in the quiet of the night. After they were out of sight, he got back into his jeep and headed back to Havana to proceed with the rest of the night's work.

Fernando waited outside of the detention jail until it was eleven thirty, when he knew the area would be left with only its skeleton crew of four guards. With a passkey, he entered through a side entrance that had a single staircase leading directly to the lowest level.

When he opened the door, it was dark with only a few small lights to guide his way to the corridor, which led to the detention area. When he reached the confinement area, there was a guard at the entrance door, sitting at a desk, reading the local paper. As Fernando approached, the soldier jumped up with surprise and saluted Fernando immediately.

"Sir," the soldier said, "I had not expected anyone here this time of night."

"I have come to look in on the soldiers. Fidel is most concerned with the one wounded, and he wanted me to check in on them before I was finished for the night. I've just returned from interrogating the two American spies at the hotel and I thought I would look in on our friends here one more time," Fernando said.

"*Si*, Colonel, I will take you to them directly, this way, sir."

As the soldier got up to open the door and lead him to the American prisoners, Fernando prepared for what was coming next. Unlike what had transpired in Miami, Fernando now had a revulsion at the thought of killing anyone. While he had done it many times in the name of the revolution, since Miami, when he killed Juan and the others for Fidel's plot, things hadn't been the same. He now hesitated at the idea of taking human life, and if it was at all possible, he intended to try and avoid killing any of these men tonight.

His plan was to first look at the Americans through the door, and when he had put on the act that he had seen what he had come for, he then intended to get the other guards all involved in conversation about what Fidel was planning to do with them next. He knew that everyone was very excited at having captured the Americans, and he felt confident they'd all want to gather about him to hear the latest. Before leaving his home, he had picked up his Glock 9 mm pistol and had it tucked in the rear of his waist band. His plan was that when he had them all together, he would pull his pistol on them and then get the first guard to open the cell holding the Americans, while he kept his gun trained on him and the other three. He figured once the American cell was opened up, that they would get the guns from the other guards and then help him tie up the soldiers and lock them into another cell.

As they approached the cell, the guard opened the small window door at the top and Fernando peered in as planned. It had been even easier than he thought, for as he went to the cell, the other three guards saw him and wandered over to see what was happening. While they were all talking, Fernando asked one of the guards if he had a cigarette. The guard reached into his fatigue jacket and pulled out a pack and offered it to Fernando.

Two of the soldiers had their guns straddled over their shoulders while the other two had set them down against the wall to light up and have a cigarette with El Colonel. After the soldier with the cigarettes gave one to Fernando, another leaned over with a match to light it after he had lit his own. With the cool and calm of a professional, Fernando reached behind his jacket and pulled out the 9 mm Glock, pointed it at them, and asked them all to drop their weapons and step back against the wall.

While it was fairly dark inside, the look of surprise on their faces truly betrayed them.

"*Por que colonel*, what are you doing?"

Fernando wasn't going to go through the explanations and just turned to them and said, "*Mi compadres, mi amigos*, you'd never understand." He then told them all to move to the same side of the hall where the Americans' cell was. While standing six feet back, he told three of them to stay where they were and the other to open the cell door. After the door was open, with a wave of his gun, he signaled the fourth soldier to move back against the wall with the others.

Henry was the first to step out of the cell and into the hall. When he came out, he turned to Fernando and said, "I don't know who the hell you are but I sure am glad to see you."

Fernando responded and said, "There is no time now for me to explain who I am but only to say I am working with your American friends and all of us will be getting out of Cuba tonight. Here, please help me. Get their guns and help me put them in this other cell. I have some rope and rags with me, get some of your other men to help."

Henry turned back to Spencer, Barry, and Joel and said, "Come on, boys, let's get it on."

With that Henry and the others helped Fernando move the four guards into an empty cell and tied them all up nice and neat before they slammed the door, and Henry turned and said, "In case we don't get the chance to tell you before the night's over, thanks."

Fernando and the others then left the confinement area and headed down the corridor for the staircase from which Fernando had arrived. Just as they were getting to the corridor entrance where the guard had been sitting, they heard someone coming. Fernando signaled with the wave of his hand for all of them to press back against the recess of the corridor wall and put his finger over his mouth, signaling them not to move and to be quiet. Eliot was a bit hard to move since he was near passed out from the obvious infection that had developed in his wound and was not able to walk or stand under his own power. Both Spencer and Barry had to hold Eliot up and cover his mouth, as he moaned unconsciously from his pain.

With all of them pressed flat into the recess of the corridor and its relative darkness, they were obscure and were well hidden from the sight of the approaching guard. As the guard approached, he saw the entryway gate open, called out to the guard who had been sitting there and said, "*Santos, donde esta, mi amigo* (where are you, my friend), I forgot my keys, *que stupido*." He then stopped at the desk, picked up his friend's paper, glanced at it, and started heading into the hallway where Fernando and the rest of them were waiting. As he walked through the gate, Spencer and Barry had let Eliot slip down the wall a bit and at the sound, the guard became alerted by the obvious silence which surrounded it. He then picked up his automatic AK-47 and holding it ready at his hip, he walked forward. He called out again to Santos as he walked in and was then directly lateral to Fernando and the group hiding in the darkness. All at once, as he came by, Henry lunged out with a swift kick to the guard's abdomen and as he doubled over, Henry thrust the palm of his hand in an upward motion hitting the guard's nose and sending the bones directly into his skull, killing him instantly.

As the guard lay sprawled out on the floor with blood running down his face, Henry turned and said, "That's for my new wave electric permanent."

They then pulled the dead guard out of the light and left him on the side of the hallway. Fernando then told them that they needed to get moving quickly, as Peter and Tess were waiting at the rendezvous point and they were only minutes away from when they were all supposed to be there. As they all snaked their way up the single small staircase with Fernando at the lead, the group struggled somewhat with Eliot. He was as before nearly out cold and offered very little help to Spencer and Barry as they carried him up the tight stairwell. When they got to the door at the head of the stairs, Fernando held up his hand, signaling for them all to hold up, and he then peeked out the door to see if anyone was in the street. At seeing the street empty, he again signaled them to follow. They made their way out to the alley and while hugging the sides of buildings, they moved down the street as they made their way to the troop carrier that Fernando had waiting only a block away.

It was not unusual in a military state to see an army troop carrier parked on the street for the night, and so as expected, when they reached the vehicle, all was quiet, and the truck was ready to go. Fernando lifted the canvas cover in the rear, and they helped Eliot in first. Henry and the rest then followed in behind. Fernando then closed the back with the canvas tarp and got into the truck to drive to the rendezvous point to pick up Peter and Tess.

As Fernando got to the rendezvous point, he flashed his lights to Peter and Tess as they had prearranged. As he pulled up, Peter ran to the back of the troop carrier and helped get Tess into the back. He then went back to the front and told Fernando, "I'll ride up here with you if you don't mind the company." Fernando waved his hand with a smile and said, "Let's go."

They made it out of the city quickly and then headed in a route Fernando had decided was the best way to keep off the main roads. There was a main highway that led from Havana through Cardenas, Santa Clara, Victoria de las Tunas all the way to Guantanamo Bay. Fernando had decided that just in case they were being followed or chased, that they would take the main highway through central Cuba until it was near light. At that time, he would head to a southern coastal road until they reached Guantanamo Bay. He felt that if an alarm went off, Castro would have watched the northern coastal roads, as they were the best launching points for an escape to the US mainland. He also figured that Fidel would have put search teams on the main highway to the southeastern tip of Cuba, where Guantanamo Bay was located.

It was about 800 kilometers, or approximately 500 miles, to the Guantanamo, and based on the roads they would be travelling on, the trip would take them the better part of the night, if not more.

He knew that on these roads, he wasn't going to make great speed and he was concerned about whether or not they were going to make it before daylight. At the last minute as they were departing Havana, he decided to change his plan and take the gamble and he'd risk the highway at least until he got to Victoria de las Tunas. That was ninety percent or more of the distance and he felt confident he could make it there by four thirty or five, which would give them perhaps the additional hour they needed to get to Guantanamo before the darkness had left them.

Back at the hotel, at about 1:30 a.m., the guards at the front entrance to the hotel had been approached by someone from the hotel front desk with some warm empanadas that he had just made for himself in the kitchen. The hotel staff often knew it was a good habit to be generous with the private guard of Fidel, for you never knew when a friendship like that could be helpful. When the hotel worker came out with the food, the plate had been stacked high with as many as perhaps twenty or thirty of these Cuban sandwich delicacies. The soldiers gratefully took them and proceeded to eat. After a few minutes, both of the guards were full and one said to the other, "Why don't you bring some of these to our friends out back and upstairs?"

With the suggestion, one of the guards brought the plate out to the rear hotel entrance, left about eight sandwiches, and then proceeded upstairs to bring the rest to the other guards outside the Americans' hotel room. When he got off the elevator and saw that no one was at the door, he dropped the plate, brought his weapon down off his shoulder, and rushed towards the room. When he got to the door, it was unlocked, and he opened it immediately. As he walked inside, there he saw his two compatriots, tied, and bound lying on the floor. He quickly went over to them and immediately pulled the rags out of their mouths. As he was untying their hands and legs, they told him how the Americans had tricked and overpowered them to escape.

Once the soldiers were untied, they headed downstairs and told the senior officer what had happened. The lieutenant then immediately called the commanding officer at the local garrison and informed him of what had taken place and told him he had better call someone to wake Fidel and tell him. Once Fidel had been awoken, all bloody hell had broken loose. He immediately called over to the detention jail and found out quickly what he had anticipated that there was no answer. He got dressed quickly, ordered his aide to bring his car and meet him downstairs as soon as he was dressed.

When they arrived at the Capitol and went downstairs to the detention area, Fidel found the captain from the garrison there with a full command of soldiers waiting for him. The captain spoke first to Fidel, once he was down the stairs. He stood erect, saluted, and then said, "There is one guard dead, sir, and the others had been just tied and bound when we arrived, my general."

Fidel was fuming and he screamed as none of them had heard him before. He told the captain to immediately call the air force and to put up several helicopters to cover the northern coast highways and then to send two troop carriers on the main highway leading towards Guantanamo Bay. He then told him to alert the lookout at point Loma Picota and to also send out some scout boats to comb the waters off their coast as far as they could, without going into American waters.

After Fidel had given all of his commands to the local garrison commander, he told his aide to call Fernando immediately and have him meet them back at the Capitol pronto. He emphasized to his aide that Fernando was to be awoken immediately and to be there quickly. Once back at his office, while pacing the floor, Fidel tried to figure out how they could have escaped. He knew they must have had help from someone, and he wondered if it was the same person who had also been the traitor who had given away his secret site where he had kept his warheads. At this point, although it was almost obvious, he still did not suspect Fernando. When the aide came back into his office and said he was not able to reach Fernando, Castro banged his fist on his desk and knew at once that he had been the traitor.

He cursed himself for having held on to Fernando as long as he had. He knew now that *Los hombres de los muertos* should have visited him a long time ago. "What a fool I have been," Castro screamed. The aide stood there frozen in the midst of Fidel's wrath and just waited for what he was to do next. Fidel then said, "We must catch them at all costs. They must not be allowed to leave this island." He then turned to his aide and told him he wanted all of his junta (the generals) assembled immediately in his office and that it was not to be more than thirty minutes.

When the generals had arrived and they were all assembled in his office, Fidel proceeded to tell them all what had taken place. He explained that the Americans must not escape or else their precious bargaining position would be gone. He made sure that each of them understood in a very subtle way that if they were not found, he would hold them all responsible. He was ragging and none of his junta had ever seen this depth of madness before. They each knew that if the Americans were not found, their lives and their positions were likely to be erased as if they had never existed. "*Adelante* (go forward)," he yelled as he finished, and they all quickly got up to do whatever it was going to take to insure that no one escaped their island.

After they left, Fidel knew that without his American captives and now with his warheads destroyed, his playing days were soon to be over. With as much anger in his heart as he hadn't felt since Operation Mongoose, when the Americans tried to assassinate him, he sat down to wait and ponder what his next move would be.

He knew he still held the trump card with his one warhead hidden in Miami, but thoughts of its use would wait until he would see whether or not they would recapture the Americans this night.

It was now 4:30 a.m. and Fernando had made it almost on perfect time to Victoria de las Tunas. During the all-night ride, he and Peter had plenty of time to kill and in the silence, Fernando had finally decided it was time to tell Peter about the nuclear warhead in Miami. He had felt that if anything were to happen to him, he had to at least make sure that the Americans knew of this and where it was located. With as much time as they had together, he told Peter all about how he had followed Fidel blindly and thought of nothing other than the revolution. He explained with great shame and regret what he had done in Miami and said that it was now something, like it or not, that he would have to live with for the rest of his life. Peter was in shock at what he had told him. First because he had developed such a bond and admiration for him that he couldn't believe that Fernando could have been capable of what he had just told him, and secondly because there was a nuclear warhead in Miami. Whatever it was about, the only thing that mattered now was that they had to let Henry know so that if they got out, he could get to his people to disarm the remaining warhead. He felt sorry for Fernando at what he had told him, but nevertheless he was more concerned now about their escape and Henry notifying the authorities about the seventh warhead in Miami.

Before they entered the Victoria de las Tunas, he turned the truck off to a side road that would bypass the town and head to the southern coast. This was the coastal road that would eventually dump them at the foot of the US Guantanamo Bay Naval Base. The road ended by the water and then turned north for about eight to ten miles, running along the perimeter of the base until it turned back into the hills.

He was surprised they had made it this far without running into anyone and decided that the big man up above must have been on their side to have been so lucky. As they got onto the side road, they found the going as rough as the dirt road was. He stopped the truck once they were clear of the town, and he and Peter got out to check on everyone in the rear. When they walked around to the back, they found everyone there intact and no worse for the wear. Fernando now explained that they were taking a side mountain road past the southern side of Loma Picota peak and that the ride was going to become a lot rougher.

Peter turned to Henry and asked how Eliot was doing. Henry told him that he wasn't doing well but he was sure they'd make it. He told Peter that although they had bandaged his wound, it seemed they must have left the bullet in, because Eliot was running a high fever and it appeared that infection must have set in. Peter then turned to Tess to see how she was doing, and her answer was, "Okay, don't worry about me, let's just worry about making it to Guantanamo." As Peter and Fernando went back to the front of the truck, Peter smiled and thought about Tess to himself and said, "What a trooper," as he climbed back into the cab of the troop carrier. "It's no wonder I'm so crazy about her."

They had been driving on the dirt road for almost an hour and were surely within just a mile or so of Guantanamo Bay. The road had been rough and steep, as it ran around the base of Loma Picota and they were finally near the end of their journey. Just as they came down a steep embankment, Fernando heard a grinding noise, and then suddenly the truck skidded and dragged on the road, leaning to its left side. He looked at Peter and then the two of them got out to look at the truck to see what had happened. When they got to the rear, they instantly saw that the axle had snapped. By then, Henry had jumped out, and he walked over to them and said, "So we're up shit's creek without a paddle huh?"

Fernando responded by saying, "It looks that way, my friend."

They all just stood there and cursed that they were so close yet so far. Henry asked Fernando how far he thought they were, and Fernando said he didn't think it was much more than a mile. He pointed to the horizon and showed them that they could see off in the distance the glare of the base camp's lights against the dark of the night sky. Henry then turned to them all and said, "Well, I don't see that we've got much choice other than to start to hoof it and hope for the best."

They all agreed and proceeded to empty out of the back of the troop carrier. Henry told Spencer and Barry to go off to cut some small trees and make two large poles to use as a stretcher for Eliot. While they went off to get the poles, he cut some of the canvas from the rear flap of the truck to form a backing to use with the two poles. When Spencer and Barry returned, they fixed up the stretcher for Eliot and they then proceeded to cross the last few miles on foot. As they left, Peter told Henry what he had learned from Fernando and suggested that as they walked, he needed to get as much info from Fernando as he could. Joel, Spencer, and Barry carried Eliot, while Peter followed up the rear walking with Tess. As they walked, he turned to her and said, "Quite an adventure, eh."

Tess agreed, "More than I ever thought would happen to me."

From there on, they all fell silent and didn't say much to each other as they continued to make their way towards the base.

It was now 5:00 a.m. and Castro was in his office, waiting for word from someone, anyone, as to the progress that they had made in their search. He had had preliminary reports during the night but each of his generals continued to say that they were still searching and that they would keep him abreast of events as they unfolded. By this time, however, Fidel knew that if they had escaped by boat, they were surely now in Miami. He called in the general in charge of the armies and asked him about reports on the main road to Guantanamo. The general told him there were none but that they were proceeding to cover the entire area up to the US base.

"How far are your two troop carriers from Loma Picota now?" Fidel asked.

"They should be near the base road just about now, sir," he answered.

Fidel told the general that all of the troops were to head directly towards the perimeter fence road of the US base and to speed there as quickly as possible. He also told the general to make sure that everyone at the observation point was ready and watching for the escaped Americans. The general then made the mistake of telling Fidel that he had already given that order and that the men were at their most ready state, when Castro turned to him and said, "They'd better be, because that's where the Americans are surely headed, I'm sure, and if they make it across, it is you that I'm going to hold personally responsible."

Unaware that the soldiers at Loma Picota were on the look-out for them, they had proceeded pretty much out in the open. There wasn't much cover to speak of, only scrub brush and some small oaks. They didn't have much of an option with Eliot hurt and two nonmilitary personnel.

They had just come in sight of the perimeter fence of the base, no more than a quarter of a mile, when automatic weapon fire rang out. They all fell to the ground and Henry took over and started to give the commands. Suddenly, they could see weapon fire coming from the US side, aiming upwards towards the top of the peak. Peter knew instantly that Fernando's family must have gotten through to the authorities and they received Tess's letter. He crawled over to Henry and told Henry that the Americans must know it's them and they're giving us fire cover.

Henry yelled at Peter for not having said anything about Fernando's family and the letter. Peter responded back explaining that he wasn't exactly a spy and in all of the adrenaline rushes he'd been through tonight, he obviously left that part out. He turned to Henry and said, "So sue me, I screwed up."

Henry returned the lash and said, "Well, at least it's a screw up that's worked in our favor, so let's just forget it and get to our side of the fence."

Although the Americans were firing up at the peak, hostile fire was still raining down on the group. Henry turned to Spencer, Joel, and Barry and said, "You guys go first, then we'll follow." With that, the three of them got up with Eliot and made what must have been a thirty-to-forty-yard dash, with two of them helping Eliot, while Barry returned fire at the rear as they ran. The distance from the peak was too far for accuracy, but it sure as hell was scaring the shit out of everyone.

After Henry saw them make it through the fence, he gave the order for the four of them to move out. As they did, Fernando heard the sound of the troop carriers and when he turned around, he saw they were almost upon them. Quickly he said, "They are now coming at us from over there," and he pointed to the dust cloud as the soldiers were jumping from the trucks. After Henry saw the troop carriers, he waved his arm and all four of them got up and ran with all that they had.

Peter was holding Tess's hand and almost dragging her at the speed he was running. As they neared the fence, the automatic weapon fire from the troop carriers was whizzing by them at something too close for comfort. Just as they reached the fence, Fernando caught a bullet directly in his back and fell no more than five feet from the fence. Peter pushed Tess ahead and then, without thought or fear for himself, turned back to grab Fernando. He grabbed his arm and dragged him the five feet or so until some marines reached over his shoulder and helped pull Fernando the rest of the way through.

As they got through the fence, they were pushed by some of the marines behind some armored personnel carriers. As soon as the Cubans had realized that the Americans had made it through, the weapon fire ceased as quickly as it had started. Peter pulled Fernando into his arms and said, "Hold on, my friend, you've made it and your new world is about to begin."

Fernando coughed up some blood and, in a wheezing breath, said, "I know I will not make this, and perhaps it is better this way. Retribution, you know, for sins against God," and he coughed again. Peter looked at him and although he had never had a man die in his arms, he knew Fernando was right, he wasn't going to make it. Fernando then weakly made the sign of the cross over his head and body and said, "You will take care to make sure my family is safe, friend."

Peter nodded and said, "Count on it, buddy, but you're going to be with them, don't worry." And with that Peter felt Fernando's body go limp and his head fell to the side. Tess put her hand on Peter, but he just sat there, holding Fernando's head in silence.

Chapter 18

The Envelope

As Raul neared the Florida coast, as expected, they were hailed, stopped, and boarded quickly by the US Coast Guard. Raul cut his engines and stood ready to receive a line from the Coast Guard Cutter. After all the lines were secure, the captain boarded the twenty-six-foot Chris Craft with two other seamen alongside. Before the captain could even open his mouth, Raul quickly handed him the envelope and started his explanation that they had escaped Cuba via his friend and that his friend was in the midst of rescuing some Americans, etc.

The captain put up his hand and said, “Hold on here, buddy. I’m in overload and I have no idea what in the blazes you’re jabbering about.”

“Please,” Raul said, “if you would just read what’s in this envelope, sir, my friend has told me it will explain everything.”

The captain opened the envelope and proceeded to read its contents. After finishing it, he turned to the other two seamen and said, “Sailors, make fast this boat, we’ll be keeping her in tow all the way in.” The captain couldn’t make heads or tails of what the letter was about. He only knew that if it were the real McCoy, he needed to get to his CO (commanding officer). The person who wrote it asked that the information be relayed immediately to a Major William B. O’Connor at the Defense Intelligence Agency over at the NSA as soon as it was in our hands. After he got back onto his ship, his first officer asked the captain what the hell was going on. The captain explained about this screwy letter they gave him and said that whatever it was, before they made any decisions, he had to get in touch with the CO at the station as soon as they got back in.

In the meantime, as they motored back to the port of Miami, he radioed ahead that if the CO was available, he wanted to speak to him immediately and said that if he was not, he was to be gotten a hold of ASAP. He ended his call into the coast guard station by saying that, if possible, he was to try and reach him by ship to shore as soon as he could get to him.

The lieutenant asked the captain, “So what’s this all about?”

“I truly don’t know. We’ve either got an elaborate story on our hands or we’ve got some Americans in some real serious trouble,” the captain said.

“Well, can’t you give me anymore on this chuck than what you’ve just told me? I mean, if there’s some Americans in trouble, I sure am curious as to what’s going on,” the lieutenant asked.

"I really can't say much of anything, Joe, in case this turns out real, who the hell knows. For all I know, this could be a fake. Listen, I promise ya, guy, when it's clear and I know what's going on, I tell ya," the captain ended it on that note.

Coming into port, they were now approximately two miles off the Miami coast, and it was two thirty in the morning. Just as they were pulling into the harbor, the lieutenant came in and said, "It's the CO chuck." The captain went to the radio room and asked that Joe wait outside until he finished his communication. When he got on with the CO, he explained about the evening's events and the letter that he received from the Cuban captain. As he went into some of the details, the CO told him to hold off on the rest, since he was almost in and he'd see the letter for himself.

When they tied up at port, the INS people were already there, as was the procedure whenever a Coast Guard Cutter radioed in that they had picked up a boatload of refugees. Raul and Fernando's family were escorted off and the captain went inside to the com center to see the CO. As he walked in, he handed the letter to the CO and said, "Here, you better read this, for all I know it's true, in which case we need to let them know at the NSA immediately."

The CO opened the envelope and it read as follows:

"To whoever receives this note, we have been on a covert operation on behalf of the DIA. We've been captured and are being held hostage. We will attempt an escape tonight over land to Guantanamo Bay. DO NOT, I repeat, DO NOT give this information to anyone other than your commanding officer as soon as you've read this. Our lives and our nation are in great danger. If we are successful this evening, we should make Guantanamo by daybreak. Contact Major William B. O'Connor as soon as you've read this. He will be standing by. The people who are bringing you this letter will have been instrumental in helping us to escape if we succeed. They are to be held and kept in safety," signed Theresa Feher.

When the CO finished reading the note, he turned to the captain and said, "I see why you didn't know what to make of this letter, it's all pretty strange."

"Well, sir, what are you going to do?" the captain asked.

"I'm going to contact my superiors and have them get to this Major William B. O'Connor. What else would you have me do, Captain?" asked the CO.

It was three fifteen in the morning when Willie got the call at home. It was one of the guys in Comm Ops who'd received the request for the major and he put them on hold and called Willie directly at home. When Willie got the bizarre message, he asked, "Can you patch him into to me here at my house now?"

"Absolutely, you should know I could do that, sir," the soldier said.

"Yeah, well, I know you can do that, what I want to know is can you do it on a safe line?" Willie asked.

"Can do, sir, coming right up."

When Willie picked up the phone he said, "Major William B. O'Connor here."

"Major, this is the commanding officer at the US Naval Coast Guard station from port of Miami calling. We picked up a boat with some Cuban refugees early this morning, and it seems they had this crazy letter on them that they gave to the captain of the ship that picked them up. The letter indicated that you were to be contacted immediately as soon as it was in our hands. I don't know if it's a hoax or not, but on the chance that it was real, we decided to contact you as the letter said, immediately," the CO said.

Willie held his breath and hoped that it was a contact of some kind from Henry. He told the CO to read it over the phone. The CO asked if he was sure he wanted him to do that, and Willie told him to just ask that the room was clear and to read it. He told the CO that the line was secure and to just go ahead. When the CO was finished, he asked who else had seen the letter and then instructed him to make sure that the captain did not share what he knew with anyone. He told the CO to stand by and have the station on alert. He said to just make it a drill and not to talk about anything else.

As Willie was hanging up, he stopped and said, "Oh, by the way, whoever these Cuban refugees are, please make sure they're made comfortable and get them back from the INS. We'll clear it from here, and they'll be released to you. Please treat them well; they may have just saved the lives of some pretty brave American heroes," Willie said.

"Don't worry, we'll take care of whatever you need here, and we'll go to alert status as requested," the CO answered. After Willie got off the phone, he called General Anderson immediately. The general was at home, pacing about in his own frantic world, just as Willie had been since the mission aborted some twenty hours ago. When the general heard the news, his voice jumped five octaves. He told Willie to make all the preparations he needed to get down to Gitmo and that he was to alert them at the base ASAP.

When Willie finished with the general, he got dressed and got over to NSA headquarters in less than an hour. It was 0400 hours when he got to his office, and to his surprise, Nan was there waiting for him.

"What are you doing here?" he asked.

"One of your friends who knew what was going on here called me. I thought in light of our current events, perhaps you could've used me, so I got dressed and here I am," Nan answered.

"Well, I guess if you found out, we're not as tight around here as I thought."

"Oh, we are. It's just that you've got some pretty close friends and I guess they figured you could use me right about now."

"Alright," Willie said, "then let's get to work. Get in touch with the commanding officer down at Gitmo and put him on the line for me, wake him up, send up a flare, just do whatever we have to do, but get 'em on the line, ASAP. I do believe our boys are going to make it after all. Then, I want you to contact Andrews and arrange for a plane to be ready to get me down to Gitmo immediately. Call General Anderson, he's standing by and he'll clear whatever we need. I want to be there when and if they make it. Tell them I want a two-sweater, F4 trainer and tell them I want to be on the base in Guantanamo Bay by 0600 hours and not a minute later, so they're to put one of their best jocks in the driver's seat. Now go and get me that CO down there and have the call patched into my car, I'm leaving for Andrews AFB now.

Willie left his office and got in his Austin Healy 3000 and tore out of the parking lot towards Andrews like a man possessed. After he left, Nan got Comm Ops to try and raise the CO at Gitmo and told them that when they did, the call was to be patched to Major O'Connor in his car. After that, Nan called Andrews and processed what she needed to make sure that a plane was fueled, standing by, and ready for the major. When she first called, they questioned her authority to requisition what she was asking for. Nan laid into the airman so hard that you could have believed her head had reached out onto the other end of the telephone.

"Listen, soldier, unless you want to answer directly to General John Anderson, the deputy director of the NSA, you do what you're told and make it happen. Do I make myself clear, soldier?" Nan asked.

The airman said, "Yes, mam, we'll be on it right away," and just before he hung up, with a voice shaking slightly on the edge of concern, he said, "And, mam, I truly am sorry, it's just that without authorization, I could be stripped of my rank or worse thrown in the brig, mam," the airman said.

"I understand, soldier, but your authorization will be there, so just get things ready, am I clear?" Nan asked again.

"Yes, mam, there'll be no more questions, and all will be ready for Major O'Connor when he arrives," and he hung up the phone.

When Nan finished, she then called the general as instructed by Willie and told him what Willie was doing. She then told him that they would need direct authorization from him to ready a jet at Andrews for the major. The general answered no problem, that as soon as they hung up, he'd make the call personally himself.

After Nan got off the phone, she sat down at the major's desk, put her feet up, and said out loud, "I can be a pretty badass mother when I want to." With that, she smiled to herself and got up to head downstairs to Comm Ops and wait on standby for whatever Willie or any of them might need next.

Chapter 19

The Race

Once the hostile fire had stopped, they all stood up and gave a cheer, a sort of yelp, the kind that signaled they'd made it. Peter was not able to join in, as he was still despondent about Fernando. Tess tried to console him but it was no use. They had developed an affection between them, that while short had been strong, nevertheless. A second lieutenant gave orders for the first squad of marines to remain at the perimeter. He then went over to his newly arrived group and asked them to get into one of the personnel carriers. He told them that they were to accompany him back to the base hospital for medical assistance for their wounds and that there was also someone arriving from stateside at any moment to see Captain St. John.

They got into the troop carrier, and all headed back to the hospital. Eliot was not much better than he was before, but Henry knew now that they'd made it and so would Eliot. He felt bad about Fernando, but obviously he barely knew him. He did however know that for whatever the reasons, he had made their escape possible and for that he sadly regretted that he had lost his life in the process. The one thing, however, that Henry knew was important now was to get to the last remaining warhead hidden in Miami before Fidel did.

When they arrived at the hospital, Eliot was taken immediately to surgery and the rest of them were then taken and ushered into a sterile white room with a large conference table at the center. A male nurse came in and the lieutenant in charge asked him to get whatever the arrivees needed. Be it clothes, food, or just something strong to drink. After the orderly left, the lieutenant said that Colonel Stevens would be in here soon to check and greet them all and that until then, they should just make themselves comfortable.

Henry assumed the person he was informed was arriving shortly was Willie and he asked if Major O'Connor had arrived yet. The lieutenant answered him, saying that they expected him to touch down any moment. While they were all waiting in the room, Peter turned to Henry and asked if Fernando had gotten him totally up to speed on what he had learned about the last warhead stashed in Miami. Henry told him that he felt it had been addressed; however, he wanted to go over the story with Peter just to make sure that the information duplicated itself as it should have.

Henry started out by telling Peter that Fernando had said it was in the deep storage area in Miami customs. He told him where Fernando had seen it last and how it had been crated up.

Peter told Henry more about the story than Fernando had obviously told him. Peter explained how they had gotten it in there and what Fernando feared Fidel's plans were. As Peter spoke, Henry now realized that Fidel had all along had this elaborate plan to use this last warhead as his fallback. Peter told him that what Fernando feared most when they made their escape was that he might send one of his agents to detonate the device. Henry and the others froze at the thought.

Peter continued and told Henry that based on the confessions that Fernando made to him during the long ride to Gitmo, our first priority had to be to get there before Fidel's men did. Peter went on to tell Henry that Fidel had a whole network of agents in Miami and that he felt sure, based on what Fernando said, that Fidel would be contacting someone to get to it immediately.

Henry asked, "Did Fernando really believe that Castro would do this?"

Peter answered that based on the way Fernando was describing Castro, he was a desperate man. That his power was near its end and Fernando didn't think that Fidel would withhold his threat to detonate the warhead.

"But doesn't he think that the world, not to mention the US, would seek retribution on him?"

"No. He feels that with the world press and all of the Middle East terrorists, that no one will be able to be sure that he was responsible for it. He also indicated that Fidel planned to plant a story with some people in the Middle East that he had sold one of the warheads over there."

The more Henry thought about it, the more he realized that Peter was right. After all, no one knew that they had had this covert operation. Everyone in the world thought Fidel was in the process of negotiating with the US for the warheads. It would be logical that Castro would figure that the outside world would just see him as trying to obtain aid in return for his weapons. Henry knew that Fernando had been right about not being able to pin it on Castro. There would be no definite proof and he'd be able to deny that he'd had anything to do with it.

Just as Henry finished his thoughts, Major Willie B. O'Connor walked into the room with Colonel Stevens. Henry looked up and saw him. Willie looked at Henry and said, "I don't think I can remember the last time I've been so happy to see your face, buddy." Henry then got up and went over for a manly embrace and said, "Hey, it's good to see you too."

Henry then asked Willie to sit down, that there was no time to waste, and he had some pretty sensitive stuff to tell him. Willie asked the colonel if he would mind leaving as this was a covert operation and what they needed to talk about was extremely sensitive.

The colonel, with a look of dismay at not being included in what was going on, asked if Willie wanted him to take the others out with him when he left. Willie told him that it wasn't necessary, that all of them worked for the agency and that they were all needed for debriefing. The colonel then left with the lieutenant, leaving the group completely alone.

After the door was shut, Henry told Willie all he had learned from Fernando and Peter about Fidel's fallback plan. Willie then said, "Well, I'd say we ain't got much time here, people, and we'd better alert the necessary people and get back to Miami as soon as possible."

Peter jumped in and said he thought they needed to first secure the deep storage area in Miami until they could get there. Willie took note of the statement and liked Peter's on-top attitude. He was about to say the same thing and was not offended by Peter's lead. Nevertheless, it was what had to be done immediately. He duly noted Peter and said that before they left, that would be the first thing he would do. After that, Willie told Peter that he was sorry, that as a civilian he would have to stay on the outside from here on in. He then turned to Henry and said, "Okay, we'd better get going if we intend to get there ahead of Castro's man, that is if he hasn't made it there already."

Henry interrupted and said, "Sir, I'd like to make a few recommendations."

"Go ahead, Henry, what is it?"

"Well, first, I think we should be using Spencer since he's already disarmed six of these rusty babies and I would think he could move on this a lot faster and more safely. Second, Mr. Kennedy and Miss Feher here have been through a lot and I'm sure they'd like to be with us to the end, if that's alright with you, sir."

Willie pondered for a moment and looked around the room at all of them and then said, "Alright, but let's get moving; we're wasting time we don't have sitting here." They then all got up and left the hospital and headed for the airstrip. As they walked, Willie spoke out loud, sort of confirming and bouncing off Henry all of his thoughts. "First, we'll need to get to the FBI and the National Guard to seal off the area and have them get ready for our arrival."

"Nan is at my office and I'll have her contact General Anderson to get a story planted, so that when the National Guard and the others show up, no one will suspect anything other than a chemical spill. Nan will know to make sure the right people are contacted with the right cover story."

"Next, we need to make tracks and get there ASAP. Spencer," Willie asked, "are you feeling okay about these babies."

"Yeah, they're rusty, but if you've done six, one more is just a piece of cake," Spencer said.

When they left the base hospital, outside was another troop carrier waiting to escort them all over to the airstrip. Before they boarded, Henry asked Willie if the colonel had said anything about Eliot's condition. The major told him not to worry, the word was that he came out fine and that within twenty-four hours, he'd be flown up to Bethesda Naval Hospital. They then boarded a Galaxy A-5 transport, seated themselves, buckled up, and sat back as the jet then began her taxi down the runway. Once in the air, beneath the roar of the engines, Henry continued to tell Willie in further detail how the whole thing had fallen apart and what had happened to all of them, including Peter and Tess.

Castro was in probably one of the worst states that any of his generals had ever seen. They assessed that this betrayal by Fernando had pretty much thrown him over the edge. No one spoke as he carried on, for fear that it might be one of their last words. After Fidel had been ranting for some thirty minutes, he suddenly stopped and walked to his window in silence. The sudden cessation of his rantings had taken all of the generals by surprise. No one was really sure what was in Fidel's mind at that moment until he finally turned away from his window and said, "All of you, I want all of you out of here now. You're all nothing more than a bunch of incompetent fools. A man would have to wonder just what type of army he had when American prisoners, held right under their noses, were capable of escaping."

One of the generals, without thinking, spoke and said, "But it was Fernando who helped them. How could we have known or stopped him? After all, he was your aide, directly reporting to you, and no one would have dared to have questioned his authority."

With that comment, Fidel stared silently at the general and paused for a long moment, looking directly into his eyes. When Fidel finished, he turned to the two guards at the door and said, "Arrest this man immediately and take him downstairs until I am ready to deal with him." At this command, each of the generals knew that to say anything more was surely a death warrant. Fidel then screamed at them all to leave.

After they had all departed, he turned to his personal aide, wrote down a telephone number, and told him to contact the number in Miami immediately. He told the aide that it was to be a routed call on a secure line that could not be traced back to Cuba. He told the aide to use one of the Russian satellite feeds they still maintained from their old Soviet friends.

A few moments later, the aide returned to Fidel's office, told him that his line was ready and waiting for him. He needed to only pick up the line and the call would go through immediately. When Fidel picked up the phone, he spoke into it and said, "I am ready, put the call through." Fidel then turned to his aide and said, "Leave." The phone rang only two times when someone picked it up and said, "Miguel here."

Fidel spoke quietly and calmly as he addressed Miguel. "Do you know who this is?" Fidel asked.

"Si," the person on the other end answered.

"I have a job for you. It is what you have been waiting for, are you ready?"

"Si, I have been waiting a long time for this call, what is it you wish for me to do for our Cuba?"

"You are first to call Ortega at the mission in New York and tell him that you're on your way. He will know the significance of the call and will take care of whatever papers you will need to return to Havana. You are to then make your reservations for the flight to New York. Next, you will go to the location where we have left our goods. It is time that we pay back the Americans for all of our years of hardship. We have been betrayed and it is not important by who. What is important now is that you are to do this task immediately, as time is very important, and the Americans will surely be able to get to our goods within the next two to three hours. When you get there, you are to set the device for a two-hour delay. You are to then leave the area immediately and head directly for Ortega in New York. Again, my comrade, you must move quickly. As soon as this call is passed, make your reservations and then proceed directly, with all speed, to our goods."

When Fidel hung up the phone, he swiveled around in his thick leather chair and returned to staring out of his window. He pondered with a rueful smile just how devastating this will be for Americans. He thought about the American ego and their pride, that except for their small terrorist escapade at the World Trade Center last year, they thought they had buttoned down their borders. As Fidel continued to ponder his thoughts, his sense of retribution seemed perfectly full.

He knew now that he needed to get to his people in Africa to make sure the right stories were leaked to the Israeli press. He felt confident that the Israelis would contact the US and also let out to the world press at large that Castro had sold a nuclear warhead to an unnamed terrorist organization in the Middle East. After all, it was in the Israelis' best interests to sound the alarm and show the world that not only did they have to contend with these fanatics but so did the rest of the world, even for the US on their own shores.

After Willie's call to Nan, it took her about half an hour to get the ball rolling with the FBI and the National Guard. It took approximately another hour for the National Guard to be mobilized before they were able to get onto the scene. Although the channels were time-consuming, with first going through General Anderson and then him getting to the FBI, still the Feds were there ahead of the Guard in just about an hour and fifteen minutes. While everyone was moving as quickly as possible, Nan personally handled getting the leak to the local and national press that there had been a chemical spill at the Miami International Airport. All and all, the entire area was secured in less than two hours.

The pilot of the Galaxy A-5 transport made the announcement of their landing at Miami International and told them all to prepare for their landing. It was about 0930 hours as they got off the plane and were whisked off in two separate government cars to the customs' deep storage area. When they came to the entrance gate at the customs' storage area, there were National

Guard soldiers stationed there and what looked like five or six Fibis standing in front of a couple government vehicles. The major told them who they were and they were sent immediately to the storage hangar dead ahead of them. When they arrived in front of the hangar, *it looked like a scene out* of *Seven Days in May.* There were bomb squad vehicles, troop carriers, soldiers, and last but not least, lots of government types in dark suits mulling about with radio pieces in their ears. Henry jumped out of the car ahead of Willie and asked who was in charge here. One of the Feds immediately responded that he was. Henry then explained who they were and asked to be taken directly inside the hangar.

The head FBI man responded back to Henry to ask if he was the senior man in charge. At that, Willie stepped forward and announced that he was and said, "Let's cut the bullshit here, buddy, and let's get to the bomb or didn't you know that's what we've got here."

"Oh, I know what we've got here, sir. I believe it's you who's not aware of what's going on."

"What do you mean by that?" Willie asked.

"It seems someone got here before any of us, sir, because when we got here, we found two dead customs agents at the front entrance and when we came back here to the hangar, we found one more dead. Based on the expertise of whoever it was who did this handy work, he's a real pro. About the only good thing you could say was that he did his work early this morning or perhaps we would have had more casualties."

Henry turned around and looked at Peter and Tess and said, "I guess our boy Fidel was ahead of us on this one." Henry then turned back to the agent and said, "Alright, whatever, but we've got to get in there quickly to see what we've got."

"I don't think our man has done anything as yet, sir, since we've found a car here and it appears that unless someone came here with him, he's not had a chance to get out," the agent said. The agent then informed Henry and Willie that they'd secured the area and kept everything on hold until they had arrived as instructed by their superiors. He went on to say that they'd also done a DMV check and the car they found is registered to one Miguel Gomez, residing at 1314 SW 144th St, in South Miami. He explained that they did an NCIC check on him and there weren't any wants or warrants out on our Mr. Gomez and that they'd already sent some agents over to his house but as expected no one was there. They did however, following standard procedure, leave a couple of the agents there to hang around just in case anyone did show up.

"So you mean no one has been inside the hangar yet," Henry said.

"No, sir. We were instructed that no one was to do anything or go inside this facility until you fellas showed up." The agent then turned to Tess and said, "Pardon me, mam, I didn't mean to be politically incorrect," the agent said with a bit of sarcasm.

Willie then turned to Henry and said, "I think you ought to carry on from here, Henry. It's been your game up to now and I don't see why that should be changing at this juncture."

Henry then turned to Spencer and told him that he thought the two of them should go in first alone to take a look at the crate and make sure all was as it should have been. He told Willie to get the bomb boys ready, not that he would need their services but perhaps Spencer might need some of their devices. He also asked Willie to get him a walkie-talkie so they can communicate directly with him while they were inside. Henry turned around to talk with Spencer, while Willie went to see the senior officer there with the National Guard. When Willie returned, he handed Henry the communicator and said, "We'll be waiting out here, anything you need, just give me a shout."

Henry and Spencer then turned around and headed into the hangar. As they were walking away, Henry turned back and called to Peter. "Hey, maybe you should at least go in here with us now just in case my understanding of where this baby is located is slightly different than what Fernando told you." With that, all three of them disappeared into the storage hangar, while everyone else waited outside in the growing heat of the morning.

Miguel had called the airport right after he'd gotten off the phone and got a direct flight to New York at 9:10 a.m. After he hung up with the airlines, he then called Ortega as instructed and then made ready for his mission. He had waited a long time for this call and now he finally would have his chance to show

Fidel just how dedicated he was to the cause. He went into his closet and took out a 45 Automatic and mounted a silencer on it. He then went to the corner of his bedroom and opened up a footlocker he had stashed under his bed. When he opened it, he rummaged through all of his electronic devices until he came upon what he really wanted, a timer. After gathering all his gear and checking it over, he left his house and got into his car to head directly for Miami International Airport.

It was now 6:45 a.m. and he didn't expect there'd be much traffic at this time of the morning. Miguel lived close to the airport, and he considered that it wouldn't take him more than twenty minutes to get there. He estimated that after he had taken care of the customs agents, he'd be able to get into the crate and set a timer in less than fifteen minutes. He was well aware at how close he'd be cutting it to the time when the morning shift would be changing, but he felt confident that he'd be done before 8:00 a.m., leaving him at least thirty minutes of safety before they switched their shifts.

When he arrived at the customs gate in the rear of the airport, he was met by two customs agents as expected. The first one came over to the car and asked if he, Miguel, was lost. Miguel told him that he was supposed to meet his cousin Tito over here at 7:15 a.m., that he was a customs agent too. The agent told him that he hadn't heard of any Tito and asked if he was sure he was to meet him over there. "Sure, I'm sure, ask your friend inside. I'm sure he must know him if you don't. I mean, he's been with the customs service for over twenty years."

"Okay, wait over here and I'll go ask my buddy," the agent said.

As the agent walked back to the control booth by the gate, Miguel got out of his car and walked behind the agent as if he was going in there with him. As the first agent approached the office, the other agent came out to see what was going on. As he came out, Miguel pulled out his magnum 45 and quickly shot them both. Two shots each in deadly silence and they were no more.

After they fell to the ground, Miguel rushed over to them and dragged them one after the other into the small office at the gate. Once he had laid them out of sight, he went back outside, moved his car up a bit, and then got out and closed the gate. He then drove directly to the hangar about three hundred yards dead ahead of him.

When he arrived in front of the hangar, he pulled to the side and saw that the agent on duty came out and started to walk towards the car. As he got close to the car, he said, "Hey, buddy, is there something I can do for you?"

Miguel began rolling down his window, speaking as he did it. "Yes, I'm looking for Tito, do you know him?" And as the agent leaned in towards the window, Miguel pulled out his 45 and shot the agent dead center in the middle of his forehead. Miguel then got out of his car, ran to the door alongside of the large hangar door, and opened it. He then ran back, grabbed the guard, and pulled him inside. He peeked out the door after laying the guard on the floor just to make sure no one had seen him or was coming, and then went back inside.

Once inside, he proceeded down the center aisle to the back of the warehouse. When he called Ortega in New York, Ortega had described the crate and told him where he would find it, based on the information he had gotten from Fernando when he had seen him in New York. He moved to the back of the aisle to the exact area where it should have been, only it wasn't there. With panic in his heart, he raced up and down the aisle checking and rechecking the notes he had taken when he spoke to Ortega. He then moved one aisle to either side of the center and checked those too. He couldn't believe it, where could it have gone. It was too large to just disappear. He was now sweating, and he was finding it hard to think clearly. What had started out to be a simple task had now left him without any idea as what to do next. With no other choice at hand, he looked at his watch and decided to continue looking until there was no more time. He figured he had at least until eight fifteen before he'd be treading on the dangerous ground.

By about eight ten, Miguel had decided he would have to cease his search. He knew that if he were caught, he would not only be held on murder charges, but he'd no longer be of any use to Fidel or his nation. When he finally could look no longer, he decided it was time to give it up. He heard noises from the front of the building as he neared the front door. He quickly ran into the small office near the front and peeked out through a small slit in the blinds. What he saw sent his mind spinning. They were military troop carriers, what looked like government-type FBI vehicles, and at least two platoons of armed soldiers.

He couldn't believe what he was seeing but nevertheless they were there. *All this for me*, he thought, but then he knew it was something else. In his heart of hearts, he sensed it had something to do with the warhead he had been searching for. With nothing else to do but hide, he proceeded to retreat to the back of the warehouse in hopes that perhaps he could elude their search and eventually make an escape.

It was now 9:00 a.m. and still no one had come into the warehouse to search for him. He couldn't understand it. After all, they must have found the bodies, what could be holding them back from entering and searching for him. Miguel was completely confounded by what was taking place, but he knew for whatever the reason, they apparently weren't coming in. He had found a place up in the roof struts, which he had considered safe, and resigned himself that as hot as it was becoming, still it appeared he would be safe here.

As Henry, Spencer, and Peter walked down the center aisle, they each sensed something was not right. Where was the man who'd killed the agents? Why had he left his car out front? Nothing was as it should have been, given the scenario that three men had obviously been killed just so someone could get in here.

Whatever it was about, time was of the essence since they had no way of knowing whether or not Castro's man had gotten to the warhead yet. Logic told Henry that if one of Castro's men had made it here, he would have used a timer to allow himself time to make a getaway. The problem they had, Henry announced to both of them, was that they didn't know how long the timer had been set for.

As they neared the spot where the crate was supposed to be, Henry spoke first, "I would think that this guy would have used a two-hour timer. That would have at least given him enough time to either start driving as far north as he could or catch a plane if that was his escape plan."

"I wouldn't think the guy would have considered driving just in case he had a problem getting out of Miami. After all, they've got as many traffic accidents or as much road construction as any city does, so I'd think we've got at least until 10:00 a.m. if we figure correctly when he could have gotten here," Peter said.

"Yeah, well, I'm not interested in guessing what time he set this baby for, I'm only interested in getting to it and disarming it as soon as we can," Spencer said.

When they reached the spot where the crate should have been, they too, like Miguel, were at a loss as to why it wasn't where it should have been. Henry turned to Peter and asked if he could have missed anything in the directions he's gotten from Fernando. Peter told him that as far as he knew too, this was the spot he was told it should have been.

"You don't think our man from Fidel could have moved this baby, do you?" Henry asked.

"No way," Peter answered.

"Hey, maybe Fernando was off by one or two aisles," Spencer said.

"Okay, whatever it is let's fan out and start looking. Time is of the essence, gentlemen, but then again we all know that already," Henry said.

Henry then spoke into the walkie-talkie and informed Willie what was going on inside. Willie asked Henry if he wanted assistance in the search, but Henry declined, saying that he was afraid that too many troops might just create havoc inside and that he was sure the three of them could cover the whole area in less than ten minutes. He ended by saying that he'd check back after they'd covered all ten aisles. All three of them then fanned out, dividing the warehouse into three sections, and proceeded to check up and down each aisle for a large square wooden crate marked "fragile" diagonally across the sides.

As they spoke, above them Miguel could hear their entire conversation. He knew now that they'd faced what he had, in the fact that for some reason the crate was not here. He also realized that with the concern for the warhead, searching for him had become a secondary priority.

While listening to their conversation, he had hoped that the lead man would have allowed the troops outside to have come in. He figured he could have then perhaps grabbed one of the soldiers and stolen his uniform, allowing him to escape unnoticed. He still however felt confident that with the caution being shown outside and the massive numbers of people, if he could somehow get out the warehouse amidst all the people outside, that he might find his way to safety.

While Henry and the others searched the aisles, Miguel decided he would attempt to get out. He started to descend from the struts he was on until he came upon the catwalk which had led him to the top. After walking along the catwalk, he came to a ladder which led to the floor at the back of the hangar. While trying to keep them in sight, he made his way down to the bottom of the ladder. Once on the floor, he could no longer see any of them. He moved behind a forklift against the wall and decided to wait until he could make out where they were before making his next move. He saw at the rear wall a window which, although high, he measured he'd be able to pull himself up to if he could get there.

Henry was at the far-left side of the warehouse and Spencer was covering the center section. Peter had been at the far-right side where Miguel had just descended and was waiting for his opportunity to make it to the window. As Peter neared the end of the last aisle against the wall, without knowing it, he was no more than ten feet from Miguel. Miguel, seeing how close he was, realized that if he didn't make a move on this one, he might be discovered, and he'd alert the others. Although risky, he decided to take the chance and take Peter out. He drew his gun and at that moment realized that in climbing to the top, he'd somehow lost the silencer off his gun. Realizing this, he decided then not to shoot but to use a rope he'd found on the floor next to him and to choke Peter quietly.

As Peter came to the very end of the aisle, he stood right in front of the forklift, pondering just how this missing crate could have come about. He was just about to call out to Henry that he too had come up empty when Miguel jumped out from behind him and slipped the rope quickly over his head and cinched it as hard as he could. Before Peter could even get a word out, he felt the rope choking his windpipe and he struggled to somehow wedge his hands between the rope and his neck. Peter kicked and flailed his body, violently trying to escape his captor's hold, while all the time feeling the strength drain from his body. Eventually Peter went limp and in the light of the noise Peter had made kicking with his feet during his struggle, Miguel released the rope and ran as quickly as he could to the rear window. Peter fell to the floor and Miguel neither cared nor had any inclination to find out whether or not Peter was dead. His only thought was escape and that was primary on his mind.

During Peter's struggle with Miguel, Spencer had already left Henry and was walking back to ask Peter what he'd found when he'd heard the noises that Peter was making while Miguel was trying to dispose of him. Spencer called out, "Peter, is that you?" When there was no response, he called back to Henry, "Henry, something's going on by Peter," and when he did, he started to run towards Peter's side of the warehouse. As he reached the rear wall where Peter was, he saw him lying on the floor and simultaneously looked up and saw Miguel running further to the rear. He called out to Miguel and ran towards him. As he did, Miguel in a panic, realizing that others would now come, saw no choice other than to reach for his gun and shoot. When he did, Spencer was hit on the first round and fell to the floor.

The shot rang out in a huge echo and was heard immediately by Henry. Henry started running towards the area of the shot and had been so surprised by its sound that he hadn't thought clearly and left his walkie-talkie on top of the nearest box.

By this time, Miguel had reached the window and was pulling himself up. Henry came flying around the corner, saw Miguel, and yelled. Miguel dropped quickly from the window ledge to the floor and moved back behind some crates to try to squeeze through the center of an aisle and get behind Henry's approaching direction. Henry was clearly not thinking in his pursuit of the killer, but such was his ire at seeing Spencer lying on the floor in a pool of blood. At losing sight of the killer, Henry slowed down and started to move in a stealthier manner.

Having been experienced and trained in hand-to-hand combat, fear was the farthest thing from his mind. Henry's only thought was to get this Bastard. As he came up to Spencer, he reached down to touch the side of his neck. As he did, Spencer spoke and said, "I, alright, just get that scumbag . . ." Slowly, in a crouch, Henry moved past Spencer and made his way to the end of the last aisle to try and get behind where he thought the killer was. There he saw Peter also lying on the ground and reached over to check him too. When he put his hand over his mouth, he could feel Peter breathing and realized he was just unconscious.

Henry called out to the killer and said, "You're trapped . . . why don't you just give it up, pal?"

Miguel responded, "There is nothing for me if I am caught, so I will just have to kill you too."

Henry answered, "Hey, I like it. That suits me just fine. It's been a long time since I've killed anyone hand-to-hand and I think I'm going to enjoy this one."

Within the few minutes that had passed since the sound of the gunshot, the FBI was getting ready to storm into the warehouse. They were only waiting until they had surrounded all of the potential exits before they were going to go in. Once they had surrounded the rear windows and were sure there was no way out other than the front door, the senior FBI agent led a team through the front door. Once through the door, about eight of them, in a crouching position, started to crawl out of the left and right. They were in no more than a twenty-foot arc when the senior agent called through a bullhorn and asked Captain St. John to respond.

Henry yelled back that he was okay but the other two were down but not dead. The FBI man told Henry not to move and to stay where he was, that they were coming in. Henry called back and said, "Stay where you are. I'll handle this scumbag, just keep the door covered so he's got no way out. This guy's all mine and I don't want anyone else in here."

The senior FBI agent signaled with his hand that everyone was to hold their positions and not to move. He then slowly moved backwards until he'd made his way back out to the front.

Once outside, he confronted Willie with what was going on in there and told him how Henry wanted everyone to keep out. Willie responded by telling him that if that's the way Henry wanted it, then that's the way it's going to be. The FBI man argued for a moment until Willie held up his hand and said, "Hey, that's my man in there, and if that's the way he wants to play it then give him the space. I'll take full responsibility on this."

Tess heard the conversation and all she could do was stand there and wonder how Willie could allow them to continue inside without any assistance. She turned to Willie after the FBI man went back inside and pleaded with him to let the FBI intercede, but Willie would have none of it. "Listen, Miss Feher, that's my man in there and I care as much about him and the others as you do. If this is the way he wants it then this is how it's going to be, so spare me the tears and let's let it be," Willie said. With that, Tess left Willie and walked over to sit in one of the Fed's cars to wait like everyone else.

When the FBI man went back into the hangar, he looked to the left and the right and said, "Hold your position, we're going to let the captain here have his guy." There were a few shrugs but all in all they just maintained the crouched stance and held their positions at the door.

Henry was cautiously moving around the rear of the last aisle and saw that his man was no longer there. He stopped for a moment to see if he could hear anything but all there was, was silence. Miguel had already squeezed through the crates as he had wanted and without Henry knowing it, he was coming up right behind him. Miguel was no more than ten feet from Henry's back when he drew out his gun, pointed it, and started to pull the trigger. Just before he did, he spoke and said, "So you were going to take me hand-to-hand, huh?" He squeezed his finger on the trigger, but as he completed the motion, Peter leaped onto his back and tackled him to the ground. The bullet, slightly off aim from Peter's tackle, missed its mark and caught Henry in his butt.

Peter's tackle had taken Miguel completely by surprise and Miguel went down easily. Peter grabbed his hair and smashed his head directly into the concrete. Although dazed, Miguel still had the power to throw Peter off to the side and allow him to lunge on top of Peter and throw a good left jab to his jaw. Peter's head jerked to the right and the pain was stiffening. He rolled with the punch and felt a sharp kick to his side as Miguel had already gotten up onto his feet. While Peter grabbed his back, Miguel once again kicked him with all that he had, and Peter's body contorted again. Miguel then saw his weapon on the floor, reached for it, and as he turned to open fire on Peter, Henry rapped him over the head with a steel bar with all that he had. Miguel went down instantly and wasn't moving a muscle.

Henry limped over to Peter and said, "Not bad for a civilian, guy."

"Yeah, well, I didn't see that I had much choice."

Peter slowly picked himself up off the floor aided by Henry and brushed himself off. He slapped Henry on the shoulder and said, "So does this mean I'm an official rogue like the rest of you guys?"

"Well, whatever it means, you saved my life and between the two of us we got this mother, and best of all, he's alive."

While the two of them were standing there congratulating each other, the senior FBI man came up with his troops trailing behind him. They handcuffed Miguel and proceeded to take him out to the front. The FBI man then asked if they were okay and Henry told him that except for his embarrassing wound, they were none the worse for wear. He told them though that Spencer had been hit and that they needed an ambulance ASAP. Henry and Peter then went over to check on Spencer and when they got there, he was sitting up holding his side.

"How are you doing, big guy? I know gunfights are not your specialty but then neither are they mine."

"I'm okay but it burns like a bitch. He got me in the side, but I don't believe he hit anything other than some of this fat I've been trying to lose for a few years. Hey, don't just stand there, how 'bout helping me up here?"

"You just sit there, buddy, there's an ambulance on its way, and they'll be taking you out of here in style, boy," Henry said.

With that, a corpsman from the National Guard came up and proceeded to bandage Spencer while they waited for the ambulance. Peter then helped Henry limp outside to the front where they saw Willie. After Spencer was in the ambulance, the rest of them followed downtown to get Henry some medical attention too.

Henry was fixed up in a matter of no time and they left Spencer there to recover a little more. Spencer had no objection to being left behind, for as far as he was concerned, he'd seen all the action he wanted to see for a long time. The rest of them left the hospital, courtesy of the FBI, and went downtown to the Federal Building where they were going to have a chance to interrogate Miguel.

After Miguel's interrogation, they found out that he had in fact been sent there to detonate the warhead, but he too wasn't able to locate it anywhere in the warehouse. Miguel was taken away by the FBI when the interrogation was over to face whatever charges the Feds had lined up for him and they were sure there were plenty.

Willie and the rest of the group then went back to the airport where they returned to the warehouse. Although they had obviously caught Miguel and he hadn't had the chance to detonate any device, the question remained, what had happened to the crate Fernando had hidden there some three or more weeks ago.

When they arrived back at the hangar, a general cleanup operation was underway and most of the guard troops had left, leaving only a skeleton crew to help pack up all of their equipment. The new customs crew was there, and Henry thought that it might be worthwhile to question these guys if they were the regular day shift agents. Henry figured that the possibility might exist that somebody remembered the crate and knew what had happened to it.

Henry approached what appeared to be the senior customs agent directing things by the large open hangar door. He asked him if he remembered the delivery of the crate a few weeks ago. He told Henry that he mainly handled the paperwork and that if he wanted information about specific crates or boxes, he needed to speak with either Tony, the floor supervisor, or Jorge, who fills in if Tony's not there. Since they worked inside and literally moved the crates into the storage aisles, Henry hoped that they might recall something.

The senior customs agent called to Tony to come over and as he did, Jorge walked with him. Henry introduced himself and after answering some of their questions, he was eventually able to drive the conversation where he wanted it. Tony recalled the crate immediately and Jorge nodded in concurrence at everything Tony told him. Henry asked what had happened to the crate and Tony wasn't really sure.

Jorge then spoke and explained that about two weeks ago, some guys came by from the DEA and wanted to remove some selected inventory that they were obviously holding for some drug interdiction case they had been working on. Jorge began, "Well, their papers were totally in order, and they then loaded up all the boxes they had on their list. When they finished, I told them that they had left a large crate that was filled with drugs. One of these DEA guys then asked me how I knew that. Well, I told him about three weeks ago some lawyer guy had come by, carrying on about his client's case and how he wanted to see this crate to make sure it hadn't been opened. So then he shows me his business card and since he wasn't taking anything, I led him to the back and showed him the crate that corresponded to the case number he had. He had a case number you know, I mean, I didn't do anything wrong. He didn't leave with anything, you know."

"So what happened then?" Henry asked.

"Like I said, I took him back inside and we looked for the box with the case number he had. I mean, I've got a record of it right here in the office. That's how the DEA guys knew which crate was the one that had the drugs in it.

"Here, come with me and I'll show you the logbook."

They went into the logbook and there was the inventory number that corresponded to the crate inside that was taken by the boys from the DEA. After looking in the book, Henry turned back to Jorge and asked, "So what happened?"

"They took it, what else?" Jorge answered.

Henry then looked at Willie and said, “I don’t know how they got a case number of what, but obviously someone switched numbers and the crate Fernando stashed here used that number. I think what we need to do next is get to the DEA boys and see if what they took for disposal isn’t in fact the goody package that we’ve been looking for.”

“You think so?” Willie asked.

“Who knows,” Henry said, “I only know what we’re looking for isn’t here and somebody’s got it.”

Henry returned to Jorge and thanked him for his help, and they all left to return back downtown to the Federal Building. On their way downtown, Joel and Barry told them to drop them off at the hospital as they wanted to check in on Spencer. Tess asked them if they minded if she went with them, as she’d had all the excitement and running around, she needed for the day. She asked Peter if he wanted to join her, but he declined saying he wanted to see this through to the end with Henry. He looked at Henry for his approval and Henry nodded, so as to say, if that’s what you want, it’s okay with me.

At the Federal Building, the three of them were waiting in a private office when a senior DEA official finally arrived. He told them that he’d been brought up to speed on everything and said that in fact some agents did remove an additional crate that day from deep storage and it was in a holding area behind the loading dock downstairs. Henry smiled at his compatriot and turned to the DEA man and said, "Lead the way, my friend," and they all left the office, hopefully to come to their journey's end.

They took an elevator downstairs and when they arrived at the loading dock, they climbed down and walked around the back of the building to an area enclosed by a razor wire fence. The DEA man opened the gate and they walked off to the left and there before their eyes was a large wooden crate with *Fragile* printed diagonally on all sides. Henry asked the man for a crowbar and, when he got it, proceeded to pry the side facing of the crate open.

As the panel fell to the floor, Henry quickly started to pull the straw packing out as fast as he could and there, staring him in the face, was a cobalt jet-black nuclear warhead standing about four feet high in front of their faces. Henry laughed and turned to Willie and Peter and said, "Even Fidel himself would never have known."

The three of them then just started laughing out loud as the DEA man stood there in silence without the slightest possibility of ever comprehending what could have been so funny about the sight of a nuclear warhead.

EPILOGUE

After a few days, the team, including Tess and Peter, were eventually reunited up at NSA headquarters in Fort Meade, Maryland. Tess and Peter truly lived through a great deal with the team and now felt, like the others, that they were nearly a part of it. They sat in Henry's office with Willie and Nan and they all enjoyed, laughed, and relished in the joke that Fidel's plan inside itself was the thing that had ruined any chance he had ever had to get at that warhead.

It turned out that when Fernando's man in Miami had used an actual drug evidence case number and that was his mistake when his man had posed as a lawyer to get his first look at the customs deep storage area. As things had turned out, by the number being attached to Fernando's crate, Jorge had no idea that he was passing off a nuclear warhead to the DEA as a crate full of contraband drugs.

Tess had decided that she was going to return to Hungary and take a post there working for the government again. Peter and Tess had both realized that they were of different worlds. They both knew that what they had shared was wonderful, but it had been borne of the moment, not of any other truth. After what she had been through, the home office was certainly amenable to give her any post that was within their ability to offer. The rest of team SIREN returned to their normal lives and Peter returned back to his world with his sons and his private consulting business. Peter and Henry had both saved each other's lives, and in those events, they had found a new bond that they knew would keep them close to each other, no matter how far their lives might drift apart in the years ahead.

The world was as it was, left as it had been before. Fidel, despite all of his efforts, remained a frustrated isolated leader and the rest of the world was led to believe that there never were any nuclear warheads, that it had all just been a false rumor circulated by radical terrorists from the Middle East. Fidel, to save himself the embarrassment, denied ever having made any offer to trade anything with the United States government.